A Mysterious Disap

Louis Tracy

Alpha Editions

This edition published in 2024

ISBN : 9789361478840

Design and Setting By
Alpha Editions
www.alphaedis.com
Email - info@alphaedis.com

Contents

CHAPTER I ....- 1 -

CHAPTER II...- 9 -

CHAPTER III ....- 16 -

CHAPTER IV ....- 22 -

CHAPTER V ....- 30 -

CHAPTER VI ....- 35 -

CHAPTER VII..- 41 -

CHAPTER VIII ....- 47 -

CHAPTER IX ....- 53 -

CHAPTER X ....- 61 -

CHAPTER XI ....- 67 -

CHAPTER XII..- 75 -

CHAPTER XIII ....- 80 -

CHAPTER XIV ....- 87 -

CHAPTER XV..- 95 -

CHAPTER XVI ....- 103 -

CHAPTER XVII..- 111 -

CHAPTER XVIII...- 119 -

CHAPTER XIX ....- 128 -

CHAPTER XX...- 134 -

CHAPTER XXI ....- 143 -

CHAPTER XXII...- 151 -

CHAPTER XXIII..- 160 -

CHAPTER XXIV ....- 167 -

CHAPTER XXV...- 174 -

CHAPTER XXVI ....- 183 -

CHAPTER XXVII ....- 189 -

CHAPTER XXVIII ....- 196 -

CHAPTER XXIX ....- 204 -

CHAPTER XXX ....- 211 -

CHAPTER XXXI ....- 219 -

CHAPTER I

"LAST SEEN AT VICTORIA!"

Alice, Lady Dyke, puckered her handsome forehead into a thoughtful frown as she drew aside the window-curtains of her boudoir and tried to look out into the opaque blackness of a November fog in London.

Behind her was cheerfulness—in front uncertainty. Electric lights, a nice fire reflected from gleaming brass, the luxury of carpets and upholstery, formed an alluring contrast to the dull yellow glare of a solitary lamp in the outer obscurity.

But Lady Dyke was a strong-minded woman. There was no trace of doubt in the wrinkled brows and reflective eyes. She held back the curtains with her left hand, buttoning a glove at the wrist with the other. Fog or no fog, she would venture forth, and she was already dressed for the weather in tailor-made costume and winter toque.

She was annoyed, but not disconcerted by the fog. Too long had she allowed herself to take things easily. The future was as murky as the atmosphere; the past was dramatically typified by the pleasant surroundings on which she resolutely turned her back. Lady Dyke was quite determined as to her actions, and a dull November night was a most unlikely agent to restrain her from following the course she had mapped out.

Moving to the light again, she took from her pocket a long, closely written letter. Its details were familiar to her, but her face hardened as she hastily ran through it in order to find a particular passage.

At last she gained her object—to make quite sure of an address. Then she replaced the document, stood undecided for a moment, and touched an electric bell.

"James," she said, to the answering footman, "I am going out."

"Yes, milady."

"Sir Charles is not at home?"

"No, milady."

"I am going to Richmond—to see Mrs. Talbot. I shall probably not return in time for dinner. Tell Sir Charles not to wait for me."

"Shall I order the carriage for your ladyship?"

"Will you listen to me and remember what I have said?"

"Yes, milady."

James ran downstairs, opened the door, bowed as Lady Dyke passed into Portman Square, and then confidentially informed Buttons that "the missus" was in a "rare old wax" about something.

"She nearly jumped down my bloomin' throat when I asked her if she would have the carriage," he said.

Her ladyship's mood did not soften when she drifted from the fixed tenure of Wensley House, Portman Square, into the chaos of Oxford Street and fog at 5.30 on a November evening.

Though not a true "London particular," the fog was chilly, exasperating, tedious. People bumped against each other without apology, 'buses crunched through the traffic with deadly precision, pair-horse vans swept around corners with magnificent carelessness.

In the result, Lady Dyke, who meant to walk, as she was somewhat in advance of the time she had fixed on for this very important engagement, took a hansom. In her present mood slight things annoyed her. Usually, the London cab-horse is a thoughtful animal; he refuses to hurry; when he falls he lies contented, secure in the knowledge that for five blissful minutes he will be at complete rest. But this misguided quadruped flew as though oats and meadow-grass awaited him at Victoria Station on the Underground Railway.

He raced down Park Lane, skidded past Hyde Park Corner, and grated the off-wheel of the hansom against the kerb outside the station within eight minutes.

In other words, her ladyship, if she would obey the directions contained in the voluminous letter, was compelled to kill time.

As she stepped from the vehicle and halted beneath a lamp to take a florin from her purse, a tall, ulster-wrapped gentleman, walking rapidly into Victoria Street, caught a glimpse of her face and well-proportioned form.

Instantly his hat was off.

"This is an unexpected pleasure, Lady Dyke. Can I be of any service?"

She bit her lip, not unobserved, but the law of Society forced her features into a bright smile.

"Oh, Mr. Bruce, is it you? I am going to see my sister at Richmond. Isn't the weather horrid? I shall be so glad if you will put me into the right train."

Mr. Claude Bruce, barrister and man about town, whose clean-cut features and dark, deep-set eyes made him as readily recognizable, knew that she would have been much better pleased had he passed without greeting. Like the footman, he wondered why she did not drive in her carriage rather than travel by the Underground Railway on such a night. He guessed that she was perturbed—that her voluble explanation was a disguise.

He reflected that he could ill afford any delay in dressing for a distant dinner—that good manners oft entail inconvenience—but of course he said:

"Delighted. Have you any wraps?"

"No, I am just going for a chat, and shall be home early."

He bought her a first-class ticket, noting as an odd coincidence that it bore the number of the year, 1903, descended to the barrier, found that the next train for Richmond passed through in ten minutes, fumed inwardly for an instant, explained his presence to the ticket-collector, and paced the platform with his companion.

Having condemned the fog, and the last play, and the latest book, they were momentarily silent.

The newspaper placards on Smith & Son's bookstall announced that a "Great Society Scandal" was on the tapis. "The Duke in the Box" formed a telling line, and the eyes of both people chanced on it simultaneously.

Thought the woman: "He is a man of the world, and an experienced lawyer. Shall I tell him?"

Thought the man: "She wants to take me into her confidence, and I am too busy to be worried by some small family squabble."

Said she: "Are you much occupied at the Courts just now, Mr. Bruce?"

"No," he replied; "not exactly. My practice is more consultive than active. Many people seek my advice about matters of little interest, never thinking that they would best serve their ends by acting decisively and promptly themselves."

Lady Dyke set her lips. She could be both prompt and decisive. She resolved to keep her troubles, whatever they were, locked in the secrecy of her own heart, and when she next spoke of some trivial topic the barrister knew that he had been spared a recital.

He regretted it afterwards.

At any other moment in his full and useful life he would have encouraged her rather than the reverse. Even now, a few seconds too late, he was sorry. He strove to bring her back to the verge of explanations, but failed, for her ladyship was a proud, self-reliant personage—one who would never dream of risking a rebuff.

A train came, with "Richmond" staring at them from the smoke and steam of the engine.

"Good-bye!" he said.

"Good-bye!"

"Shall I see you again soon?"

"I fear not. It is probable that I shall leave for the South of France quite early."

And she was gone. Her companion rushed to the street, and almost ran to his Victoria Street chambers. It was six o'clock. He had to dress and drive all the way to Hampstead for dinner at 7.30.

At ten minutes past nine Sir Charles Dyke entered Wensley House. A handsome, quiet, gentlemanly man was Sir Charles. He was rich—a Guardsman until the baronetcy devolved upon him, a popular figure in Society, esteemed a trifle fast prior to his marriage, but sobered down by the cares of a great estate and a vast fortune.

His wife and he were not well-matched in disposition.

She was too earnest, too prim, for the easy-going baronet. He respected her, that was all. A man of his nature found it impossible to realize that the depths of passion are frequently coated over with ice. Their union was irreproachable, like their marriage settlements; but there are more features in matrimony than can be disposed of by broad seals and legal phrases.

Unfortunately, they were childless, and were thus deprived of the one great bond which unites when others may fail.

Sir Charles was hurried, if not flurried. His boots were muddy and his clothes splashed by the mire of passing vehicles.

"I fear I am very late for dinner," he said to the footman who took his hat and overcoat. "But I shall not be five minutes in dressing. Tell her ladyship—"

"Milady is not at home, Sir Charles."

"Not at home!"

"Milady went out at half-past five, saying that she was going to Richmond to see Lady Edith Talbot, and that you were not to wait dinner if she was late in returning."

Sir Charles was surprised. He looked steadily at the man as he said:

"Are you quite sure of her ladyship's orders?"

"Quite sure, Sir Charles."

"Did she drive?"

"No, Sir Charles. She would not order the carriage when I suggested it."

The baronet, somewhat perplexed, hesitated a moment. Then he appeared to dismiss the matter as hardly worth discussion, saying, as he went up stairs:

"Dinner almost immediately, James."

During the solitary meal he was preoccupied, but ate more than usual, in the butler's judgment. Finding his own company distasteful, he discussed the November Handicap with the butler, and ultimately sent for an evening paper.

Opening it, the first words that caught his eye were, "Murder in the West End." He read the paragraph, the record of some tragic orgy, and turned to the butler.

"A lot of these beastly crimes have occurred recently, Thompson."

"Yes, Sir Charles. There's bin three since the beginning of the month."

After a pause. "Did you hear that her ladyship had gone to Richmond?"

"Yes, Sir Charles."

"Do you know how she went?"

"No, Sir Charles."

"I wanted to see her to-night, *very* particularly. Order the brougham in ten minutes. I am going to the Travellers' Club. I shall be home soon—say eleven o'clock—when her ladyship arrives."

The baronet was driven to and from the club by his own coachman, but on returning to Wensley House was told that his wife was still absent.

"No telegram or message?"

"No, Sir Charles."

"I suppose she will stay with her sister all night, and I shall have a note in the morning to say so. Just like a woman. Now if I did that, James, there would be no end of a row. Anxiety, and that sort of thing. Call me at 8.30."

An hour later Sir Charles Dyke left the library and went to bed.

At breakfast next morning the master of the house rapidly scanned the letters near his plate for the expected missive from his wife. There was none.

A maid was waiting. He sent her to call the butler.

"Look here, Thompson," he cried, "her ladyship has not written. Don't you think I had better wire? It's curious, to say the least, going off to Richmond in this fashion, in a beastly fog, too."

Thompson was puzzled. He had examined the letters an hour earlier. But he agreed that a telegram was the thing.

Sir Charles wrote: "Expected to hear from you. Will you be home to lunch? Want to see you about some hunters"; and addressed it to his wife at her sister's residence.

"There," he said, turning to his coffee and sole. "That will fetch her. We are off to Leicestershire next week, Thompson. By the way, I am going to a sale at Tattersall's. Send a groom there with her ladyship's answer when it comes."

He had not been long at the sale yard when a servant arrived with a telegram.

"Ah, the post-office people are quick this morning," he said, smiling. He opened the envelope and read:

"Want to see you at once.—DICK."

He was so surprised by the unexpected nature of the message that he read the words aloud mechanically. But he soon understood, and smiled again.

"Go back quickly," he said to the man, "and tell Thompson to send along the next telegram."

A consignment of Waterford hunters was being sold at the time, and the baronet was checking the animals' descriptions on the catalogue, when he was cheerily addressed:

"Hallo, Dyke, preparing for the shires, eh?"

Wheeling round, the baronet shook hands with Claude Bruce.

"Yes—that is, I am looking out for a couple of nice-mannered ones for my wife. I have six eating their heads off at Market Harborough now."

Bruce hesitated. "Will Lady Dyke hunt this season?" he asked.

"Well, hardly that. But she likes to dodge about the lanes with the parson and the doctor."

"I only inquired because she told me last night that she would probably winter in the South of France."

"Told you—last night—South of France!" Sir Charles Dyke positively gasped in his amazement.

"Why, yes. I met her at Victoria. She was going to Richmond to see her sister, she said."

"I am jolly glad to hear it."

"Glad! Why?"

"Because I have not seen her myself since yesterday morning. She went off mysteriously, late in the afternoon, leaving a message with the servants. Naturally I am glad to hear from you that she got into the train all right."

"I put her in the carriage myself. Have you not heard from her?"

"No. I wired this morning, and expect an answer at any moment. But what is this about the South of France? We go to Leicestershire next week."

"I can't say, of course. Your wife seemed to be a little upset about something. She only mentioned her intention casually—in fact, when I asked if we would meet soon."

The other laughed, a little oddly in the opinion of his astute observer, and dismissed the matter by the remark that the expected message from his wife would soon clear the slight mystery attending her movements during the past eighteen hours.

The two men set themselves to the congenial task of criticizing the horses trotting up and down the straw-covered track, and Sir Charles had purchased a nice half-bred animal for forty guineas when his groom again saluted him.

"Please, sir," said the man, "here's another telegram, and Thompson told me to ask if it was the right one."

Sir Charles frowned at the interruption—a second horse of a suitable character was even then under the hammer—but he tore open the envelope. At once his agitation became so marked that Bruce cried:

"Good heavens, Dyke, what is it? No bad news, I hope?"

The other, by a strong effort, regained his self-control.

"No, no," he stammered; "it is all right, all right. She has gone somewhere else. See. This is from her sister, Mrs. Talbot. Still, I wish Alice would consider my natural anxiety a little."

Bruce read:

"I opened your message. Alice not here. I have not seen her for over a week. What do you mean by wire? Am coming to town at once.—EDITH."

The baronet's pale face and strained voice betrayed the significance of the thought underlying the simple question.

"What do you make of it, Claude?"

Bruce, too, was very grave. "The thing looks queer," he said; "though the explanation may be trifling. Come, I will help you. Let us reach your house. It is the natural centre for inquiries."

They hailed a hansom and whirled off to Portman Square. They did not say much. Each man felt that the affair might not end so happily and satisfactorily as he hoped.

CHAPTER II

INSPECTOR WHITE

Lady Dyke had disappeared.

Whether dead or alive, and if alive, whether detained by force or absent of her own unfettered volition, this handsome and well-known leader of Society had vanished utterly from the moment when Claude Bruce placed her in a first-class carriage of a Metropolitan Richmond train at Victoria Station.

At first her husband and relatives hoped against hope that some extraordinary tissue of events had contributed to the building up of a mystery which would prove to be no mystery.

Yet the days fled, and there was no trace of her whereabouts.

At the outset, the inquiry was confined to the circle of friends and relatives. Telegrams and letters in every possible direction suggested by this comparatively restricted field showed conclusively that not only had Lady Dyke not been seen, but no one had the slightest clue to the motives which might induce her to leave her home purposely.

So far as her distracted husband could ascertain, she did not owe a penny in the world. She was a rich woman in her own right, and her banking account was in perfect order.

She was a woman of the domestic temperament, always in close touch with her family, and those who knew her best scouted the notion of any petty intrigue which would move her, by fear or passion, to abandon all she held dear.

The stricken baronet confided the search only to his friend Bruce. He brokenly admitted that he had not sufficiently appreciated his wife while she was with him.

"She was of a superior order to me, Claude," he said. "I am hardly a home bird. Her ideals were lofty and humanitarian. Too often I was out of sympathy with her, and laughed at her notions. But, believe me, we never had the shadow of a serious dispute. Perhaps I went my own way a little selfishly, but at the time, I thought that she, on her part, was somewhat straight-laced. I appreciate her merits when it is too late."

"But you must not assume even yet that she is dead." The barrister was certain that some day the mystery would be elucidated.

"She is. I feel that. I shall never see her on earth again."

"Oh, nonsense, Dyke. Far more remarkable occurrences have been satisfactorily cleared up."

"It is very good of you, old chap, to take this cheering view. Only, you see, I know my wife's character so well. She would die a hundred times if it were possible rather than cause the misery to her people and myself which, if living, she knows must ensue from this terrible uncertainty as to her fate."

"Scotland Yard is still sanguine." This good-natured friend was evidently making a conversation.

"Oh, naturally. But something tells me that my wife is dead, whether by accident or design it is impossible to say. The police will cling to the belief that she is in hiding in order to conceal their own inability to find her."

"A highly probable theory. Are your servants to be trusted?"

"Y—es. They have all been with us some years. Why do you ask?"

"Because I am anxious that nothing of this should get into the papers. I have caused paragraphs to be inserted in the fashionable intelligence columns that Lady Dyke has gone to visit some friends in the Midlands. For her own sake, if she be living, it is best to choke scandal at its source."

"Well, Bruce, I leave everything to you. Make such arrangements as you think fit."

The barrister's mobile face softened with pity as he looked at his afflicted friend.

In four days Sir Charles Dyke had aged many years in appearance. No one who was acquainted with him in the past would have imagined that the loss of his wife could so affect him.

"I have done all that was possible, yet it is very little," said Bruce, after a pause. "You are aware that I am supposed to be an adept at solving curious or criminal investigations of an unusual class. But in this case, partly, I suspect, because I myself am the last person who, to our common knowledge, saw Lady Dyke alive on Tuesday night, I am faced by a dead wall of impenetrable fact, through which my intellect cannot pierce. Yet I am sure that some day this wretched business will be intelligible. I will find her if living; I will find her murderer if she be dead."

Not often did Claude Bruce allow his words to so betray his thoughts.

Both men were absorbed by the thrilling sensations of the moment, and they were positively startled when a servant suddenly announced:

"Inspector White, of Scotland Yard."

A short, thick-set man entered. He was absolutely round in every part. His sturdy, rotund frame was supported on stout, well-moulded legs. His bullet head, with close-cropped hair, gave a suggestion of strength to his rounded face, and a pair of small bright eyes looked suspiciously on the world from beneath well-arched eyebrows.

Two personalities more dissimilar than those of Claude Bruce and Inspector White could hardly be brought together in the same room. People who are fond of tracing resemblances to animals in human beings would liken the one to a grey-hound, the other to a bull-dog.

Yet they were both masters in the art of detecting crime—the barrister subtle, analytic, introspective; the policeman direct, pertinacious, self-confident. Bruce lost all interest in a case when the hidden trail was laid bare. Mr. White regarded investigation as so many hours on duty until his man was transported or hanged.

The detective was well acquainted with his unprofessional colleague, and had already met Sir Charles in the early stages of his present quest.

"I have an important clue," he said, smiling with assurance.

"What is it?" The baronet was for the moment aroused from his despondent lethargy.

"Her ladyship did not go to Richmond on Tuesday night."

Inspector White did not wait for Bruce to speak, but the barrister nodded with the air of one who knew already that Lady Dyke had not gone to Richmond.

Mr. White continued. "Thanks to Mr. Bruce's remembrance of the number of the ticket, we traced it at once in the clearing office. It was given up at Sloan Square immediately after the Richmond train passed through."

Bruce nodded again. He was obstinately silent, so the detective questioned him directly.

"By this means the inquiry is narrowed to a locality. Eh, Mr. Bruce?"

"Yes," said the barrister, turning to poke the fire.

Mr. White was sure that his acuteness was displeasing to his clever rival. He smiled complacently, and went on:

"The ticket-collector remembers her quite well, as the giving up of a Richmond ticket was unusual at this station. She passed straight out into the square, and from that point we lost sight of her."

"You do, Mr. White?" said Bruce.

"Well, sir, it is a great thing to have localized her movements at that hour, isn't it?"

"Yes, it is. To save time I may tell you that Lady Dyke returned to the station, entered the refreshment room, ordered a glass of wine, which she hardly touched, sat down, and waited some fifteen minutes. Then she quitted the room, crossed the square, asked a news-vendor where Raleigh Mansions were, and gave him sixpence for the information."

His hearers were astounded.

"Heavens, Claude, how did you learn all this?" cried the baronet.

"Thus far, it was simplicity itself. On Wednesday evening when no news could be obtained from your relatives, I started from Victoria, intending to call at every station until I found the place where she left the train. The railway clearing officer was too slow, Mr. White. Naturally, the hours being identical in the same week, the first ticket-collector I spoke to gave me the desired clue. The rest was a mere matter of steady inquiry."

"Then you are the man whom the police are now searching for?" blurted out the detective.

"From the railway official's description? Possibly. Pray, Mr. White, let me see the details of my appearance as circulated through the force. It would be interesting."

The inspector was saved from further indiscretions by Sir Charles Dyke's plaintive question:

"Why did you not tell me these things sooner, Claude?"

"What good was there in torturing you? All that I have ascertained is the A B C of our search. We are at a loss for the motive of your wife's disappearance. Victoria, Sloane Square, or Richmond—does it matter which? My belief is that she intended to go to Richmond that night. Why, otherwise, should she make to the footman and myself the same unvarying statement? Perhaps she did go there?"

"But these houses, Raleigh Mansions. What of them?"

"Ah, there we may be forwarded a stage. But there are six main entrances and no hall porters. There are twelve flats at each number, seventy-two in all, and all occupied. That means seventy-two separate inquiries into the history and attributes of a vastly larger number of persons, in order to find some possible connection with Lady Dyke and her purposely concealed visit. She may have remained in one of those flats five minutes. She may be in one of them yet. Anyhow, I have taken the necessary steps to obtain the fullest knowledge of the inhabitants of Raleigh Mansions."

"Scotland Yard appears to be an unnecessary institution, Mr. Bruce," snapped the detective.

"By no means. It is most useful to me once I have discovered a criminal. And it amuses me."

"Listen, Claude, and you, Mr. White," pleaded the baronet. "I implore you to keep me informed in future of developments in your search. The knowledge that progress is being made will sustain me. Promise, I ask you."

"I promise readily enough," answered Bruce. "I only stipulate that you prepare yourself for many disappointments. Even a highly skilled detective like Inspector White will admit that the failures are more frequent than the successes."

"True enough, sir. But I must be going, gentlemen." Mr. White was determined to work the new vein of Raleigh Mansions thoroughly before even his superiors were aware of its significance in the hunt for her lost ladyship.

When the detective went out there was silence for some time. Dyke was the first to speak.

"Have you formed any sort of theory, even a wildly speculative one?" he asked.

"No; none whatever. The utter absence of motive is the most puzzling element of the whole situation."

"Whom can my wife have known at Raleigh Mansions? What sort of places are they?"

"Quite fashionable, but not too expensive. The absence of elevators and doorkeepers cheapens them. I am sorry now that I mentioned them to White."

"Why?"

"He will disturb every one of the residents by injudicious inquiries. Each housemaid who opens a door will be to him a suspicious individual, each butcher's boy an accomplice, each tenant a principal in the abduction of your wife. If I have a theory of any sort, it is that the first reliable news will come from Richmond. There cannot be the slightest doubt that she was going there on Tuesday night."

"It will be very odd if you should prove to be right," said Sir Charles.

Again they were interrupted by the footman, this time the bearer of a telegram, which he handed to his master.

The latter opened it and read:

"What is the matter? Are you ill? I certainly am angry.—DICK."

He frowned with real annoyance, crumpling up the message and throwing it in the fire.

"People bothering one at such a time," he growled.

Soon afterwards Bruce left him.

True to the barrister's prophecy, Inspector White made life miserable to the denizens of Raleigh Mansions. He visited them at all hours, and, in some instances, several times. Although, in accordance with his instructions, he never mentioned Lady Dyke's name, he so pestered the occupants with questions concerning a lady of her general appearance that half-a-dozen residents wrote complaining letters to the company which owned the mansions, and the secretary lodged a protest at Scotland Yard.

Respectable citizens object to detectives prowling about, particularly when they insinuate questions concerning indefinite ladies in tailor-made dresses and fur toques.

At the end of a week Mr. White was nonplussed, and even Claude Bruce confessed that his more carefully conducted inquiries had yielded no result.

Towards the end of the month a sensational turn was given to events. The body of a woman, terribly disfigured from long immersion in the water and other causes, was found in the Thames at Putney.

It had been discovered under peculiar circumstances. A drain pipe emptying into the river beneath the surface was moved by reason of some sanitary alterations, and the workmen intrusted with the task were horrified at finding a corpse tightly wedged beneath it.

Official examination revealed that although the body had been in the water fully three weeks, the cause of death was not drowning. The woman had been murdered beyond a shadow of a doubt. A sharp iron spike was driven into her brain with such force that a portion of it had broken off, and remained imbedded in the skull.

If this were not sufficient, there were other convincing proofs of foul play.

Although her skirt and coat were of poor quality, her linen was of a class that could only be worn by some one who paid as much for a single undergarment as most women do for a good costume; but there were no laundry marks, such as usual, upon it.

On the feet were a pair of strong walking boots, bearing the stamped address of a fashionable boot-maker in the West End. Among a list of customers to whom the tradesman supplied footgear of this size and character appeared the name of Lady Dyke.

Not very convincing testimony, but sufficient to bring Sir Charles to the Putney mortuary in the endeavor to identify the remains as those of his missing wife.

In this he utterly failed.

Not only was this poor misshapen lump of distorted humanity wholly unlike Lady Alice, but the color of her hair was different.

Her ladyship's maid called to identify the linen—even the police admitted the outer clothes were not Lady Dyke's—was so upset at the repulsive nature of her task that she went into hysterics, protesting loudly that it could not be her mistress she was looking at.

Bruce differed from both of them. He quietly urged Sir Charles to consider the fact that a great many ladies give a helping hand to Nature in the matter of hair tints. The chemical action of water would—

The baronet nearly lost his temper.

"Really, Bruce, you carry your theories too far," he cried. "My wife had none of these vanities. I am sure this is not she. The mere thought that such a thing could be possible makes me ill. Let us get away, quick."

So a coroner's jury found an open verdict, and the poor unknown was buried in a pauper's grave.

The newspapers dismissed the incident with a couple of paragraphs, though the iron spike planted in the skull afforded good material for a telling headline, and within a couple of days the affair was forgotten.

But Claude Bruce, barrister and amateur detective, was quite sure in his own mind that the nameless woman was Alice, Lady Dyke.

He was so certain—though identification of the body was impossible—that he bitterly resented the scant attention given the matter by the authorities, and he swore solemnly that he would not rest until he had discovered her destroyer and brought the wretch to the bar of justice.

CHAPTER III

THE LADY'S MAID

The first difficulty experienced by the barrister in his self-imposed task was the element of mystery purposely contributed by Lady Dyke herself. To a man of his quick perception, sharpened and clarified by his legal training, it was easy to arrive at the positive facts underlying the trivial incidents of his meeting with the missing lady at Victoria Station.

Briefly stated, his summary was this: Lady Dyke intended to go to Richmond at a later hour than that at which his unexpected presence had caused her to set out. She had resolved upon a secret visit to some one who lived in Raleigh Mansions, Sloane Square—some person whom she knew so slightly as to be unacquainted with the exact address, and, as the result of this visit, she desired subsequently to see her sister at Richmond.

Sir Charles Dyke was apparently in no way concerned with her movements, nor had she thought fit to consult him, beyond the mere politeness of announcing her probable absence from home at the dinner hour.

To one of Bruce's analytical powers the problem would be more simple were it, in a popular sense, more complex. In these days, it is a strange thing for a woman of assured position in society to be suddenly spirited out of the world without leaving trace or sign. He approached his inquiry with less certainty, owing to Lady Dyke's own negative admissions, than if she had been swallowed up by an earthquake, and he were asked to determine her fate by inference and deduction.

It must be remembered that he was sure she was dead—murdered, and that her body had been lodged by human agents beneath an old drain-pipe at Putney.

What possible motive could any one have in so foully killing a beautiful, high-minded, and charming woman, whose whole life was known to her associates, whom the breath of scandal had never touched?

The key of the mystery might be found at Raleigh Mansions, but Bruce decided that this branch of his quest could wait until other transient features were cleared up.

He practically opened the campaign of investigation at Putney. Mild weather had permitted the workmen to conclude their operations the day before the barrister reached the spot where the body had been found—that is to say, some forty-eight hours after he had resolved neither to pause nor deviate in his search until the truth was laid bare.

A large house, untenanted, occupied the bank, a house with solid front facing the road, and a lawn running from the drawing-room windows to the river. Down the right side of the grounds the boundary was sharply marked by a narrow lane, probably a disused ferry road, and access to this thoroughfare was obtained from the lawn by a garden gate.

A newly marked seam in the roadway showed the line of the drainage work, and Bruce did not glance at the point where the pipe entered the Thames, as the structural features here were recent.

He went to the office of the contractor who had carried out the alterations. An elderly foreman readily answered his questions.

"Yes, sir. I was in charge of the men who were on the job. It was an easy business. Just an outlet for rain from the road. An old-fashioned affair; been there thirty or forty years, I should think; all the pipes were crumbling away."

"Why were the repairs effected at this moment?"

"Well, sir, the house was empty quite a while. You see it used to be a school, a place where young gents were prepared for the army. It was closed about a year ago, and it isn't everybody as wants so many bedrooms. I do hear as how the new tenant has sixteen children."

"The incoming people have not yet arrived?"

"No, sir."

"Can you tell me the name of the schoolmaster?"

"Oh, yes. When I was younger I have done a lot of carpenter's work for him. He was the Reverend Septimus Childe."

Bruce made a note of the name, and next sought the local police-inspector.

"No, nothing fresh," said the latter, in reply to a query concerning the woman "found drowned."

"I suppose these things are soon lost sight of?" said Bruce casually.

"Sometimes they are, and sometimes they aren't. It's wonderful occasionally how a matter gets cleared up after years. Of course we keep all the records of a case, so that the affair can be looked into if anything turns up."

"Ah, that brings me to the most important object of my visit. A small piece of iron was found imbedded in the woman's skull."

The inspector smiled as he admitted the fact.

"May I see it? I want either the loan of it for a brief period, or an exact model."

Again the policeman grinned.

"I don't mind telling you that you are too late, sir."

"Too late! How too late?"

"It's been gone to Scotland Yard for the best part of a week."

So others besides the barrister thought that the Putney incident required more attention than had been bestowed upon it.

Bruce concluded his round by a visit to the surgeon who gave evidence at the inquest.

The doctor had no manner of doubt that the woman had been murdered before being placed in the water, the state of the lungs being proof positive on that point.

"It was equally indisputable that she was put to death by malice aforethought?"

"Oh, yes. A small iron spike was absolutely wedged into the brain through the hardest part of the skull."

"What was the nature of the injuries that caused death?"

"This piece of iron penetrated the occipital bone at the lowest part, and injured the cerebellum, damaging all the great nerve centres at the base of the brain."

"Would death ensue instantly?"

"Yes. Such a blow would have the effect of a high voltage electric current. Complete paralysis of the nerve centres means death."

"Then I take it that great force must have been used?"

"Not so much, perhaps, as the nature of the wound seems to imply; but considerable—sufficient, at any rate, to break the piece of iron."

"It was broken, you say? Was it cast-iron?"

"Yes, of good quality. Off some ornament or design, I should imagine. But it snapped off inside the head at the moment of the occurrence."

"Curious, is it not, for a person to be killed in such a manner by such an instrument?"

"I have never before met such a case. Were it not for the way in which the body was jammed beneath a hidden drain-pipe, and the effective means taken to destroy the identity, I should have inclined to the belief that some strange accident had happened. At any rate, the murderer must have committed the crime on the spur of the moment, and seized upon the first weapon to hand."

"You say she was forcibly placed where found?"

"Yes; the workmen's description left no other idea."

"Could not the tide have done this?"

"Hardly. One cannot be quite emphatic, as such odd things do happen. But it seems to be almost impossible for the tide at Putney to pack a body beneath a jutting drain-pipe in such a manner that the waist, or narrowest part, should be beneath the pipe and the body remain securely held."

"Yet it is not so marvellous as the coincidence that this particular drain should need repairs at the precise period when this tragedy happened."

"Quite so. It is exceedingly strange. Are you interested in the case? Have you reason to believe that this poor woman—?"

"I hardly know," broke in the barrister. "I have no data to go upon, but I feel convinced that I shall ultimately establish her identity. You, doctor, can help me much by telling me your surmises in addition to the known facts."

The medico looked thoughtfully through the window before he exclaimed: "I am certain that the woman found in the Thames came from the upper walks of life. Notwithstanding the disfiguring effects of the water and rough usage, any medical man can rapidly appreciate the caste of his subject. She was, I should say, a woman of wealth and refinement, one who led an orderly, well-regulated life, whose surroundings were normal and healthy."

Bruce thanked his informant and hurried back to London. A telegram to Inspector White preceded him. He had not long reached his Victoria-street chambers when the detective was announced. He soon made known his wishes. "I want you to give me that small piece of iron found in the head of the woman at Putney," he said. "If necessary, I will return it in twenty-four hours."

Mr. White's face showed some little sign of annoyance. "It is against the rules," he began; but Bruce curtly interrupted him.

"Very well, I will make direct application to the Commissioner."

"I was going to say, Mr. Bruce, that although not strictly in accordance with orders, I will make an exception in your case." And the detective slowly produced the *piece de conviction* from a large pocket-book.

In sober fact, the police officer was somewhat jealous of the clever lawyer, who saw so quickly through complexities that puzzled his slower brain. He was in nowise anxious to help the barrister in his inquiries, though keenly wishful to benefit by his discoveries, and follow out his theories when they were defined with sufficient clearness.

Bruce did not at first take the proffered article.

"Let me understand, Mr. White," he said. "Do you object to my presence in this inquiry? Are you going to hinder me or help me? It will save much future misunderstanding if we have this point settled now."

The detective flushed at this direct inquiry. "I will be candid with you, Mr. Bruce. It is true I have been vexed at times when you have overreached me; but I regret it immediately. It is foolish of me to try and solve problems by your methods. Kindly forget my momentary disinclination to hand over the only genuine link in the case."

"In what case?"

"In the case of Lady Dyke's disappearance."

"Ah! Then you think it is in some way connected with the woman found at Putney?"

"I am sure of it. The woman at Putney, whether Lady Dyke herself or not I cannot tell, wore some of her ladyship's clothes. When we have ascertained the means and the manner of the death of the woman buried at Putney we shall not be far from learning what has become of Lady Dyke."

"How have you identified the clothes?"

"I managed to gain the confidence of the lady's maid, who gave evidence at the inquest. She, of course, is quite positive that the body was not that of her mistress, but when I had examined some of Lady Dyke's linen I no longer doubted the fact."

"If you knew all this, how comes it that more did not transpire at the coroner's inquiry?"

"In such affairs an inquest is rather a hindrance to the police. It is better to lull the guilty person or persons into the belief that the crime has passed into oblivion. They know as well as we do that Lady Dyke is buried at Putney. We have failed to establish her identity by the evidence of the husband and servants. The linen and clothes, our sole effective testimony, remain in our possession; so, taking everything into consideration, I prefer that matters should remain as they are for the present."

"Really, Mr. White, I congratulate you. You will perhaps pardon me for saying that some of your colleagues do not usually take so sensible a view."

The policeman smiled at the compliment. "I am learning your method, Mr. Bruce," he said.

As he spoke, Smith entered with a note endorsed "Urgent."

It was in the handwriting of Sir Charles Dyke, and even the imperturbable barrister could not resist an exclamation of amazement when he read:

"MY DEAR BRUCE,—My wife's maid has vanished. She has not been near the house for three days. The thing came to my ears owing to gossip amongst the servants. There is something maddening about these occurrences. I really cannot stand any more. Do come to see me, there's a good fellow."

"Well, I'm jiggered!" said the detective. "The blessed girl must have been spirited away a few hours after I saw her. Maybe, Mr. Bruce, we are all wrong. Has she gone to join her mistress?"

"Possibly—in the next world."

Nothing would shake the barrister's belief that Alice, Lady Dyke, was dead.

CHAPTER IV

NO. 61 RALEIGH MANSIONS

Really, the maid deserved to have her ears pulled.

People in her walk in life should not ape their betters. Lady Dyke, owing to her position, was entitled to some degree of oddity or mystery in her behavior. But for a lady's maid to so upset the entire household at Wensley House, Portman Square, was intolerable.

Sir Charles became, if possible, more miserable; the butler fumed; the housekeeper said that the girl was always a forward minx, and the footman winked at Buttons, as much as to say that he knew a good deal if he liked to talk.

The police were as greatly baffled by this latter incident as by its predecessor. The movements of the maid were quite unknown. No one could tell definitely when she left the house. Her fellow-servants described the dress she probably wore, as all her other belongings were in her bedroom; but beyond the fact that her name was Jane Harding, and that she had not returned to her home in Lincolnshire, the police could find no further clue.

So, in brief, Jane Harding quickly joined Lady Dyke in the limbo of forgetfulness.

Bruce, however, forgot nothing. Indeed, he rejoiced at this new development.

"The greater the apparent mystery," he communed, "the less it is in reality. We now have two tracks to follow. They are both hidden, it is true, but when we find one, it will probably intersect the other."

The new year was a few days old when Bruce made his first step through the bewildering maze which seemed to bar progress on every side. He received a report from the man, a pensioned police-officer, who had conducted a painstaking search into the history and occupation of every inhabitant of Raleigh Mansions.

Two items the barrister fastened on to at once.

"At No. 12, top floor right, entrance by first door on Sloane Square side, is a small flat occupied by a man named Sydney H. Corbett. He passes as an American, but is probably an Englishman who has resided in the United States. He does not mix with other Americans in London, and is of irregular habits. He frequents race meetings and sporting clubs, is reported to belong to a Piccadilly club where high play is the rule, and has no definite occupation. He occasionally visits a lady who lives at No. 61, same mansions, ground floor, and sixth door. They have been heard to quarrel seriously, and the dispute appears always to have concerned money. Corbett went to Monte Carlo early in December. His address there is 'Hotel du Cercle,' and the local post-office has a supply of stamped and addressed envelopes in which to forward his correspondence.

"At No. 61, as already described, resides Mrs. Gwendoline Hillmer. She lives in good style, rents a brougham and a victoria, and is either a wealthy widow or maintained by some one of means. She dresses well, and goes out a good deal to theatres, but otherwise leads a rather lonely life. Her most frequent visitor is, or was, a gentleman who looked like an officer in the Guards, and, much less often, the aforesaid Sydney H. Corbett. Her servants, except the maid, live out. The maid, who is a sort of companion, is talkative, but does not know much, or, if she does, will not speak."

Bruce weighed these statements very carefully. They did not contain any positive facts that promised well for the elucidation of Lady Dyke's visit to the mansions on that fateful November evening, but the absolute colorlessness of the reports concerning the other occupants rendered them quite impossible of individual distinction.

After an hour of puzzled thought the barrister finally decided upon a course of action. He would see Mrs. Gwendoline Hillmer, and trust to luck in the way of discoveries.

A quiet smile lit up his handsome, regular features as he proceeded to array himself in the most fashionable clothes he possessed, paying the utmost attention to every detail in a manner that amazed his valet.

When at last that worthy was despatched to the nearest florist's for a *boutonniere*, he communicated his bewilderment to the hall-porter.

"My guv'nor's going out on the mash," he said confidentially. "I thought he would never look at a woman; but, bless you, Jim, we're all alike. When the day comes we all rush after a petticoat."

It was nearly six o'clock when Bruce walked down Victoria Street. For some reason, he did not call a hansom, and it was almost with a start that he found himself purchasing a ticket to Sloane Square at the Underground Railway office. At this precise hour and place he had last seen Lady Alice on earth. The memory nerved him to his purpose.

A few minutes later he pressed the electric bell of No. 61 Raleigh Mansions. As he listened to the slight jar of the indicator within, he smiled at the apparent fatuity of his mission.

He had one card, perhaps a weak one, to play, it was true, but he hoped that circumstances might prevent this from being tabled too early in the game.

The door opened, and a youthful housemaid stood before him, the simple wonder in her eyes showing that such visitors were rare.

"Is Mrs. Hillmer at home?" he said.

"I'll see sir, if you give me your name."

"Surely you know whether or not she is at home?"

The girl stammered and blushed at this unexpected query. "Well, sir," she said, "my mistress is in, but I do not know if she can receive any one. She is dressed to go out."

"Ah! that's better. Now, take her my card, and say that while I will not detain her, my business is very important." This with a sweet smile that put the flurried maid entirely at her ease.

The girl withdrew, after hesitating for a moment to decide the important question as to whether or not she should close the door in his face.

Another smile, and she did not.

He was thus free to note the luxurious and tasteful air of the general appointments, for the entrance hall usually reveals much of the characteristics of the inmates. Here was every evidence of refinement and wealth. All the display had not been lavished on the drawing-room.

As he waited, conscious of the fact that his colloquy with the servant had been overheard, a lady crossed from one room to the other at the end of the passage. Her smart but simple dress, and the quick scrutiny she gave him, as though discovering his presence accidentally, caused him to believe—rightly, as it transpired—that this was the maid-companion described by his assistant.

Not only had she obviously made her appearance in order to look at him, but the housemaid had carried his message to a different section of the flat.

The girl returned. "My mistress will see you in a few minutes," she said. "Will you kindly step into the dining-room?"

He followed her, sat down in a position where the strong glare of the electric lamps would fall on any one who stood opposite, and waited developments.

The furniture was solid and appropriate, the carpet rich, and the pictures, engravings for the most part, excellent. This pleasant room, warmed by a cheerful fire, impressed Bruce as a place much used by the household. Books and work-baskets were scattered about, and a piano, littered with music, filled a corner. There were a few photographs of persons and places, but he had not time to examine these before the lady of the house entered.

Her appearance, for some reason inexplicable to the barrister himself, took him by surprise. She was tall, graceful, extremely good-looking, and dressed in a style of quiet elegance. Just the sort of woman one would expect to find in such a well-appointed abode, yet more refined in manner than Bruce, from his knowledge of the world, thought he would meet, judging by the hasty inferences drawn from his subordinate's report. She was self-possessed, too. With calm tone, and slightly elevated eyebrows, she said:

"You wish to see me, I understand?"

"Yes. Allow me first to apologize for the hour at which I have called."

"No apology is necessary. But I am going out. Perhaps you will be good enough not to detain me longer than is absolutely necessary."

She stood between the table and the door. Bruce, who had risen at her entrance, was at the other side of the room. Her words, no less than her attitude, showed that she desired the interview to be brief. But the barrister resolved that he would not be repelled so coolly.

Advancing, with a bow and that fascinating smile of his, he said, pulling forward a chair:

"Won't you be seated?"

The lady looked at him. She saw a man of fine physique and undoubted good breeding. She hesitated. There was no reason to be rude to him, so she sat down.

Claude drew a chair to the other side of the hearthrug, and commenced:

"I have ventured to seek this interview for the purpose of making some inquiries."

"I thought so. Are you a policeman?" The words were blurted out impetuously, a trifle complainingly, but Bruce gave no sign of the interest they had for him.

"Good gracious, no," he cried. "Why should you think that?"

"Because two detectives have been bothering me, and every other person in these mansions, about some mysterious lady who called here two months ago. They don't know where she called, nor will they state her name; as if any one could possibly know anything about it. So I naturally thought you were on the same errand."

"Confound that rascal White," growled he to himself.

But Mrs. Hillmer went on: "If that is not your business, would you mind telling me what it is?"

Now Bruce's alert brain had been actively engaged during the last few seconds. This woman was not the clever, specious adventuress he had half expected to meet. It seemed more than ever unlikely that she could have any knowledge of Lady Dyke or the causes that led to her disappearance. He was tempted to frame some excuse and take his departure. But the certainty that his missing friend had visited Raleigh Mansions, and the necessity there was for exploiting every line of inquiry, impelled him to adopt this last resource.

"It is not concerning a missing lady, but concerning a missing gentleman that I have come to see you."

The shot went home.

Why, for the life of him, he could not tell, but his companion was manifestly disturbed at his words.

"Oh," she said.

Then, after a little pause: "May I ask his name?"

"Certainly. He is known as Mr. Sydney H. Corbett."

She gave a slight gasp.

"Why do you put it in that way? Is not that his right name?"

"I have reason to believe it is not."

Mrs. Hillmer was so obviously distressed that Bruce inwardly reviled himself for causing her so much unnecessary suffering. In all probability, the source of her emotion had not the remotest bearing upon his quest.

Then came the pertinent query, after a glance at his card, which she still held in her hand:

"Who are you, Mr.—Mr. Claude Bruce?"

"I am a member of the Bar, of the Inner Temple. My chambers are No. 7 Paper Buildings, and my private residence is given there."

"And why are you interested in Mr. Sydney Corbett?"

"Ah, in that respect I am at this moment unable to enlighten you."

"Unable, or unwilling?"

He indulged in a quiet piece of fencing:

"Really, Mrs. Hillmer," he said, "I am not here as in any sense hostile to you. I merely want some detailed information with regard to this gentleman, information which you may be able to give me. That is all."

All this time he knew that the woman was scrutinizing him narrowly—trying to weigh him up as it were, not because she feared him, but rather to discover the true motive of his presence.

Personally, he had never faced a more difficult task than this make-believe investigation. He could have laughed at the apparent want of connection between Lady Dyke's ill-fated visit to Raleigh Mansions and this worrying of a beautiful, pleasant-mannered woman, who was surely neither a principal nor an accomplice in a ghastly crime.

"Well, I suppose I may consider myself in the hands of counsel. Tell me what it is you want to know!" Mrs. Hillmer pouted, with the air of a child about to undergo a scolding.

"Are you acquainted with Mr. Corbett's present address?" he said.

"No. I have neither seen him nor heard from him since early in November."

"Can you be more precise about the period?"

"Yes, perhaps." She arose, took from a drawer in the sideboard a packet of bills—receipted, he observed—searched through them and found the document she sought. "I purchased a few articles about that time," she explained, "and the account for them is dated November 15. I had not seen my—" She blushed, became confused, laughed a little, and went on. "I had not seen Mr. Corbett for at least a week before that date—say November 8th or 9th."

Lady Dyke disappeared on the evening of the 6th!

Bruce swallowed his astonishment at the odd coincidence of dates, for he said, with an encouraging laugh, "Out with it, Mrs. Hillmer. You were about to describe Mr. Corbett correctly when you recollected yourself."

Mrs. Hillmer, still coloring and becoming saucily cheerful, cried, "Why should I trouble myself when you, of course, know all that I can tell you, and probably more? He is my brother, and a pretty tiresome sort of relation, too."

"I am obliged for your confidence. In return, I am free to state that your brother is now in the South of France."

"As you are here, Mr. Bruce," she said, "I may as well get some advice gratis. Can people writ him in the South of France? Can they ask me to pay his debts?"

"Under ordinary circumstances they can do neither. Certainly not the latter."

"I hope not. But they sometimes come very near to it, as I know to my cost."

"Indeed! How?"

Mrs. Hillmer hesitated. Her smile was a trifle scornful, and her color rose again as she answered: "People are not averse to taking advantage of circumstances. I have had some experience of this trait in debt-collectors already. But they must be careful. You, as a legal man, must know that demands urged on account of personal reasons may come very near to levying blackmail."

"Surely, Mrs. Hillmer, you do not suspect me of being a dun. Perish the thought! You could never be in debt to me."

"Very nice of you. Don't you represent those people on Leadenhall Street, then?"

"What people?"

"Messrs. Dodge & Co."

"No; why do you ask?"

"Because my brother entered into what he called a 'deal' with them. He underwrote some shares in a South African mine, as a nominal affair, he told me, and now they want him to pay for them because the company is not supported by the public."

"No, I do not represent Dodge & Co."

"Is there something else then? Whom do you represent?"

"To be as precise as permissible, I may say that my inquiries in no sense affect financial matters."

"What then?"

"Well, there is a woman in the case."

Mrs. Hillmer was evidently both relieved and interested.

"No, you don't say," she said. "Tell me all about it. I never knew Bertie to be much taken up with the fair sex. I am all curiosity. Who is she?"

He did not take advantage of the mention of a name which in no way stood for Sydney. Besides, perhaps the initial stood for Herbert. He resolved to try another tack.

Glancing at his watch he said: "It is nearly seven o'clock. I have already detained you an unconscionable time. You were going out. Permit me to call again, and we can discuss matters at leisure."

He rose, and the lady sighed: "You were just beginning to be entertaining. I was only going to dine at a restaurant. I am quite tired of being alone."

Was it a hint? He would see. "Are you dining by yourself, then, Mrs. Hillmer?"

"I hardly know. I may bring my maid."

Claude now made up his mind. "May I venture," he said, "after such an informal introduction, to ask you to dine with me at the Prince's Restaurant, and afterwards, perhaps, to look in at the Jollity Theatre?"

The lady was unfeignedly pleased. She arranged to call for him in her brougham within twenty minutes, and Bruce hurried off to Victoria Street in a hansom to dress for this unexpected branch of the detective business.

When he told his valet to telephone to the restaurant and the theatre respectively for a reserved table and a couple of stalls, that worthy chuckled.

When his master entered a brougham in which was seated a fur-wrapped lady, the valet grinned broadly. "I knew it," he said. "The guv'nor's on the mash. Now, who would ever have thought it of him?"

CHAPTER V

AT THE JOLLITY THEATRE

By tacit consent, Claude and his fair companion dropped for the hour the rôles of inquisitor and witness.

They were both excellent talkers, they were mutually interested, and there was in their present escapade a spice of that romance not so lacking in the humdrum life of London as is generally supposed to be the case.

Bruce did not ask himself what tangible result he expected from this quaint outcome of his visit to Sloane Square. It was too soon yet. He must trust to the vagaries of chance to elucidate many things now hidden. Meanwhile a good dinner, a bright theatre, and the society of a smart, nice-looking woman, were more than tolerable substitutes for progress.

As a partial explanation of his somewhat eccentric behavior, he volunteered a lively account of a recent *cause celebre*, in which he had taken a part, but the details of which had been rigidly kept from the public. He more than hinted that Mr. Sydney Corbett had figured prominently in the affair; and Mrs. Hillmer laughed with unrestrained mirth at the unwonted appearance of her brother in the character of a Lothario.

"Tell me," said Bruce confidentially, when a couple of glasses of Moët '89 had consolidated friendly relations, "what sort of a fellow is this brother of yours?"

"Not in any sense a bad boy, but a trifle wild. He will not live an ordinary life, and at times he has been hard pressed to live at all. As a matter of fact, it is this scrape he blundered into with Messrs. Dodge & Co. that induced him to masquerade temporarily under an assumed name."

"Then what is his real name?"

"Ah, now you are pumping me again. I refuse to tell."

"But there are generally serious reasons when a man disguises himself in such fashion."

"The reason he gave me was that he dreaded being writted for liability regarding the shares I mentioned to you. It was good enough. Now you come with this story of meddling with somebody else's wife. Surely this is an additional reason. I supplied him with funds until we quarrelled, and then he went off in a huff."

"What did you quarrel about?"

"That concerns me only." Mrs. Hillmer was so emphatic that Bruce dropped the subject.

When they drove to the theatre Mrs. Hillmer, on alighting at the entrance, said to her coachman, "You may return home now, and bring Dobson to meet me at 11.15."

"May I venture to inquire who Dobson is?" said Claude.

"Certainly. Dobson is my maid."

This woman puzzled him the more he saw of her. He was now quite positive that she lived on the fringe of Society. Her status was, at the best, dubious. Yet he had never heard of her before, nor met her in public. None of his friends were known to her, and she mentioned no one beyond those popular personages who are *connu* of all the world. She was obviously wealthy and refined, with more than a spice of unconventionality. At times, too, beneath her habitual expressions of lively and vivacious interest, there was a touch of melancholy.

For an instant her face grew sad when her eyes rested on a typical family party of father, mother, and two girls who occupied seats in the row of stalls directly in front of her.

For some reason Bruce felt sorry for Mrs. Hillmer. He regretted that the exigencies of his quest forced him to make her his dupe, and he resolved that, if by any chance her scapegrace brother were concerned in Lady Dyke's death, Mrs. Hillmer should, if possible, be spared personal humiliation or disgrace.

Indeed, he had formed such a favorable opinion of her that he had made up his mind to conduct his future investigations without causing her to assist involuntarily in putting a halter around her relative's neck.

Nevertheless, it was impossible to avoid getting some further information, as the lady herself paved the way for it. Her comments betrayed such an accurate acquaintance with the technique of the stage that he said to her, "You must have acted a good deal?"

"No," she said, "not very much. But I was stage struck when young."

"But you have not appeared in public?"

"Yes, some six years ago. I worked so hard that I fell ill, and then—then I got married."

"Do you go out much to theatres, nowadays?"

"Very little. It is lonely by oneself, and there are so few plays worth seeing."

Bruce wondered why she insisted so strongly upon the isolation of her existence. In his new-found sympathy he forebore to question, and she continued:

"When I do visit a theatre I amuse myself mostly by silent criticism of the actors and actresses. Not that I could do better than many of them, or half so well, but it passes the time."

"I hope you do not regard killing time as your main occupation?"

"It is so, I fear, however hard I may strive otherwise." And again that shadow of regret darkened the fair face.

Some one in front turned round and glared at them angrily, for the famous comedian, Mr. Prospect Ricks, was singing his deservedly famous song, "It was all because I buttoned up her boots," so the conversation dropped for the moment.

Claude focussed his opera-glasses on the stage. While his eyes wandered idly over the pretty faces and shapely limbs of the coryphées his brain was busy piecing together all that he had heard. The odd coincidence of the dates of Lady Dyke's murder and the speedy departure of the self-styled Sydney Corbett for the Riviera would require a good deal of explanation by the latter gentleman.

True, it was not the barrister's habit to jump at conclusions. There might be a perfectly valid motive for the journey. If the man did not desire his whereabouts to be known, why did he leave his address at the post-office?

And, then, what possible reason could Lady Dyke have in visiting him voluntarily and secretly at his chambers in Raleigh Mansions? This virtuous and high-principled lady could have nothing in common with a careless adventurer, taking the most lenient view of his sister's description of him. And as Bruce's subtle brain strove vainly to match the queer fragments of the puzzle, his keen eyes roved over the stage in aimless activity.

Suddenly they paused. His power of vision and mental analysis were alike inadequate to the new and startling fact which had obtruded itself, unasked and unsought for, upon his sight.

Among the least prominent of the chorus girls, posturing and moving with the stiffness and visible anxiety of the novice, who is not yet accustomed to the glare of the footlights upon undraped limbs, was one in whose every gesture Bruce took an absorbing interest.

He was endowed in full measure with that prime requisite in the detection of criminals, an unusually good memory for faces, together with the artistic faculty of catching the true expression.

Hence it was that, after the whirl of a dancing chorus had for a few seconds brought this particular member of the company close to the proscenium, Bruce became quite sure of having developed at least one branch of his inquiry within measurable distance of its conclusion.

The girl on the stage was Jane Harding, Lady Dyke's maid.

When her features first flashed upon his conscious gaze he could hardly credit the discovery. But each instant of prolonged scrutiny placed the fact beyond doubt. Not even the make-up and the elaborate wig could conceal the contour of her pretty if insipid face, and a slight trick she had of drooping the left eyelid when thinking confirmed him in his belief.

So astounded was he at this sequel to his visit to the theatre, that he utilized every opportunity of a full stage to examine still further the appearance and style of this strange apparition.

When the curtain fell and Jane Harding had vanished, he was brought back to actuality by Mrs. Hillmer's voice.

"Fie, Mr. Bruce. You are taking altogether too much notice of one of the fair ladies in front. Which one is it? The tall standard bearer or the little girl who pirouettes so gracefully?"

"Neither, I assure you. I was taken up by wondering how a young woman manages to secure employment in a theatre for the first time."

"I think I can tell you. Influence goes a long way. Talent occasionally counts. Then, a well-known agent may, for a nominal fee, get an opening for a handsome, well-built girl who has taken lessons from either himself or some of his friends in dancing or singing, or both."

"Is such a thing possible for a domestic servant?"

"It all depends upon the domestic servant's circle of acquaintances. As a rule, I should say not. A theatre like this requires a higher average of intelligence."

This, and more, Bruce well knew, but he was only making conversation, while he thought intently, almost fiercely, upon the latest phase of his strange quest.

During the third act he devoted more time to Mrs. Hillmer. If that sprightly dame were a little astonished at the celerity with which he conducted her to her carriage and the waiting Dobson, it was banished by the nice way in which he thanked her for the pleasure she had conferred.

"The enjoyment has been mostly on my side," she cried, as he stood near the window of her brougham. "Come to see me again soon."

He bowed, and would have said something if an imperious policeman had not ordered the coachman to make way for the next vehicle. So Mrs. Hillmer was whisked into the traffic.

From force of habit, he glanced casually at the crowd struggling through the exit of the theatre, and he caught sight of Mr. White, who, too late, averted his round eyes and strove to shield his portly form in the portico of a neighboring restaurant.

He did not want to be bothered by the detective just then. He lit a cigarette, and Mr. White slid off quietly into the stream of traffic, finally crossing the road and jumping on to a Charing Cross 'bus.

"So," said Claude to himself, "White has been watching Raleigh Mansions, and watching me too. 'Pon my honor, I shouldn't wonder if he suspected me of the murder! I'm glad I saw him just now. For the next couple of hours I wish to be free from his interference."

Waiting a few moments to make sure that White had not detailed an aide-de-camp to continue the surveillance, he buttoned his overcoat to the chin, tilted his hat forward, and strolled round to the stage door of the Jollity Theatre.

CHAPTER VI

MISS MARIE LE MARCHANT

The uncertain rays of a weak lamp, struggling through panes dulled by dirt and black letters, cast a fitful light about the precincts of the stage-door.

Elderly women and broken-down men, slovenly and unkempt, kept furtive guard over the exit, waiting for the particular "super" to come forth who would propose the expected adjournment to a favorite public-house. Some smart broughams, a four-wheeler, and a few hansoms, formed a close line along the pavement, which was soon crowded with the hundred odd hangers-on of a theatre—scene-shifters, gasmen, limelight men, members of the orchestra, dressers, and attendants—mingling with the small stream of artistes constantly pouring out into the cold night after a casual inquiry for letters at the office of the doorkeeper.

This being a fashionable place of amusement there were not wanting several representatives of the gilded youth, some obviously ginger-bread or "unleavened" imitations, others callow specimens of the genuine article.

Bruce paid little heed to them as they impudently peered beneath each broad-leafed and high-feathered hat to discover the charmer honored by their chivalrous attentions.

Yet the presence of this brigade of light-headed cavaliers helped the barrister far more than he could have foreseen or even hoped.

At last the ex-lady's maid appeared, dressed in a showy winter costume and jaunty toque. She was on very friendly terms with two older girls, on whom the stage had set its ineffaceable seal, and the reason was soon apparent.

"Come along," she cried, her words being evidently intended to have an effect on others in the throng less favored than those whom she addressed; "let us get into a hansom and go to Scott's for supper. Here, cabby!"

She was on the step of a hansom when a tall, good-looking boy, faultlessly dressed, and with something of Sandhurst or Woolwich in his carriage, darted forward.

"Hello, Millie," he said to one of Jane Harding's companions. "How are you? A couple of fellows have come up with me for the night. Let's all go and have something to eat at the Duke's," thereby indicating a well-known club usually patronized by higher class artistes than this trio.

After a series of introductions by Christian names, among which Bruce failed to catch the word "Jane," the party went off in three hansoms, a pair in each.

Claude was not a member of the "Duke's," though he had often been there. But there was a man close at hand who was a member of everything in London that in any way pertained to things theatrical. Every one knew Billy Sadler and Billy Sadler knew every one. A brief run in a cab to a theatre, a restaurant, and another restaurant, revealed the large-hearted Billy, drinking a whisky and soda and relating to a friend, with great gusto and much gesticulation, the very latest quarrel between the stage-manager and the leading lady. He hailed Claude with enthusiasm.

"'Pon my soul, Bruce, old chap, haven't seen you for an age. Where have you bin? An' what's the little game now?"

Mr. Sadler was fully aware of the barrister's penchant for investigating mysteries. The two had often foregathered in the past.

"Are you 'busy'"? said Bruce.

"Not a bit. By-bye, Jack. See you at luncheon to-morrow at the Gorgonzola. Well, what is it?"

"I want you to come with me to the 'Duke's.' There's a young lady there I'm interested in."

Billy squeezed round in the hansom, which was now bowling across a corner of Trafalgar Square.

"You," he cried. "After a girl! Is she in the profession? Is mamma frightened about her angel? The correct figure for a breach just now, my boy, is five thou'."

"Oh, it's nothing serious. I will tell you all about it when matters have cleared a bit. It is a mere item in a really big story. But, here we are. Take me straight to the supper-room."

As they entered the comfortable, brightly lit club the strains of a band came pleasantly to their ears, and in a minute they were installed at a corner table in the splendid room devoted to the most cheery of all gatherings—a Bohemian meal when the labors of the night are past.

Bruce soon marked his quarry. Jane Harding was in great form—eating, drinking, and talking at the same time.

"Who is that, Billy?" he said, indicating the girl.

Sadler carefully balanced his *pince-nez* on his well-defined nose, gazed, and laughed: "Goodness knows. She's a new-comer, and not much at the best. Do you know where she carries a banner?"

"At the Jollity."

"Oh! then here's our man"—for a Mephistophelian gentleman was passing at the moment. "Say, Rosenheim, who's the new coryphée over there?"

Mephistopheles halted, looked at Jane and laughed, too. "Her name is Miss Marie le Marchant; but as she happened to be born in London she pronounces it Mahrie Lee Mahshuns, with the accent on the 'Mahs.' Anything else you would like to know?"

"Yes, I'm stuck on her! Where did you pick her up?"

"She's a housemaid, or something of the sort. Came into money. Wants to knock 'em on the stige. The rest is easy."

"Has she been with you long?" put in Claude, as their informant was the under-manager of the Jollity.

Mr. Rosenheim glanced at him. Sadler, he knew, had no interest in the girl, and the barrister did not quite possess the juvenile appearance that warranted such solicitude.

"She joined us just before Christmas. What's up? Is she really worth a lot of 'oof?"

"I should imagine not," laughed Bruce; and Mr. Rosenheim joined another group.

Supper ended, Marie and Millie, and eke Flossie, attended by their swains, discussed coffee and cognac in the *foyer*.

Chance separated Miss le Marchant, as she may now be known, momentarily from the others, and Bruce darted forward.

"Good-evening," he said. "I am delighted to meet you here."

The girl recognized him instantly. She would have denied her identity, but her nerve failed her before those steadfast, penetrating eyes. Moreover, it was not an ill thing for such a well-bred, well-dressed man to acknowledge her so openly.

"Good-evening, Mr. Bruce," she said, with a smile of assurance, though her voice faltered a little.

He resolved to make the situation easy.

"We have not met for such a long time," he said; "and I am simply dying to have a talk with you. I am sure your friends will pardon me if I carry you off for five minutes to a quiet corner."

With a simper, Miss le Marchant took his proffered arm, and they went off to an unoccupied table.

"Now, Jane Harding," said he, with some degree of sternness in his manner, "be good enough to explain to me why you are passing under a false name, and the reasons which led you to leave Sir Charles Dyke's house in such a particularly disagreeable way."

"Disagreeable? I only left in a hurry. Who had any right to stop me?"

"No one, in a sense, except that Sir Charles Dyke may feel inclined to prosecute you."

"For what, Mr. Bruce?"

This emancipated servant girl was not such a simpleton as she looked. It was necessary to frighten her and at the same time to force her to admit the facts with reference to her sensational flight from Wensley House.

"You must know," he said, "that Sir Charles Dyke can proceed against you in the County Court to recover wages in lieu of notice, and this would be far from pleasant for you in your new surroundings."

"Yes, I know that. But why should Sir Charles Dyke, or you, or any other gentleman, want to destroy a poor girl's prospects in that fashion?"

"Surely, you must feel that some explanation is due to us for your extraordinary behavior?"

"No, I don't feel a bit like it."

"But why did you go away?"

"To suit myself."

"Could you not have given notice? Why was it necessary to create a further scandal in addition to the disappearance of your unfortunate mistress?"

"I am sorry for that. It was thoughtless, I admit. If I had to act over again I should have done differently. But what does it matter now?"

"It matters this much—that the police must be informed of your existence, as they are searching for you, believing that you are in some way mixed up with Lady Dyke's death."

The girl started violently, and she flushed, rather with anger than alarm, Bruce thought, as he watched her narrowly.

"The police, indeed," she snorted; "what have the police to do with me? A nice thing you're saying, Mr. Bruce."

"I am merely telling you the naked truth."

"All right. Tell them. I don't care a pin for them or you. Have you anything else to say, because I wish to join my friends?"

The girl's language and attitude mystified him more than any preceding feature of this remarkable investigation. She was, of course, far better educated than he had imagined, and the difference between the hysterical witness at the coroner's inquiry and this pert, self-possessed young woman was phenomenal.

Rather than risk an open rupture, the barrister temporized. "If you are anxious to quarrel with me, by all means do so," he said; "but that was not my motive in speaking to you here to-night."

Miss le Marchant shot a suspicious glance at him. "Then what was your motive," she said.

"Chiefly to reassure my friend, your former master, concerning you; and, perhaps, to learn the cause of your very strange conduct."

"Why should Sir Charles bother his head about me?"

"As I have told you. Because of the coincidence between your departure and Lady—"

"Oh yes, I know that." Then she added testily: "I was a fool not to manage differently."

"So you refuse me an explanation?"

"No, I don't. I have no reason to do so. I came in for some money, and as I have longed all my life to be an actress I could not wait an hour, a moment, before I—before I—"

"Before you tried to gratify your impulse."

"Yes, that is what I wanted to say."

"But why not at least have written to Sir Charles, telling him of your intentions?"

The fair Marie was silent for a moment. The question confused her. "I hardly know," she replied.

"Will you write to him now?"

"I don't see why I should."

"Indeed. Not even when it was you who gave some of your mistress's underclothing to Mr. White, by which means he was able to identify the body found at Putney as that of Lady Dyke?"

"Mr. White told you that, did he?"

"He did."

"Then you had better get him to give you all further information, Mr. Bruce, as not another word will you get out of me."

She bounced up, fiery red, pluming herself for the fray.

"Will you not communicate with Sir Charles?" he said, utterly baffled by Miss le Marchant's uncompromising attitude.

"Perhaps I will and perhaps I won't. Mr. White, indeed!" And she ran off to join her friends.

The barrister drove quietly homewards. This was his summary of the evening's events: "I have found two women. When I know all about them I shall be able to lay my hand on the person who killed Lady Dyke."

CHAPTER VII

IN THE CITY

Messrs. Dodge & Co., of Leadenhall Street, possessed business premises of greater pretensions than Bruce had pictured to himself from Mrs. Hillmer's description of their transactions with her brother.

Not only were their offices commodious and well situated, but a liberal display of gold lettering, intermingled with official brass plates marking the registering offices of many companies, gave evidence of some degree of importance—whether fictitious or otherwise Bruce could not determine, as he scrutinized the exterior of the building on the following morning.

Moreover, workmen were even then busy in substituting the title "Dodge, Son & Co., Ltd.," for "Messrs. Dodge & Company," the suggestive nature of the latter designation having perhaps proved a stumbling-block in the way of the guileless investor.

When the barrister entered the office, a busy place, a hive of many clerks, and adorned with gigantic maps of the Rand, West Australia, Cripple Creek, and Klondike, he asked for "Mr. Dodge."

His card procured him ready admission. He was shown into an elaborately upholstered apartment of considerable size. At the farther end, seated in front of a gorgeous American desk, was a young man who ostentatiously finished a letter and then motioned the barrister to a seat.

Bruce was curious on the question of the age of the head of the firm.

"Are you Mr. Dodge, or the son?" he said, with the utmost gravity.

The other was taken back by this unexpected method of opening the conversation. It annoyed him.

"I am the representative of the firm, sir, and fully able to deal with your business, whatever it may be," he replied.

"No doubt. But it will simplify matters if I know exactly to whom I am addressing myself."

After an uneasy shuffling in his seat—he could not guess what this keen-faced, earnest-eyed lawyer might want—the representative of Messrs. Dodge, Son & Co. (Limited) explained that he was Dodge, and the name of the firm had been adopted for general purposes.

"Then there is no 'son,' I take it."

"Yes, there is, sir,"—this with a snort of anger.

"How old is he?"

"What the Dickens has that got to do with it? Will you kindly tell me what you want, sir, as my time is fully occupied?"

"Just now I want to know how old the 'son' is?"

This calm persistence irritated Mr. Dodge beyond endurance.

"Three years, confound you, and his sister is four months. Can I oblige you with any more details concerning my family affairs?"

Having purposely raised this man to boiling point by this harmless method of examination, Claude tackled the real business in hand. He was quite sure that a financial sharper in a temper was far more likely to blurt out the truth than if he were approached in a matter-of-fact manner.

"To begin with," he explained, never taking his eyes off the furious face of Mr. Dodge, "I have called to ask for information with regard to your dealings with Mr. Sydney H. Corbett, of Raleigh Mansions, Sloane Square."

"I never heard of him in my life. You have evidently come to the wrong office, Mr. Bruce."

"Are you quite sure?"

"Well, nearly so. However, I can tell you in a moment, as it is impossible for me to carry every name connected with several companies in my memory."

Mr. Dodge recovered his temper now that he saw a chance of disconcerting his caustic visitor. He touched an electric bell, and told the answering youth to send Mr. Hawkins.

"My correspondence clerk," he explained loftily when Hawkins entered. "Are we in communication with any one named Sydney H. Corbett, Mr. Hawkins?"

"No, sir."

"Have you ever heard the name?"

"No, sir."

"That will do. You may go. You see you have come to the wrong shop, Mr. Bruce."

"Yes, so I see."

The barrister kept looking at the back of Mr. Dodge's head, but made no move.

Mr. Dodge became puzzled.

"Now, Mr. Bruce," he cried, "you know the age of my son, and the extent of my information about Mr. Corbett. Is there anything else in which I may be of service?"

"Yes. You do a great deal of underwriting, mostly for the flotation of gold-mining companies?"

"Y—yes. That is a branch of our business."

"I am interested in this class of undertaking, and I was given to understand that Mr. Corbett has had some dealings with you in a similar respect for a considerable sum of money."

"The name is absolutely unknown to me."

"Of course. So I gather. I am sorry to hear it. Several clients of mine have money to invest in that way, and I naturally came to a firm whose name apparently figured largely in the transactions of Mr. Corbett."

It was good to see the manner in which Mr. Dodge metaphorically kicked himself for his previous attitude. His emotion was painful. For quite an appreciable time he could not trust his sentiments to words.

At last he struggled to express himself.

"Really, Mr. Bruce, if you had only put things differently. Don't you see, it rather upset me when you came in and began jawing about the youngsters. And then you spring Mr. Corbett's name on me—a man of whom I have no sort of knowledge. It must have been my firm of which your friends heard. There is absolutely no other Dodge in Leadenhall Street. Indeed, we are the only financial Dodges—that is—er—Messrs. Dodge, Son & Co. (Limited) are the only firm of the name dealing with financial matters—in the city."

By this time Bruce had assured himself that Mr. Dodge did not know Mr. Corbett's identity, and if Mrs. Hillmer's brother had changed his name to conceal himself from Dodge, it was likely to be successful.

"Anyhow, I am here, Mr. Dodge," he said cheerfully, "so I may as well enter into negotiations with you. Have you any good things in hand at this moment?"

"Some of the best. We are just waiting for the market to ease a bit, and we shall have at least five splendid properties to place before the public. By the way, do you smoke?"

Bruce did smoke; and Mr. Dodge produced a box of excellent cigars. Then he warmed to his work.

"Here is the prospectus of the Golden Halo Mine, capital £150,000, for which the vendors are asking £140,000 in cash, with a working capital of £10,000. The ore now in sight is estimated to produce two millions sterling, and the mine is not one-tenth developed. We are offering underwriters ten per cent in cash, and there is not the slightest risk, as the shares will stand at a high premium within a few days after the lists—"

"It sounds most promising," said Bruce; "but my principals are more interested in taking up concerns which have been already established, but in which, for want of sufficient capital, the vendors' shares have, by a process of reconstruction, come into the market. If you have anything of that kind—"

"The very thing," interrupted Dodge excitedly. "The Springbok Mine will just suit 'em. After all is said and done, Golden Halos are a bit in the air, between you and me. But the Springbok is a genuine article. It was capitalized for a quarter of a million, and the directors went to allotment on a subscription list of about £14,000. This money has been expended, but twice the amount is necessary to develop the property properly. A call was made on the shares, but no one paid up, and there is a talk of compulsory reconstruction. Believe me, money put into it now will yield two hundred per cent in dividends within twelve months."

"There is a whiff of scent on this trail," said Claude to himself. He added aloud: "That looks promising. Can you give me details?"

"By all means. Here is the original prospectus." Bruce glanced through the document, which dealt with the Springbok claims on the Rand with more candor than is usually exhibited in such compilations. Judging from the reports of several mining engineers of repute it really looked as if, this time, Mr. Dodge were speaking with some degree of accuracy.

"This reads well," said Bruce. "What proportion of share capital is falling in on the reconstruction scheme?"

"I hold fifty thousand shares myself," cried Dodge, "and though my money is locked up just now I am so convinced about this mine that I will manage to pay the call myself. Roughly speaking, there are one hundred and fifty thousand shares to be underwritten at, say, three shillings each."

"And who are the present holders?"

The barrister asked the question in the most unconcerned way imaginable, yet upon the answer depended the whole success or otherwise of this hitherto unproductive mission.

Mr. Dodge was manifestly anxious.

"I take it that we are talking with a definite view to business?" he said.

The barrister hesitated. Even in the detection of a crime a man does not care to tell a deliberate lie, and Dodge's attitude so far had been candid enough. The Springbok Mine honestly looked to be a good speculative investment, so he resolved to place the proposition before one or two friends who dealt with similar matters, and who were fully able to look after their own interests.

"Yes," he answered, "I am here for that purpose. If my principals like this thing they will go in for it."

"Then here is the vendors' list," said Mr. Dodge, taking a foolscap sheet from a drawer.

Claude perused it nonchalantly. His quick eyes took in each name and address out of half-a-dozen, and rejected all as being in no way connected with the man whose antecedents he was seeking.

Yet, where possible, he left nothing to chance.

"Have you any objection to a copy being made?" he asked.

Mr. Dodge hummed doubtfully.

"You see," went on the barrister, "it is best to be quite candid with people whom you wish to bring into risky if apparently high promising ventures. I presume these gentlemen are moneyless. If so, it is a factor in favor of your scheme. Should any of them be men of means, my principals would naturally ask why they did not themselves underwrite the shares."

Mr. Dodge was convinced. "From that point of view," he cried emphatically, "they are above suspicion. Jot them down, sir."

The barrister armed himself with the necessary documents, and they parted with mutual good wishes. It was only after reflection that Mr. Dodge saw how remarkably little he had got out of the interview. "He was a jolly smart chap," communed the company promoter. "I wonder what he was really after. And who the dickens is Mr. Sydney H. Corbett? Anyhow, the Springbok business is quite above board. How can I raise the wind for my little lot?"

If Mr. Bruce had probed more deeply Mr. Dodge's holding, he would have been saved much future perturbation. But, clever as he was, he did not know all the methods of financial juggling practised by experts on the Stock Exchange.

A hansom brought him quickly to Portman Square. In fulfilment of his promise, he was about to place Sir Charles Dyke in possession of his recent discoveries.

When the door of Wensley House opened, the butler, Thompson, who happened to be in the hall, anticipated the footman's answer to Bruce's inquiry.

"Sir Chawles left yesterday for Bournemouth, sir. 'E was that hovercome by the weather an' his trouble that 'e has gone for a few days' rest at the seaside. If you called, sir, I was to tell you 'e would be glad to see you there should you find it convenient to run down. And, sir, you'll never guess who came 'ere this morning, as bold as brass."

"Jane Harding."

"Now, 'ow upon earth can you 'it upon things that way, sir? It was 'er, 'er very self. And you ought to 'ave seen her airs. 'Thompson,' sez she, 'is Sir Chawles at 'ome?' 'No, 'e isn't,' sez I; 'but you're wanted at the polis station.' She was in a keb, and she 'ad asked a butcher's boy to pull the bell, so 'im and the cabby larfed. 'Thompson,' she said, very red in the face, 'I'll 'ave you dismissed for your impidence.' An' off she went. Did you ever 'ear anythink like it, sir?"

"No, Thompson, Miss Harding is certainly a cool hand."

Bruce walked to his chambers, and his stroll through the parks was engrossed by one subject of thought. It was not Mrs. Hillmer, nor Corbett, nor Dodge who troubled him. What puzzled him more than all else was the "impidence" of Jane Harding.

———————

CHAPTER VIII

THE HOTEL DU CERCLE

Bruce did not go to Bournemouth.

He quitted London by the next mail, and after a wearisome journey of thirty-six hours, found himself in the garden courtyard of the Hotel du Cercle at Monte Carlo.

Refreshed by a bath and an excellent *déjeuner*, he decided to go quietly to work and search the visitors' book for himself without asking any questions. The Hotel du Cercle was a popular resort, and it took him some time, largely devoted to the elucidation of hieroglyphic signatures, before he was quite satisfied that no one even remotely suggestive of the name of Sydney H. Corbett had recorded his presence in the hotel since the first week in November.

The barrister, for the first time, began to doubt Mrs. Hillmer. Twice had her statements not been verified by facts. It was with an expression of keen annoyance at his own folly in trusting so much to a favorable impression that he turned to the hotel clerk to ask if the name of Mr. Sydney H. Corbett was familiar to him.

The courteous Frenchman screwed up his forehead into a reflective frown before he answered: "But yes, monsieur. Me, I have not seen the gentleman, but he exists. There have been letters—two, three letters."

"Ah, letters! Has he received them?"

The attendant examined a green baize-covered board, decorated with diamonds of tape, in which was stuck an assortment of letters, mostly addressed to American tourists.

"They were here! They have gone! Then he has taken them!"

"Yes," cried Bruce; "but surely you know something about him?"

"Nothing. This hall is open to all the world."

"Do you tell me that any one can come here and take any letters which may be stuck in that rack?"

"Will the gentleman be pleased to consider? Many persons give their address here days and weeks before they come to arrive. Some persons, in the manner of Monte Carlo, do not wish their names to be known of everybody. We cannot distinguish. We do not allow the address of the hotel to be used improperly, if we know it; but there are no complaints."

The barrister did not argue the matter further. He only said: "Perhaps you can tell me thus far, as I am very anxious to meet Mr. Corbett. About how long is it since the last letter came for him?"

"But certainly. It came yesterday. It was re-addressed from some place in London. If possible, with the next one I will keep watch for Mr. Corbett."

So Mrs. Hillmer had not misled him. The so-called Corbett was in Monte Carlo, but had possibly disguised himself under another name. Again did Bruce consult the hotel register, this time with the aid of the vendors' list in the Springbok Mine, but without result.

There was nothing for it but to familiarize himself with Monte Carlo and its *habitués*, awaiting developments in the chase of Corbett. In January, when London alternates between fog and sleet, it is not an intolerable thing to remain in forced idleness amid the sunshine and flowers of the Riviera. There are two ways of "doing" Monte Carlo. You may live riotously, lose your substance at the Casino, and go home on a free ticket supplied by the proprietors of the gambling saloons, or you may enjoy to the utmost the keen air, magnificent scenery, fine promenades, and excellent music—the two latter provided by the same benevolent agency.

It is needless to say which of these alternatives appealed to Claude Bruce. Being a rich man, it was of no consequence to him to lose a few louis in backing the red for a five minutes' bit of excitement. Being a sensible one, he then quitted the Casino and went for a stroll in the gardens.

Fashion, backed by the doctors, has decreed that no longer shall the northern littoral of the Mediterranean be the only haven of rest for those afflicted with pulmonary complaints. Weak-chested and consumptive people are now banished to the windless and icy altitudes of Switzerland; so of recent years a walk through Nice, Mentone, or Monte Carlo itself is not such a depressing experience as it was when every second person encountered was a hopeless invalid.

A pigeon-shooting match was in progress, and, as Bruce fell in with a friend who took a prominent part in local life, the two entered the club grounds to watch the contest.

At the moment a handsome, well-set-up young Englishman was shooting off a tie with a Russian count. A very pretty girl, with a delicate and refined beauty enhanced by a pleasant expression, was taking a most unfeminine interest in the slaughter of the pigeons by the Englishman.

Her eyes spoke her thoughts. It was as if they said: "I do not want the birds to be killed, but I want a certain person to win."

Nine birds each had been grassed, and the Russian was growing impatient. The Englishman was cool, his fair backer keenly excited. The Count fired and missed his tenth. Up rose the Englishman's bird, and the girl could not restrain an impetuous "Now!"

So the Englishman missed also.

Amidst the buzz of comment which arose, Bruce said to his companion: "What's going on?"

"This is the final tie in the International. It is a big prize, and each man has backed himself heavily. The two are Albert Mensmore and Count Bischkoff. The girl has taken all the nerve out of Mensmore. Bar accident, he is a goner."

The cynic was right. In the thirteenth round the count alone scored, and smiled largely in response to his antagonist's quiet congratulations. As for the girl, it was with difficulty she restrained her tears.

"I think that we have witnessed a tragedy," said Bruce's acquaintance as they walked off; and the barrister agreed with him. He was sorry for Mensmore and his pretty supporter. Mayhap the loss of the match meant a great deal to both of them.

That night he learned by chance that Mensmore lived at the Hotel du Cercle. He met him in the billiard-room and tried to inveigle him into conversation. But the young fellow was too miserable to respond to his advances. Beyond a mere civil acknowledgement of some slight act of politeness, Bruce could not draw him out.

Next morning he saw Mensmore again. If the man looked haggard the previous evening his appearance now was positively startling, that is, to one of Bruce's powers of observation. Ninety-nine men out of a hundred would have seen that Mensmore had not slept well. Bruce was assured that, for some reason, the other's brain was dominated by some overwhelming idea, and one which might eventuate in a tragic manner were it to be allowed to go unchecked.

For some reason he took a good deal of interest in his unfortunate fellow-countryman, and determined to help him if the opportunity presented itself.

It came, with dramatic rapidity.

During dinner he noticed that Mensmore was in such a state of mental disturbance that he ate and drank with the air of one who is feverishly wasting rather than replenishing his strength.

Soon after eight o'clock, at the hour when frequenters of the Casino go there in order to secure a seat for the evening's play, Mensmore quitted the dining-room. Bruce followed him unobstrusively, and was just in time to see him enter the lift.

The barrister waited in the hall, having first secured his hat and overcoat from the bureau, where he happened to have left them.

Even while he noted the descending lift, in which he could see Mensmore, who had donned a light covert coat, the breast of which bulged somewhat on the left side, the hotel clerk came to him, triumphantly holding a letter.

"And now, monsieur," cried the clerk, "we shall see what we shall see."

The missive was addressed to the mysterious Sydney H. Corbett, and had been forwarded by the Sloane Square Post-Office.

With a clang the door of the lift swung open and Mensmore hastened out. Bruce had to decide instantly between the chance of seeing Corbett with his own eyes and pursuing the fanciful errand he had mapped out in imagination with reference to the stranger who so interested him.

"Thank you," he said to the clerk. "I am going to the Casino for an hour; you will greatly oblige me by keeping a sharp lookout for any one who claims the letter."

"Monsieur, it shall have my utmost regard."

The barrister had not erred in his surmise as to Mensmore's destination. The young man walked straight across the square and entered the grounds of the famous Casino.

Indoors, an excellent band was playing a selection from "The Geisha." The spacious *foyer* was fast filling with a fashionable throng; without, the silver radiance of the moon, lighting up gardens, rocks, buildings, and sea, might well have added the last link to the pleasant bondage that would keep any one from the gambling saloon that night; but Mensmore heeded none of these things.

He passed the barrier, closely followed by Bruce, crossed the *foyer*, and disappeared through the baize doors that guard the magnificent room in which roulette is played.

Round several of the tables a fairly considerable crowd had gathered already. The more, the merrier, is the rule of the Casino. There is something curiously fascinating for the gambler in the presence of others. It would seem to be an almost ridiculous thing for a man to stalk solemnly up to a deserted board and stake his money on the chances of the game merely for the edification of the officials in charge.

Bruce entered the room soon after Mensmore, and saw the latter elbowing his way to a seat about to be vacated by a stout Spanish lady, who had rapidly lost the sum she allowed herself to stake each day.

She was one of those numerous players who bring to the Casino a certain amount daily, and systematically stop playing when they have either lost their money or won a previously determined maximum.

This method, in fact, when combined with a careful system, is the only one whereby even a rich individual can indulge in a costly pastime, and, at the same time, escape speedy ruin. With a fair share of luck it may be made to pay; with continuous bad fortune the loss is spread over such a period that common sense has some opportunity to rescue the victim before it is too late.

Claude took up a position from which he could note the actions of the stranger in whom he was so interested. At first, Mensmore staked nothing. He placed a small pile of gold in front of him; he seemed to listen expectantly to the *croupier's* monotonous cry—"*Vingt-sept, rouge, impair, passe,*" or "*Dixhuit, noir, pair, manque,*" and so on, while the little ivory ball whirred around the disc, and the long rakes, with unerring skill, drew in or pushed forward the sums lost or won.

The dominant expression of Mensmore's face as he sat and listened was one of disappointment. Something for which he waited did not happen. At last, with a tightening of his lips and a gathering sternness in his eyes, he placed five louis on the red, the number previously called being thirteen.

Black won.

For the next three attempts, each time with a five louis stake on the board, Mensmore backed the red, but still black won.

Next to him, an Italian, betting in notes of a thousand francs each, had quadrupled his first bet by backing the black.

Both men rose simultaneously, the Italian grinning delightedly at a smart Parisienne, who joyously nodded her congratulations, the Englishman quiet, utterly unmoved, but slightly pallid.

He passed out into the *foyer* and stopped to light a cigarette. Bruce noticed that his hand was steady, and that all the air of excitement had gone.

These were ill signs. There is no man so calm as he who has deliberately resolved to take his own life. That Mensmore was ruined, that he was hopelessly in love with a woman whom he could not marry, and that he was about to commit suicide, Bruce was as certain as though the facts had been proved by a coroner.

But this thing should not happen if he could prevent it.

The band was now playing one of Waldteufel's waltzes. Mensmore listened to the fascinating melody for a moment. He hesitated at the door of the writing-room; but he went out, puffing furiously at his cigarette. A guard looked at him as he turned to the right of the entrance, and made for the shaded terraces overlooking the sea.

"A silent Englishman," thought the man; and he caught sight of Bruce, also smoking, preoccupied, and solitary.

"Another silent Englishman. *Mon Dieu!* What miserable lives these English lead!"

And so the two vanished into the blackness of the foliage, while, within the brilliantly lighted building, the *frou-frou* of silk mingled with soft laughter and the sweet strains of music.

If it be true that extremes meet, then this was a night for a tragedy.

CHAPTER IX

BREAKING THE BANK

There were not many people in this part of the Casino gardens. A few love-making couples and a handful of others who preferred the chilly quietude of Nature to the throng of the interior promenade, made up the occupants of the winding paths that cover the seaward slope.

At last Mensmore halted. There was no one in front, and he turned to look if the terrace were clear behind him. He caught sight of Bruce, but did not recognize him, and leant against a low wall, ostensibly to gaze at the sea until the other had passed.

Claude came up to him and cried cheerily:

"Hello! Is that you, Mr. Mensmore? Isn't it a lovely night?"

Mensmore, startled at being thus unexpectedly addressed by name, wheeled about, stared at the new-comer, and said, very stiffly:

"Yes; but I felt rather seedy in the Casino, so I came here to be alone."

"Of course," answered the barrister. "You look a little out of sorts. Perhaps got a chill, eh? It is dangerous weather here, particularly on these heavenly evenings. Come back with me to the hotel, and have a stiff brandy and soda. It will brace you up."

Mensmore flushed a little at this persistence.

"I tell you," he growled, "that I only require to be left in peace, and I shall soon recover from my indisposition. I am awfully obliged to you, but—"

"But you wish me to walk on and mind my own business?"

"Not exactly that, old chap. Please don't think me rude. I am very sorry, but I *can't* talk much to-night."

"So I understand. That is why I think it is best for you to have company, even such disagreeable companionship as my own."

"Confound it, man," cried the other, now thoroughly irritated; "tell me which way you are going and I will take the other. Why on earth cannot you take a polite hint, and leave me to myself?"

"It is precisely because I am good at taking a hint that I positively refuse to leave you until you are safely landed at your hotel. Indeed, I may stick to you then for some hours."

"The devil take you! What do you mean?"

"Exactly what I say."

"If you don't quit this instant I will punch your head for you."

"Ah! You are recovering already. But before you start active exercise take your overcoat off. That revolver in the breast pocket might go off accidentally, you know. Besides, as I shall hit back, I might fetch my knuckles against it, and that would be hardly fair. Otherwise, I can do as much in the punching line as you can, any day."

This reply utterly disconcerted Mensmore.

"Look here," he said, avoiding Bruce's steadfast gaze, "what are you talking about? What has it got to do with you, anyhow?"

"Oh, a great deal. My business principally consists in looking after other people's affairs. Just now it is my definite intention to prevent you from blowing out your brains, or what passes for them."

"Then all I can say is that I wish you were in Jericho. It is your own fault if you get into trouble over this matter. Had you gone about your business I would have waited. As it is—"

It so happened that the guard, having nothing better to do, strolled along the terraces by the same path that Mensmore and Bruce had followed. The first sight that met his astonished eyes, when in the flood of moonlight he discovered their identity, was the spectacle of these two springing at each other like a pair of wild cats.

"*Parbleu*," he shouted, "the solitary ones are fighting!"

He ran forward, drawing his short sword, ready to stick the weapon into either of the combatants if the majesty of the law in his own person were not at once respected.

In reality, the affair was simple enough. Mensmore made an ineffectual attempt to draw his revolver, and Bruce pinioned him before he could get his hand up to his pocket. Both men were equally matched, and it was difficult to say how the struggle might have ended had not the sword-brandishing guard appeared on the scene.

Claude, even in this excited situation, kept his senses. Mensmore, blind with rage and the madness of one who would voluntarily plunge into the Valley of the Shadow, took heed of naught save the effort to rid himself of the restraining clutch.

"Put away your sword. Seize his arms from behind. He is a suicide," shouted the barrister to the gesticulating and shrieking Frenchman.

Fortunately, Bruce was an excellent linguist. The man caught Mensmore's arms, put a knee in the small of his back, and doubled him backwards with a force that nearly dislocated his spine. In the same instant Claude secured the revolver, which he promptly pocketed.

"It is well," he said to the guard. "Here is a louis. Say nothing, but leave us."

"Monsieur understands that the honor of a French policeman—"

"I understand that if there is any report made of this affair to the authorities you will be dismissed for negligence. Had this lunatic been left to your care he would now have been lying here dead. Do you doubt me?"

The guard hesitated. "Monsieur mentioned a louis," he said, for Bruce's finger and thumb had returned the coin to his waistcoat pocket.

This transaction satisfactorily ended, Bruce accosted Mensmore, who was awkwardly twisting himself to see if his backbone were all right.

"You are not hurt, I hope?"

"It is matterless. Why could you not let me finish the business in my own way?"

"Because the world has some use for a man like you. Because you are a moral coward, and require support from a stronger nature. Because I did not want to think of that girl crying her eyes out to-morrow when she read of your death, or heard of it, as she assuredly would have done."

Mensmore, though still furious at his fellow-countryman's interference, was visibly amazed at this final reference.

"What do you know about her?" he cried.

"Nothing, save what my eyes tell me."

"They seem to tell you a remarkable lot about my affairs."

"Possibly. Meanwhile I want you to give me your word of honor that you will not make any further attempt on your life during the next seven days."

"The word of honor of a disgraced man! Will you accept it?"

"Most certainly."

"You are a queer chap, and no mistake. Very well, I give it. At the same time, I cannot help dying of starvation. I lost my last cent to-night at roulette. I am hopelessly involved in debts which I cannot pay. I have no prospects and no friends. You are not doing me a kindness, my dear fellow, in keeping me alive, even for seven days."

"You might have obtained your fare to London from the authorities of the Casino?"

"Hardly. I lost very little at roulette. I am not such a fool. My losses are nearly all in bets over the pigeon-shooting match which I ought to have won. I was backing myself at a game where I was apparently sure to succeed."

"Until you were beaten by a woman's voice."

"Yes, wizard. I am too dazed to wonder at you sufficiently. Yet I would have lost fifty times for her sake, though it was for her sake that I wanted to win."

"Come, let us smoke. Sit down, and tell me all about it."

They took the nearest seat, lighting cigarettes. The guard, watching them from the shade of a huge palm-tree, murmured:

"Holy Virgin, what madmen are these English! They move apart, unknown; they fight; they fraternize; they consume tobacco—all within five minutes."

And he lovingly felt for the louis to assure himself that he was not dreaming.

"There is not much to tell," said Mensmore, who had quite recovered his self-control, and was now trying to sum up the man who had so curiously entered his life at the moment when he had decided to do away with it. "I came here, being a poor chap living mostly on my wits, to go in for the pigeon-shooting tournaments. I won several, and was in fair funds. Then I fell in love. The girl is rich, well-connected, and all that sort of thing. She is the first good influence that has crossed my life, so I thought that perhaps my luck was now going to turn. I backed myself for all I was worth, and more, to win the championship. If it came off I should have won over £3,000. As it is, I owe £500, which must be paid on Monday. My total assets, after I settled my hotel bill and sent a cheque to a chum who took some of my bets in his own name, was £16. Now I have nothing. So you see—"

"Yes," interrupted Bruce, "it is a hard case. But death is no settlement. Nobody gets paid, and everybody is worried."

"My dear fellow, my life is in your keeping for seven days. After that, I presume, I take myself in charge again."

The barrister took thought for a while before he inquired:

"Why did you go to the Casino to-night, if you did not patronize the tables as a rule?"

The other colored somewhat and laughed sarcastically.

"Just a final bit of folly. I dreamt that my luck had turned."

"Dreamt?"

"Yes, last night. Three times did I imagine that I was playing roulette, and that after a certain number—whether thirteen or twenty-three I was uncertain—turned up, there was a run of seventeen on the red. The funny thing is that I had an impression that the number was twenty-three, but with a doubt that it might be thirteen. I remember, during a sub-conscious state in the third dream, resolving to listen and look more carefully to discover the exact number. But again things got blurred. The only clear point was that the run of seventeen on the red commenced at once."

"Well?"

"Well, I took my remaining cash, went to the Casino, became a bit impatient when neither number turned up for quite a while, and when thirteen appeared I backed the red. But four times it was the black that won."

"So I saw."

"Have you been keeping guard over me?"

"Yes, in a sort of way."

"You are a queer chap. I can't help saying that I am obliged to you. But it won't do any good. I am absolutely dead broke."

"Now listen to me. I will pay your fare back to London and give you something to live on until I return a week hence. Then you must come to see me, and I will help you into some sort of situation. But you must once and for all abandon this notion of suicide."

"What about my debts?"

"Confound your debts. Tell people to wait until you are able to pay them."

"And—and the girl?"

"If she is worth having she will give you a chance of making a living sufficient to enable you to marry her. She is of age, I suppose, and can marry any one she likes."

Mensmore puffed his cigarette in silence for fully a minute. Then he said:

"You are a very decent sort, Mr.—"

"Bruce—Claude Bruce is my name."

"Well, Mr. Bruce, you propose to hand me £10 for my railway fare, and, say, £5 for my existence, until we meet again in London, in exchange for which you purchase the rights in my life indefinitely, accidents and reasonable wear and tear excepted."

"Exactly!"

"Make it £20, with five louis down, and I accept."

"Why the stipulation?"

"I want to back my dream. The number is twenty-three. It evidently was not thirteen. I want to see that thing through. I will back the red after twenty-three turns up, and if I lose I shall be quite satisfied."

"What if I refuse?"

"Then I don't care a bit what happens during the next seven days. After that, *au revoir*, should we happen to meet across the divide. Please make up your mind quickly. That run on the red may come and go while we are sitting here."

Bruce opened his pocket-book. "Here," he said with a smile, "I will give you four hundred francs. You will reach the maximum more quickly if you are right."

Mensmore's face lit up with excitement. "By Jove, you are a brick," he said. "So you really trust me?"

"Yes."

"Then give me back my revolver."

Without a word, Bruce handed him the weapon.

Mensmore extracted the cartridges and threw them into a clump of shrubs.

"Come," he cried; "come with me to the Casino. You will see something. This is not my own luck; it is borrowed. Come, quick!"

They raced off, Bruce himself being more fired with the zest of the thing than he cared to admit. Within the Casino all the tables were now crowded, but Mensmore hurried to that at which he sat during his earlier visit.

"It was here that I played in my dream," he whispered, "soon after I came to it."

He edged through the onlookers, closely followed by Bruce. Neither cared for the scowls and injured looks cast at them by the people whom they forced out of the way.

The Italian, the winner of half an hour ago, had come back like a moth to the candle. Now he was getting his wings singed. At last, with a groan, he hastily rose, but as a final effort flung the maximum, six thousand francs, on the black.

The disc whirled and slowly slackened pace, the ball rested in one of the little squares, and the *croupier's* monotonous words came:

"*Vingt-trois, rouge, impair, et passe!*"

Out bounced the Italian, and Mensmore seized his chair, turning to Bruce with white face as he murmured:

"You hear! Twenty-three!"

The barrister nodded, and placed his hands on Mensmore's shoulders as though to steady him.

Mensmore staked his ten louis on the red. They became twenty, then forty. Another whirl and they were eighty. A fourth made them one hundred and sixty.

Mensmore was now so agitated that the table and the players swam before his eyes. But Bruce, under the stress of exciting circumstances, had the gift of remaining preternaturally cool.

At the fifth coup the sum to Mensmore's credit was £256. He would have left it all on the table had not Bruce withdrawn £16 in notes, as the maximum is £240.

When Mensmore won the sixth and seventh coups a buzz of animated interest passed around the board. People began to note the run on the red, together with the fact that a man was staking the maximum each time. Even the *croupiers* cast fleeting glances at the new-comer, when, several times in succession, the long rake pushed across the table the little pile of money and notes.

Thenceforth Mensmore sat in a state of stupor more pronounced now that he was playing and awake than when he dreamt he was playing.

Each time he mechanically staked the maximum and received back twice as much, while the eager onlookers now burst into cries of wonder that brought others running from all parts of the room.

But Bruce did not lose count.

When the red had turned up seventeen times, and the amount to Mensmore's credit was £3,128, he shook the latter violently as he was about to shove forward another maximum, and, of his own volition, placed the money on the black.

"*Douze, noir, pair et manque*," sang out the *croupier*, and Bruce hissed into Mensmore's ear:

"Get up at once."

His strangely made acquaintance obeyed, gathered up his gold and notes, fastened them securely in an inner pocket, and the pair quitted the Casino amid extravagant protestations of good-will and friendship from all the voluble foreigners present, having attracted not a little attention from the less demonstrative Americans and English in the room.

It was some time before the roulette tables began their orderly round again, for Mensmore's sensational performance was in everybody's mouth.

The highest recorded sum is twenty-three on the black, but a run of eighteen on the red is sufficiently remarkable to keep Monte Carlo in talk for a week.

Albert Mensmore certainly could not complain that the events of the particular evening were dull. For one hour at least he lived in the fire that consumes, for he stepped back from the porch of dishonored death to find himself the possessor of a sum more than sufficient for his reasonable requirements.

The pace was rapid and almost fatal.

CHAPTER X

SOME GOOD RESOLUTIONS

Once safe in the seclusion of Claude's sitting-room Mensmore almost collapsed. The strain had been a severe one, and now he had to pay the penalty by way of reaction.

The barrister forced him to swallow a stiff brandy and soda, and then wished him to retire to rest, but the other protested with some show of animation.

"Let me talk, for goodness' sake!" he cried. "I cannot be alone. You have seen me through a lot of trouble to-night. Stick to me for another hour, there's a good fellow."

"With pleasure. Perhaps it is the best thing you can do, after all. Let us see how much you have won."

Bruce made a calculation on a sheet of paper and said: "Exclusive of the original stake of ten louis you ought to have £3,128."

Mensmore pulled out of his pocket the crumpled bundle of notes and bills. Claude's notes were among them, and he tossed them across the table with a smile.

"There's your capital. I will see if the total is all right before we go shares."

Claude nodded, and Mensmore began to jot down the items of his valuable package. He bothered with the figures for some time but could not get them right. Finally he tossed everything over to the other, saying:

"No matter how I count, I can't get this calculation straight. Seventeen coups, beginning with ten louis, work out at £3,128 all right enough. But in this lot there is £3,368, and they don't pay twice at the Casino."

The barrister thought for a moment, and then laughed heartily. "I remember now," he said; "I kept careful count of the series of seventeen, or eighteen, to be exact. On my own account, as you were too dazed to notice anything, I put a maximum on the black. Your dream turned up trumps, as the series stopped and black won. Hence the odd £240."

"Then that is yours," said the other gravely. "I will take £1,128 to square all my debts, and we go shares in the balance, a thousand each, if you think that fair. If not I will gladly hand over the lot, after paying my debts, I mean."

Mensmore's seriousness impressed the barrister more than any other incident of that dramatic evening.

"You forget," he replied, "that I told you I had money in plenty for my own needs. You must keep every farthing except my own £8, which you do not now need. No. Please do not argue. I will consent to no other course. This turn of Fortune's wheel should provide you with sufficient capital to branch out earnestly in your career, whatever it be. I will ask my interest in different manner."

"I can never repay you, in gratitude, at any rate. And there is another who will be thankful to you when she knows. Ask anything you like. Make any stipulation you please. I agree to it."

"It is a bargain. Sign this."

Bruce took a sheet of notepaper, bearing the crest of the Hotel du Cercle, dated it, and wrote:

"I promise that, for the space of twelve months, I will not make a bet of any sort, or gamble at any game of chance."

When Mensmore read the document his face fell a little. "Won't you except pigeon-shooting?" he said. "I am sure to beat that Russian next time."

"I can allow no exceptions."

"But why limit me for twelve months?"

"Because if in that time you do not gain sense enough to stop risking your happiness, even your life, upon the turn of a card or the flight of a bird, the sooner thereafter you shoot yourself the less trouble you will bring upon those connected with you."

"You are a rum chap," murmured Mensmore, "and you put matters pretty straight, too. However, here goes. You don't bar me from entering for sweepstakes."

He signed the paper, and tossed it over to Bruce, while the latter did not comment upon the limitation of his intentions imposed by Mensmore's final sentence. The man undoubtedly was a good shot, and during his residence in the Riviera he might pick up some valuable prizes.

"And now," said the barrister, "may I ask as a friend to what use you intend to put your newly found wealth?"

"Oh, that is simple enough. I have to pay £500 which I lost in bets over that beastly unlucky match. Then I have a splendid 'spec,' into which I will now be able to place about £2,000—a thing which I have good reason to believe will bring me in at least ten thou' within the year, and there is nearly a thousand pounds to go on with. And all thanks to you."

"Never mind thanking me. I am only too glad to have taken such a part in the affair. I will not forget this night as long as I live."

"Nor I. Just think of it. I might be lying in the gardens now, or in some mortuary, with half my head blown off."

"Tell me," said Bruce, between the contemplative puffs of a cigar, "what induced you to think of suicide?"

"It was a combination of circumstances," replied the other. "You must understand that I was somewhat worried about financial and family matters when I came to Monte Carlo. It was not to gamble, in a sense, that I remained here. I have loafed about the world a good deal, but I may honestly say I never made a fool of myself at cards or backing horses. At most kinds of sport I am fairly proficient, and in pigeon-shooting, which goes on here extensively, I am undoubtedly an expert. For instance, all this season I have kept myself in funds simply by means of these competitions."

His hearer nodded approvingly.

"Well, in the midst of my minor troubles, I must needs go and fall over head and ears in love—a regular bad case. She is the first woman I ever spoke two civil words to. We met at a picnic along the Corniche Road, and she sat upon me so severely that I commenced to defend myself by showing that I was not such a surly brute as I looked. By Jove, in a week we were engaged."

The barrister indulged in a judicial frown.

"No. It's none of your silly, sentimental affairs in which people part and meet months afterwards with polite inquiries after each other's health. I am not made that way; neither is Phil—Phyllis is her name, you know. This is for life. I am just bound up in her, and she would go through fire and water for me. But she is rich, the only daughter of a Midland iron-master with tons of money. Her people are awfully nice, and I think they approve of me, though they have no idea that Phil and I are engaged."

He paused to gulp down a strong decoction of brandy and soda. The difficult part of his story was coming.

"You can quite believe," he continued, "that I did not want to ask her father, Sir William Browne—he was knighted by the late Queen for his distinguished municipal services—to give his daughter to a chap who hadn't a cent. He supposes I am fairly well off, living as I do, and I can't bear acting under false pretences. I hate it like poison, though in this world a man often has to do what he doesn't like. However, this time I determined to be straight and above board. It was a very odd fact, but I just wanted £3000 to enable me to make a move which, I tell you, ought to result in a very fair sum of money, sufficient, at any rate, to render it a reasonable proposition for Phil and me to get married."

Claude was an appreciative listener. These love stories of real life are often so much more dramatic than the fictions of the novel or the stage.

"The opportunity came, to my mind, in this big tournament. I had no difficulty of getting odds in six or seven to one to far more than I was able to pay if I lost. Phil came into the scheme with me—she knows all about me, you know—and we both regarded it as a certainty. Then the collapse came. She wanted to get the money from her mother to enable me to pay up, but I would not hear of it. I pretended that I could raise the wind some other way. The fact is I was wild with myself and with my luck generally. Then there was the disgrace of failing to settle on Monday, combined with the general excitement of that dream and a fearfully disturbed night. To make a long story short, I thought the best thing to do was to try a final plunge, and if it failed, to quit. I even took steps to make Phil believe I was a bad lot, so that she might not fret too much after me."

Mensmore's voice was a little unsteady in this last sentence. The barrister tried to cheer him by a little bit of raillery:

"I hope you have not succeeded too well?" he laughed.

"Oh, it is all right now. I mean that I left her some papers which would bring things to her knowledge that, unexplained by me, would give any one a completely false impression."

The subject was evidently a painful one, so Bruce did not pursue it.

"About this speculation of yours," he said. "Are you sure it's all right, and that you will not lose your money?"

"It is as certain as any business can be. It is a matter I thoroughly understand, but I will tell you all about it. If you will pardon me a moment I will bring you the papers, as I should like to have your advice, and it is early yet. You don't want to go to bed, I suppose?"

"Not for hours."

Mensmore rose, but before he reached the door a gentle tap heralded the appearance of the hall-porter.

"There is a letter for the gentleman. Monsieur is not in his room. He is reported to be here, so I bring it."

Mensmore took the note, read it with a smile and a growing flush, and handed it to the barrister, saying: "Under the circumstances I think you ought to see this. Isn't she a brick?"

The tiny missive ran:

"*Dearest One*,—You must forgive me, but we are both so miserable about that wretched money that I told mother everything. She likes you, and though she gave me a blowing up, she has promised to give me £500 to-morrow. We can never thank her sufficiently. Do come around and see me for a minute. I will be in the verandah until eleven.

"Ever yours,
"PHYLLIS."

Claude returned the note.

"Luck! you're the luckiest fellow in the South of France!" he said. "Why, here's the mother plotting with the daughter on your behalf. Sir William hasn't the ghost of a chance. Off you go to that blessed verandah."

When Mensmore had quitted the hotel Bruce descended to the bureau to take up the threads of his neglected quest. The letter to Sydney H. Corbett was still unclaimed, and he thought he was justified in examining it. On the reverse of the envelope was the embossed stamp of an electric-lighting company, so the contents were nothing more important than a bill.

An hour later Mensmore joined him in the billiard-room, radiant and excited.

"Great news," he said. "I squared everything with Lady Browne. Told her I was only chaffing Phil about the five hundred, because she spoiled my aim by shrieking out. Sir William has chartered a steam yacht to go for a three weeks' cruise along the Gulf of Genoa and the Italian coast. They have put him up to ask me in the morning to join the party. Great Scott! what a night I'm having!"

They parted soon afterwards, and next morning Bruce was informed that his friend had gone out early, leaving word that he had been summoned to breakfast at the Grand Hotel, where Sir William Browne was staying.

During the afternoon Mensmore came to him like a whirlwind. "We're off to-day," he said. "By the way, where shall I find you in London?"

The barrister gave him his address, and Mensmore, handing him a card, said, "My permanent address is given here, the Orleans Club, St. James's. But I will look you up first. I shall be in town early in March. And you?"

"Oh, I shall be home much sooner. Good-bye, and don't let your good luck spoil you."

"No fear! Wait until you know Phyllis. She would keep any fellow all right once he got his chance, as I have done. Good-bye, and—and—God bless you!"

During the next three days Bruce devoted himself sedulously to the search for Corbett. He inquired in every possible and impossible place, but the man had utterly vanished.

Nor did he come to claim his letter at the Hotel du Cercle. It remained stuck on the baize-covered board until it was covered with dust, and the clerk of the bureau had grown weary of watching people who scrutinized the receptacle for their correspondence.

Others came and asked for Corbett—sharp-featured men with imperials and long moustaches—the interest taken in the man was great, but unrequited. He never appeared.

At last the season ended, the hotel was closed, and the mysterious letter was shot into the dustbin.

CHAPTER XI

THEORIES

Bruce announced his departure from Monte Carlo by a telegram to his valet.

Nevertheless, he did not expect to find that useful adjunct to his small household—Smith and his wife comprised the barrister's *ménage*—standing on the platform at Charing Cross when the mail train from the Continent steamed into the station.

Smith, who had his doubts about this sudden trip to the Riviera, was relieved when he saw his master was alone. "Sir Charles Dyke called this afternoon, sir," he explained. "I told Sir Charles about your wire, sir, and he is very anxious that you should dine with him to-night. You can dress at Portman Square, and if I come with you—"

"Yes; I understand. Bundle everything into a four-wheeler."

"Sir Charles thought you might come, sir, so he sent his carriage."

London looked dull but familiar as they rolled across Leicester Square and up Regent Street. Your true Cockney knows that he is out of his latitude when the sky is blue overhead. Let him hear the tinkle of the hansoms' bells through a dim, fog-laden atmosphere, and he knows where he is. There is but one London, and Cockneydom is the order of Melchisedek. Claude's heart was glad within him to be home again, even though the band was just gathering in the Casino gardens, and the lights of Monaco were beginning to gleam over the moon-lit expanse of the Mediterranean.

At Wensley House the traveller was warmly welcomed by the baronet, who seemed to have somewhat recovered his health and spirits.

Nevertheless, Bruce was distressed to note the ineffaceable signs of the suffering Sir Charles Dyke had undergone since the disappearance of his wife. He had aged quite ten years in appearance. Deep lines of sorrowful thought had indented his brow, his face was thinner, his eyes had acquired a wistful look; his air was that of a man whose theory of life had been forcibly reversed.

At first both men fought shy of the topic uppermost in their minds, but the after-dinner cigar brought the question to Dyke's lips:

"And now, Claude, have you any further news concerning my wife's—death?"

The barrister noted the struggle before the final word came. The husband had, then, resigned all hope.

"I have none," he answered. "That is to say, I have nothing definite. I promised to tell you everything I did, so I will keep my promise, but you will, of course, differentiate between facts and theories?"

The baronet nodded an agreement.

"In the first place," said Bruce, "let me ask you whether or not you have seen Jane Harding, the missing maid?"

"Yes. It seems that she called here twice before she caught me at home. At first she was very angry about a squabble there had been between Thompson and herself. I refused to listen to it. Then she told me how you had found her at some theatre, and she volunteered an explanation of her extraordinary behavior. She said that she had unexpectedly come into a large sum of money, and that it had turned her head. She was sorry for the trouble her actions had caused, so, under the circumstances, I allowed her to take away certain clothes and other belongings she had left here."

"Did she ask for these things?"

"Yes. Made quite a point of it."

"Did you see them?"

"No."

"So you do not know whether they were of any value, or the usual collection of rubbish found in servants' boxes."

"I have not the slightest notion."

"Have they ever been thoroughly examined by any one?"

"'Pon my honor, I believe not. Now that you remind me of it I think the girl seemed rather anxious on that point. I remember my housekeeper telling me that Harding had asked her if her clothes had been ransacked by the detectives."

"And what did the housekeeper say?"

"She will tell you herself. Let us have her up."

"Don't trouble her. If I remember aright the police did not examine Jane Harding's room. They simply took your report and the statements of the other servants, while the housekeeper was responsible for the partial search made through the girl's boxes for some clue that might lead to her discovery."

"That is so."

The barrister smoked in silence for a few minutes, until Sir Charles broke out rather querulously:

"I suppose I did wrong in letting Harding take her traps?"

"No," said Bruce. "It is I who am to blame. There is something underhanded about this young woman's conduct. The story about the sudden wealth is all bunkum, in one sense. That she did receive a bequest or gift of a considerable sum cannot be doubted. That she at once decided to go on the stage is obvious. But what is the usual course for a servant to pursue in such cases? Would she not have sought first to glorify herself in the sight of her fellow-servants, and even of her employers? Would there not have been the display of a splendid departure—in a hansom—with voluble directions to the driver, for the benefit of the footman? As it was, Jane Harding acted suddenly, precipitately, under the stress of some powerful emotion. I cannot help believing that her departure from this house had some connection, however remote, with Lady Dyke's disappearance."

"Good heavens, Claude, you never told me this before."

"True, but when we last met I had not the pleasure of Miss Marie le Marchant's acquaintance. I wish to goodness I had rummaged her boxes before she carried them off."

"And I sincerely echo your wish," said Sir Charles testily. "It always seems, somehow, that I am to blame."

"You must not take that view. I really wonder, Dyke, that you have not closed up your town house and gone off to Scotland for the fag-end of the shooting season. You won't hunt, I know, but a quiet life on the moors would bring you right away from associations which must have bitter memories for you."

"I would have done so, but I cannot tear myself away while there is the slightest chance of the mystery attending my wife's fate being unravelled. I feel that I must remain here near you. You are the only man who can solve the riddle, if it ever be solved. By the way, what of Raleigh Mansions?"

The baronet obviously nerved himself to ask the question. The reason was patent. His wife's inexplicable visit to that locality was in some way connected with her fate, and the common-sense view was that some intrigue lay hidden behind the impenetrable wall of ignorance that shrouded her final movements.

Bruce hesitated for a moment. Was there any need to bring Mrs. Hillmer's name into the business? At any rate, he could fully answer Sir Charles without mentioning her at this juncture.

"The only person in Raleigh Mansions who interests me just now is one who, to use a convenient bull, is not there."

"Yes?"

"This person occupies a flat in No. 12, his name is Sydney H. Corbett, and he left his residence for the Riviera two days after your wife was lost."

"Now, who on earth can *he* be? I am as sure as a man may be of anything that no one of that name was in the remotest way connected with either my wife or myself for the last—let me see—six years, at any rate."

"Possibly. But you cannot say that Lady Dyke may not have met him previously?"

The baronet winced at the allusion as though a whip had struck him. "For heaven's sake, Claude," he cried, "do not harbor suspicions against her. I cannot bear it. I tell you my whole soul revolts at the idea. I would rather be suspected of having killed her myself than listen to a word whispered against her good name."

"I sympathize with you, but you must not jump at me in that fashion. One hypothesis is as wildly impossible as the other. I did not say that Lady Dyke went to Raleigh Mansions on account of some present or bygone transgression of her own. I would as soon think of my mother in such a connection. But a pure, good woman will often do on behalf of others what she will not do for herself. Really, Dyke, you must not be unjust to me, especially when you force me to tell you what may prove to be mere theories."

"Others? What others?"

"I cannot say. I wish I could. If I once lay hold of the reason that brought Lady Dyke to Raleigh Mansions, I will, within twenty-four hours, tell you who murdered her. Of that I am as certain as that the sun will rise to-morrow."

And the barrister poked the fire viciously to give vent to the annoyance that his friend's outburst had provoked.

"Pardon me, Bruce. Do not forget how I have suffered—what I am suffering—and try to bear with me. I never valued my wife while she lived. It is only now that I feel the extent of my loss. If my own life would only restore her to me for an instant I would cheerfully give it."

If ever man meant his words this man did. His agitation moved the kindly hearted barrister to rise and place a gentle hand on his shoulder.

"I am sorry, Dyke," he said, "that the conversation has taken this turn. These speculative guesses at potential clues distress you. If you took my advice, you would not worry about events until at least something tangible turns up."

"Perhaps it is best so," murmured the other. "In any event, it is of little consequence. I cannot live long."

"Oh, nonsense. You are good for another fifty years. Come, shake off this absurd depression. You can do no good by it. I wish now I had taken you with me to Monte Carlo. The fresh air would have braced you up while I hunted for Corbett."

"Did you find him?"

"No, but I dropped in for an adventure that would cheer the soul of any depressed author searching vainly for an idea for a short story."

"What was it?"

Claude, who possessed no mean skill as a *raconteur*, gave him the history of the Casino incident, and the thrilling *dénouement* so interested the baronet that he lit another cigar.

"Did you ascertain the names of the parties?" he said.

"Oh yes. You will respect their identity, as the sensational side of the affair had better now be buried in oblivion, though, of course, all the world knows about the way we scooped the bank. The lady is a daughter of Sir William Browne, a worthy knight from Warwickshire, and her rather rapid swain is a youngster named Mensmore."

"Mensmore!" shouted the baronet. "A youngster, you say?" and Sir Charles bounced upright in his excitement.

"Why, yes, a man of twenty-five. No more than twenty-eight, I can swear. Do you know him?"

"Albert Mensmore?"

"That's the man beyond doubt."

Dyke hastily poured out some whiskey and water and swallowed it. Then he spoke, with a faint smile: "You didn't know, Bruce," he said, "that you vividly described the attempted self-murder of a man I know intimately."

"What an extraordinary thing! Yet I never remember hearing you mention his name."

"Probably not. I have hardly seen him since my marriage. We were schoolboys together, though I was so much his senior that we did not chum together until later, when we met a good deal on the turf. Then he went off, roughing it in the States. It must be he. It is just one of his pranks. And he is going to marry, eh? Is she a nice girl?"

The baronet was thoroughly excited. He talked fast, and helped himself liberally to stimulants.

"Yes, unusually so. But I cannot help marvelling at this coincidence. It has upset you."

"Not a bit. I was interested in your yarn, and naturally I was unprepared for the startling fact that an old friend of mine filled the chief part. What a fellow you are, Claude, for always turning up at the right time. I have never been in a tight place personally, but if I were I suppose you would come along and show me the way out. Sit down again and give me all the details. I am full of curiosity."

Bruce had never before seen Sir Charles in such a hysterical mood. The anguish of the past three months had changed the careless, jovial baronet into a fretful, wayward being, who had lost control of his emotions. Undoubtedly he required some powerful tonic. The barrister resolved to see more of him in the future, and not to cease urging him until he had started on a long sea voyage, or taken up some hobby that would keep his mind from brooding upon the everlasting topic of his wife's strange death.

Dyke's fitful disposition manifested itself later. After he had listened with keen attention to all that Bruce had told him concerning Mensmore and Phyllis Browne, he suddenly swerved back to the one engrossing thought.

"What are you going to do about Corbett?" he asked.

"Find him."

"But how?"

"People are always tied to a centre by a string, and no matter how long the string may be, it contracts sooner or later. Corbett will turn up at Raleigh Mansions, and before very many weeks have passed, if I mistake not."

"And then?"

"Then he will have to answer me a few pertinent questions."

"But suppose he knows nothing whatever about the business?"

"In that case I must confess the clue is more tangled than ever."

"It would be curious if Corbett and Jane Harding were in any way associated."

"If they were, it would take much to convince me that one or both could not supply at least some important information bearing on my—on our quest. If Mr. White even knew as much as I do about them he would arrest them at sight."

"Oh, he's a thick-headed chap, is White. By the way, that reminds me. He got hold of the maid, it seems, before she had bolted, and made her give him some of my wife's clothes. By that means he established some sort of a theory about—"

"About a matter on which we differ," put in Bruce quietly. "Let us talk of something else."

The other moved restlessly in his chair, but yielded. For the remainder of the evening they discussed questions irrelevant to the course of this narrative.

It was late when they separated, but Bruce found Smith sitting up for him at home.

That faithful servitor bustled about, stirring the fire and turning up the lights. Finally he nervously addressed his master:

"Pardon me, sir, but there was a policeman here asking about you to-night, sir."

"A policeman!"

"Well, sir, a detective—Mr. White, of Scotland Yard. I knew him, sir, though he did not think it. He came about ten o'clock, and asked where you were."

"Did you tell him?"

"Well, sir," and Smith shifted from one foot to the other, "I thought it best to let him know the truth, sir."

"Good gracious, Smith, he is not going to handcuff me. You did quite right. What did he say?"

"Nothing, sir; except that he would call again. He wouldn't leave his name, but I know'd him all right."

"Thank you. Good-night. It was unnecessary that you should have remained up. But I am obliged to you all the same."

The barrister laughed as he went to his room. "Really," he said to himself, still highly amused, "White will cap all his previous feats by trying to arrest me. I suspect he has thought of it for a long time."

And Mr. White *had* thought of it.

CHAPTER XII

WHO CORBETT WAS

"Inexorable Fate!" is a favorite phrase with the makers of books; but Fate, being feminine according to the best authorities, is also somewhat fickle in disposition. Not only is she not invariably inexorable, but at times she delights to play with her poor subjects, to dazzle them with surprise, as it were, to stupefy them with the sense of their sheer inability to foresee or understand her vagaries.

It was Bruce's turn to receive the sharpest lesson in this respect that he ever remembered.

At breakfast the next morning he selected from a packet of unimportant letters one which required immediate attention. The financiers to whom he had written in conformity with his implied promise to Mr. Dodge had replied favorably with reference to the reconstruction of the Springbok Mine.

They informed Bruce confidentially that a thoroughly reliable man in Johannesburg, to whom they had cabled, reported very strongly in favor of the property. They would await his written statement before finally committing themselves. Meanwhile, if Messrs. Dodge, Son & Co. (Limited) were anxious to get the business advanced a stage, there was no reason why he (Bruce) should not assure them that, subject to the first satisfactory report being confirmed, his clients would underwrite the shares. The whole thing would thus go through in about three weeks. As for Bruce himself, they proposed to give him a commission of five per cent in fully paid shares for the introduction.

"Well, I never!" he laughed. "Now who would have thought such a thing possible? Why, if that rascal Dodge is right and this company is really a sound undertaking, my share of the deal will be £10,000. It seems wildly incredible, yet my friends know what they are writing about as a rule."

An hour later he was in the city.

A smart brougham stood in front of the now thoroughly renovated offices of Dodge, Son & Co. (Limited), and out of it, at the moment the barrister detached himself from the chaos of Leadenhall Street, stepped the head of the firm.

He was making up the steps when Claude cried:

"Hello, Mr. Dodge, how is the junior partner?"

Dodge stopped, focussed Bruce with his sharp eyes, and smiled:

"Oh, it is you, is it? The young 'un is all right, thanks. Are you coming in?"

"That was my intention."

"Come along then. I was hoping I would see you one of these days."

"Has business improved recently?" inquired Bruce, as they entered the inner office.

"Yes, somewhat; but money is very tight still. However, we generally look for a spurt early in the New Year. Why do you ask?"

"No valid reason. A mere hazard."

"Was it because you saw me drive up in a carriage?"

"Mr. Dodge, I never dreamt that self-consciousness was a failing of the members of the Stock Exchange."

"Then that *was* the cause. I guessed it. I have been making inquiries about you, Mr. Bruce, and there is no use in trying to fool you, not a bit."

"Have you another Springbok proposition on hand?"

"No; bar chaffing. You were the man who ferreted out the truth about that West Australian combination when everybody else had failed. And, now I think of it, you made me talk a lot the last time you were here. However, I am ready. Fire away! I will tell you the truth, the whole truth, and nothing but the truth, so help me—"

"Sh-s-sh! Do not perjure yourself for the sake of alliteration. Besides, it is I who have come to talk this time."

"About Springboks?"

"Yes. The people I mentioned to you at my previous visit are prepared to underwrite the shares, provided that their agent's report is as favorable in its entirety as a telegraphic summary leads them to believe."

"Eh? That's good news! When will they be in a position to complete?"

"As soon as they hear from South Africa by post. Say three weeks."

"So long! But suppose I get an offer from some other quarter in the meantime? I cannot keep the proposal open indefinitely."

"I have not asked you to do so, Mr. Dodge. Let me see—three shillings per share on, say, two hundred thousand shares is £30,000. It is a good deal of money. If any one likes to hand you a cheque for that amount without preliminary investigation, take it by all means."

The notion tickled Dodge immensely.

"All right, Mr. Bruce. When people of that sort turn up we don't sell 'em Springboks in the City. But there is no harm in you telling me your clients' names."

"Not in the least. They are the Anglo-African Finance Corporation."

Mr. Dodge whistled. "By Jove, they're the best backing I could have. This is a good turn, Mr. Bruce, and I shan't forget it. You see, we're a young firm, and association with well-known houses is good for us in every sense. I'm jolly glad now that Springboks are all right. It would never have done for me to introduce them to a risky piece of business. I am really much obliged to you. And now, how do we stand?"

"Kindly explain."

"How much 'com' do you want?"

"Nothing."

Mr. Dodge moved his chair backward several feet in sheer amazement. "Nothing, my dear sir! Nonsense! It is a big affair. Shall we say one per cent in cash, or two in shares. I am not very well off just now, or—"

"Pray don't trouble yourself. I have already secured my commission—five per cent in fully paid shares."

"But the people who put up the money don't pay for the privilege as a rule."

"That I know quite well. This case is different. I am not, nor ever have been, a financial go-between."

"Didn't you come to see me about the deal in the first instance?"

It was Bruce's turn to hesitate.

"Not exactly," he said. "I really wanted to know something about Mr. Corbett, and the Springbok business arose out of it."

"Ah, that chap Corbett. I have been thinking about him. I wonder who he can be? Anyhow, I owe him my best wishes, as the mention of his name has had such excellent results."

"Well, that is all," said Bruce rising.

"Yes, thanks. I must now see about raising the money to pay my own call. I am interested in fifty thousand shares, you know."

"Then you require some £7,500?"

"Yes. But that will be easy when I can say that the Anglo-African Finance people are with me. Besides, this morning—queer you should call immediately afterwards—I have had some wholly unexpected news."

"Indeed?" Mr. Dodge was in a talkative vein, and Bruce was in no hurry.

"The very best!" went on Dodge gleefully. "You see, there is another man in this affair with me. I thought he was as stony-broke as I am myself—speaking confidentially, you know—when he suddenly writes to me saying that he had won a pot of money at Monte Carlo and could spare me £2,000. What's the matter? Beastly trying weather, isn't it? Try a nip of brandy."

For once in his life the self-possessed barrister had blanched at a sudden revelation. But this was too much. He felt as though a meteorite had fallen on his head. Nevertheless, he grappled with the situation.

"Ill! No!" he cried. "How stupid of me. I have forgotten my morning smoke. May I light a cigar?"

"With pleasure. You know these. Try one."

"You were saying—"

"That's all. This young fellow, Mensmore his name is, got mixed up with me over a Californian mine. I thought he had lots of coin, so when Springboks came along he and I went shares in underwriting them. The public didn't feed, so we were loaded. I tried all I knew to get him to pay up, but he absolutely couldn't. And now at the very moment affairs look promising he writes offering £2,000. More than that, he says, if necessary, he can get the remainder of his half, £1750, from somebody. Where is his letter?"

Mr. Dodge looked on his table. "Oh, here it is. Addressed from 'Yacht *White Heather*,' if you please. Quite swell, eh? Sir William Browne! That's the covey. I think I will let Sir William have 'em. It's a good, solid sort of name to have on the share register."

"I would if I were you," said Bruce, hardly conscious of his surroundings.

"If *you* think so, I will. By Jove, this has been a good morning for me. Come and have lunch."

"No, thanks. I have a lot to attend to. By the way, where did Mensmore live?"

"I don't know. His address was always at the Orleans Club."

Somehow, Bruce reached the street and a hansom. As the vehicle rolled off westward he crouched in a corner and tried to wrestle with the problem that befogged his brain.

Was Albert Mensmore Sydney H. Corbett? Was he Mrs. Hillmer's brother? The "Bertie" she had spoken of meant Albert as well as a hypothetical Herbert. Mensmore was an old schoolfellow of Sir Charles Dyke's. In all probability he knew Lady Dyke as well. He lived in Raleigh Mansions under an assumed name, and quitted his abode two days after the murder.

Every circumstance pointed to the terrible assumption that at Mensmore's hands the unfortunate lady met her death. And Bruce had sworn to avenge her memory!

He laughed with savage mirth as he reflected that he himself had helped this man to escape the punishment of Providence, self-inflicted. It was, indeed, pitifully amusing to think how the clever detective had used his powers to befool himself. The very openness of the clue had helped to conceal it the more effectually. Were it not for Dodge and his Springboks he might have gone on indefinitely covering up the criminal's tracks by his own friendly actions. The situation was maddening, intolerable. Bruce wanted to seize the reins and flog the horse into a mad gallop through the traffic as a relief to his feelings.

Blissfully unconscious of the living volcano he carried within, the cabby on the perch did not indulge in any such illegal antics. He quietly drove along the Embankment and delivered his seething fare at his Victoria-street chambers.

Quite oblivious of commonplace affairs, the barrister threw a shilling to the driver and darted out.

The man gazed at his Majesty's image with the air of one who had never before seen such a coin. It might have been a Greek obolus, so utter was his blank astonishment.

But Bruce was across the pavement, and cabby had to find words, else it would be too late.

"Here guv'nor," he yelled, "what the ballyhooley do you call this?"

"What's the matter?" was the impatient query.

"Matter!" The cabman looked towards the sky to see if the heavens were falling. "Matter!" in a higher key, as a crowd began to gather. "I tykes him from Leaden'all Street to Victoria. 'E gives me a bob, an' 'e arsks me wot's the matter. I'd been on the ranks four bloomin' hours—"

"Oh, there you are!" and Bruce threw him half-a-crown before he disappeared up the steps.

Mr. White was watching for Bruce's arrival. He wondered why the barrister was so perturbed, and resolved to strike while the iron was hot. So he, too, vanished into the interior.

CHAPTER XIII

A QUESTION OF PRINCIPLE

"If any one calls, I am out," cried Claude to his factotum, as he crossed the entrance-hall of his well-appointed flat, and flung open the door of his library.

"The guv'nor's in a tantrum," observed Smith to his wife, and he settled himself to renew the perusal of Grand National training reports. He had just noticed the interesting fact that last year's winner had "jumped in for the last mile" in a gallop given to a rank outsider, when the electric bell upset his calculations.

"My master is out," he said, as he opened the door to find Mr. White standing on the mat.

He was about to close the door again, but the detective planted his foot against the jamb.

"Your master is not out," he answered. "I saw him come in a minute since. Tell him Mr. White wants to see him."

Smith's dignity was superb. "My master may be hin," he cried, "but 'e told me to say 'e was hout to callers." The aspirates supplied emphasis.

"Tell him what I say at once," and Mr. White gave him his best "accessory-after-the-crime" glance.

"I don't see why I should," snarled Smith, but the squabble ended when Bruce's voice was heard—

"Show him in, Smith, but admit nobody else."

With an air of armed neutrality Smith ushered the representative of Scotland Yard into the library.

"You're not looking very well, sir," said White, his round eyes fixed on Bruce with all their power.

"Was it to ask about my health that you came?"

"No, sir, not exactly. But I haven't seen you for quite a while, and as we are both interested in the same matter I thought I would look you up and compare notes."

Bruce was annoyed by the interruption. He wanted to think, not to be bothered by official theories. He looked hard at Mr. White, wondering whether he should tell him all he knew and wash his own hands clear of the investigation in future. But there was a second picture before his eyes. He saw Phyllis Browne's face, not as it was that day at the Tir aux Pigeons, but with the light of happiness in it, with the joyousness of requited and undisturbed love, with the glow reflected from dancing waves, and the tremulous smile of innocent pleasure.

It was hard to believe that such a woman could place her heartfelt trust in a man who was possibly a cold-blooded murderer. Such a combination was unnatural and horrible. Already Bruce was beginning to doubt the evidence of his analytical senses.

Mr. White meanwhile flattered himself by the thought that the other was trying to read his thoughts by looking at him fixedly.

"I have been away from home," said Bruce at last. "I had occasion to go to the South of France."

"I thought so. I was sure of it. How do you manage always to get ahead of us?" Mr. White was enthusiastic in his admiring divination.

"You have heard about Sydney H. Corbett?" said the barrister, still keeping that inscrutable, calculating gaze upon the policeman.

"Yes. I am on his track. We may be slow, but we are sure in Scotland Yard. May I ask what luck you have had, sir?"

"In what respect?"

"As if you didn't go to Monte Carlo to find Corbett yourself! Really, Mr. Bruce, the scent is too hot this time. You might as well give a 'View halloa' if you have seen him."

"Seen Sydney H. Corbett, you mean?"

"That is the gentleman."

For an instant Mensmore's future trembled in the balance. Bruce almost framed the words which would have led to his immediate arrest at the next port touched by the *White Heather*. But the memory of Phyllis Browne, of her agony, of the fearful scandal that must fly through Society on the Riviera, restrained him. There was no hurry. He must have time to think.

"I certainly went to Monte Carlo to discover the identity of that interesting personage, but I came back, Mr. White, as wise as I went. The only trace I found of him was an undelivered letter awaiting him at the Hotel du Cercle."

"A letter! Wasn't he there?" Mr. White's face, notwithstanding its official decorum, betrayed its disappointment. This was an unlooked-for check.

"He had been there. Other letters came for him earlier, and he had received them."

"But the hotel people—"

"Did not know him. In fact, there cannot be the slightest doubt that Mr. Corbett concealed his identity at Monte Carlo under another name."

"It doesn't matter much," growled the detective. "We will nab him all the same, if he had fifty names."

"Possibly. But it is wonderful how a man may be under your very nose, and yet you may miss him."

During the next few minutes neither man spoke. Bruce smiled cynically at the thought that he was actually shielding Lady Alice's probable slayer from the minions of the law. He marvelled at himself for his irresolution. Nevertheless, he would wait. Mensmore could not escape him now. Perhaps the business might be managed without the dramatic features which would accompany an immediate arrest. And there were some things that required explanation. If his Monte Carlo acquaintance really killed Lady Dyke, then he was the strangest criminal whom Bruce had ever encountered during the course of his varied career.

The policeman misinterpreted his expression.

"You can't laugh at us this time, Mr. Bruce," he cried. "Scotland Yard and yourself evolved the same theory, eh? And we can't fly off to the South of France as readily as you."

"Your skill is profound, no doubt. Indeed, I wonder at it, considering the mysterious way in which the missing man left his address at the post-office."

The other reddened. "That was simple enough, I know; but we were on his track before that."

"By watching me when I visited his sister."

"You saw me outside the Jollity Theatre, then?"

"Of course. What did you expect?"

Mr. White recovered his placidity. "There's no use quarrelling about it," he laughed. "I did get that wrinkle from you. But how on earth were we to know what to do, when there were seventy-one flats occupied by respectable people, and one closed for months, the caretaker told us."

"I hope you have ceased your surveillance so far as I am concerned."

"Honor bright, sir. I won't do it again. Besides, we must lay hands on Corbett sooner or later."

"What steps are you taking?"

"The Monte Carlo police are making inquiries. They have his description. It has also gone to America."

"Why America?"

"Because he spent some time there. He only returned from the States early last year. His sister has not seen him for years, and a rare old row they had when he turned up. He had not much money, so she helped him, and he settled down for a time in the same mansions as herself."

"Who told you all this?"

"Mrs. Hillmer, and a precious lot of trouble she gave me. She is a clever woman that."

"It was rather too bad to pester her about it, poor lady."

"I only followed your lead, sir."

This was so true that Claude changed the conversation.

"What sort of man is Corbett? Have you his description?"

"Yes. Here it is." Mr. White produced a copy of the *Police Gazette*, a publication never seen by the public, but of a large circulation among the police of the United Kingdom. The details were fairly accurate as to Mensmore's personal appearance, but there was no photograph. Oddly enough, Bruce was pleased on noting this serious deficiency.

"You did not secure his picture?"

"No. Mrs. Hillmer declared that she had not a single photograph of her brother in her possession."

"Did she—tell you his real name?" the barrister had almost said, but he deflected the question. "Did she give you any hint as to a possible cause for this apparently unnecessary crime?"

"Not a word."

"Then you did not mention Lady Dyke to her?"

"No. Sir Charles has always implored me to keep his wife's name out of my inquiries until it became absolutely impossible to conceal it in view of a public prosecution. He wants to know definitely when that time comes."

"Why?"

The detective did not reply for a moment. When he spoke he leaned forward and subdued his voice. "I am as sure as I am sitting here, sir, that Sir Charles will not live if any disgrace should come to be attached to his wife's memory."

"Do you mean that he will kill himself?"

"I do. He has changed a great deal since this affair happened. He is not the same man. He appears to be always mooning about her. And people say that they were not so devoted to one another when she was alive."

Again did the barrister switch off their talk from an unpleasant topic.

"This description of Corbett is not much use," he said. "It applies to every athletic young Englishman of good physique and gentlemanly appearance."

"Quite true. I don't depend on that for his arrest, but it will be valuable for identification. 'Blue eyes, light brown hair, fresh, clear complexion, well-modelled nose and chin.' Some of these things can be changed by tricks, but not all. For instance, there would be no use in smoking a man with black eyes and irregular features."

"'Smoking' him?"

"Oh, that's our way of putting it. Following him, it means."

"Suppose the French police don't succeed in catching him?"

"We will get him at Raleigh Mansions. He is sure to think that Lady Dyke's fate has never been determined, and he will return when the inquiry has blown over, to all appearance."

"You have quite made up your mind, then, that Sydney H. Corbett is the murderer?"

"It looks uncommonly like it. At any rate, he knows something about it. If not, why did he bolt to France two days after the crime? Why has he concealed his identity? Why does he take pains to receive his correspondence in the manner he has adopted? And, by Jove! suppose he isn't in Monte Carlo at all, but in London all the time!"

The inspector glowed with his sudden inspiration, but Bruce kept him to the lower level of realities.

"Corbett is, or was, in Monte Carlo. Of that you may be sure. He, and none other, got the letters sent to the Hotel du Cercle. I cannot for the life of me imagine why he did not take the last one. But let us look at what we know. Lady Dyke, we will say, went to Corbett's chambers, secretly and of her own accord. That may be taken as fairly established. Thence there is a blank in our intelligence until she appears as a hardly recognizable corpse, stuffed by hands beneath an old drain-pipe in the Thames at Putney. How do you fill up that gap, Mr. White?"

"Simply enough. Corbett, or some other person, persuaded her to voluntarily accompany him to Putney. She was killed there, and not in London. It would be almost a matter of impossibility for any man to have conveyed her lifeless body from Raleigh Mansions to Putney without attracting some notice. One man could *not* do it. Several might, but it is madness to imagine that a number of people would join together for the purpose of killing this poor lady."

"The seemingly impossible is often accomplished."

"Do you really believe, then, that she met her death in London?"

"I have quite an open mind on the question."

"You forget that she had resolved early that day to visit her sister at Richmond, and Putney is on the direct road. What more reasonable than to assume—"

"Beware of assumptions! You are assuming all the time that Corbett was a principal in her murder."

"Very well, Mr. Bruce. Then I ask you straight out if you don't agree with me?"

"I do not."

This declaration astounded the barrister himself. Often the mere utterance of one's thoughts is a surprise. Speech seems to stiffen the wavering outlines of reflection, and the new creation may differ essentially from its embryo. It was so with Bruce in this instance.

Ever since Mr. White's arrival had aroused him from the positive stupor caused by the stock-broker's unwitting revelation, Claude Bruce had been slowly but definitely deciding that Mensmore did not kill Lady Dyke. He had seen him, unprepared, facing death as preferable to dishonor. At such moments a man's soul is laid bare. With the shadow of a crime upon his conscience Mensmore's actions could not have been so genuine and straightforward as they undoubtedly were.

Mensmore, of course, might in some way be bound up with the mystery surrounding Lady Dyke's movements. His very utterance in Bruce's room at the Hotel du Cercle implied as much. That was another matter. It would receive his (Bruce's) most earnest attention. But the major hypothesis, so quickly jumped at by the police, needed much more substantiation than it had yet obtained.

That it was plausible was demonstrated by the barrister's readiness to adopt it at the outset. Even now that his impulse to fasten the crime on Mensmore had weakened he wondered at his eagerness to defend him.

The detective was even more surprised.

"I don't see how you can take that view," he cried. "Corbett's behavior is, to say the least, unaccountable. If he is an innocent man, then he must be a foolish one. Besides, why should he necessarily be innocent? This is the first gleam of light we have had in a very dark business, and I mean to follow it up."

The vindictive emphasis of his tone showed that the detective was annoyed at the other's impassive attitude. He even went so far as to dimly evolve a theory that the barrister wished to throw him off Corbett's trail on account of his sympathy for Mrs. Hillmer, but Claude rapidly dispelled this notion.

"You are here, I suppose, to ask my advice in pursuance of our understanding that we are working together in the matter, as it were?" he said.

"Well, something of the kind, sir."

"Then I recommend that we see the inside of that closed flat in Raleigh Mansions at the earliest moment."

"Do you mean by a search warrant?"

"Certainly not. Do you want the whole neighborhood to know of it? You have probably heard of locks being picked before to-day. You and I, and none other, must have a quiet look around the place without anyone being the wiser."

Mr. White hesitated, but the prospect was attractive. "I think I can manage it," he said, smiling reflectively. "Will six this evening suit?"

"Admirably."

"Then I will call for you."

After a parting glance at Smith, who returned it, nose in air, the inspector ran down the stairs, murmuring, "Blest if I can understand Mr. Bruce. But this is a good move. We may learn something."

CHAPTER XIV

NO 12 RALEIGH MANSIONS

When the door of Corbett's or Mensmore's flat swung open before the skilful application of a skeleton key, a gust of cold air swept from the interior blackness, and whirled an accumulation of dust down the stairs.

It is curious how a disused house seems to bottle up, as it were, an atmospheric accumulation which always seeks to escape at the first available moment. Emptiness is more than a mere word; it has life and the power of growth. A residence closed for a week is less depressing than if it has not been inhabited for a month. If the period of neglect be lengthened into a year, the sense of dreariness is magnified immeasurably.

In this instance, the mysterious abode might have been the abiding-place of disembodied spirits, so cold was its aspect, so uninviting the dim vista that sprung into uncertain vision under the flickering rays of a wax vesta struck by the detectives.

But neither the policeman nor his companion was a nervous subject.

They entered at once, closed the door by its latch, and, aided by other matches, found the switch of the electric light.

In this brighter radiance the indefinable vanished. The flat became a cosy, fairly well appointed bachelor's "diggings," neglected and untidy, yet not without a semblance of comfort, which only needed the presence of a sturdy housemaid and a fire to be converted into the ordinary chambers with which the locality abounds.

Their first care was to draw down all the blinds, the neglect of which housewifely proceeding argued the careless departure of a mere male when the place was vacated.

A rapid preliminary survey followed, and drew from Bruce the remark:

"Furnished by a woman, but occupied by a man."

Mr. White agreed, but he didn't know why, so he put a tentative question on the point.

"Don't you see," said Bruce, "that the carpets match the upholstery of the furniture, that the beds have valances, that the spare bedroom for a guest is even more elaborate than that used by the tenant, that care has been taken in fitting up the kitchen, and taste displayed in the selection of pieces of bric-a-brac? Only a woman attends to these things. On the other hand, a card tray has been used as a receptacle for a cigar ash, the pictures—no woman ever buys a picture—have been picked up promiscuously from shops where they sell sporting prints, and the sides of the mantelpieces are chipped by having feet propped against them. There are plenty of other signs, but these suffice."

Thenceforth the two men devoted themselves to their task, each after his kind.

The representative of Scotland Yard hunted for documents, photographs, torn envelopes; he looked at the covers of books to see if they were inscribed; he opened every drawer, ransacked every corner, peered into the interior of jars, pots, and ovens; appraised the value of furniture, noted its age, and was specially zealous in studying the appearance of the only bedroom which had been occupied so far as he could judge.

Bruce, having given a casual glance around, entered the sitting-room, selected the most comfortable chair, and proceeded to envelope himself in smoke.

He had not spent two minutes in Mensmore's flat before he made a striking discovery.

The dwelling consisted of a central passage, dividing two equal portions from the other. That on the right contained a drawing-room and a large bedroom, with dressing-room attached. On the left were another bedroom, a dining-room, a kitchen, and a store-room. At the end of the passage, which terminated in the transverse corridor, were the bathroom, a pantry, and a small room, empty now, but apparently designed for a servant's bedroom.

The furniture, as has been stated, was good in quality and sufficient for its purposes. But the fact which immediately impressed this skilled observer was that the arrangement of the sitting-room differed essentially from the other details of the flat.

The same care had not been taken in the disposition of the articles. They had been dumped down anyhow, without taste or regard for suitable position. The carpet had not been bought for this special apartment like the carpets elsewhere. A handsome ebony cabinet stood in the wrong place. The blue china ornaments obviously intended to fill its shelves were littered about the mantelpiece or on small tables, while the Satsuma ware meant for the over-mantel was stiffly disposed on the cabinet.

Small matters these, but Bruce thought them more fruitful of accurate theory than the detective's hunt for a written history of the crime!

So, as he smoked, he mused and examined.

"The drawing-room was the last place to be furnished," he thought. "The usual course. It remained empty for some time probably. The rest of the flat was arranged by a woman—Mrs. Hillmer in all likelihood—before the arrival of her brother. Then he came and tackled the vacant room. The history of the place is as plain as though I were present. More than that, a woman— Mrs. Hillmer again, let us say—fixed upon these latter purchases, but without measurements. She did not personally see to their adaptability, and she certainly did not supervise their final arrangement. Now, why was that? Again, these things are more worn than those in the other rooms. Were they bought second-hand? If so, why? A woman thinks most of her drawing-room. It is the last place in which she would economize."

Mr. White entered, anxious and puzzled.

"Found anything?" inquired Claude, without looking at him.

"Not a rag, not a piece of old newspaper with a date on it. A lot of papers were burned in the kitchen grate, but from the remnants I judge that they were mostly bills."

"The place has been systematically cleared, eh?"

"It looks like it."

"Going to hunt here?"

"Yes. You don't seem to take much interest in the premises, Mr. Bruce, though you persuaded me to do a bit of house-breaking in order to get here."

"I find the quietude good for thought, Mr. White. Be good enough not to make more noise than is absolutely necessary."

The other sniffed. He was disappointed. He hoped for something tangible from this visit, and the outlook was far from promising.

"This room appears to have been lived in a good deal," he growled.

"That is one way of looking at it."

"Is there any other way?" His voice snapped out the question as if he held the barrister personally responsible for his failure to gain a clue.

"No, Mr. White, I should have guessed your point of view exactly."

"My point of view, indeed! Do you want me to draw up another chair and light a pipe? Should we be enlightened by tobacco smoke?"

"I cannot trust your tobacco. Try a cigar."

The detective angrily thumped a Chesterfield lounge to see if it betrayed aught suspicious.

At that instant Bruce's glance rested on the fireplace. The grate contained the ashes of a fire,—a fire not long lighted. This, combined with the undrawn blinds, argued a departure early in the morning.

"He went to Monte Carlo by the day Channel service," mused Bruce. "He may have departed a few hours after Lady Dyke's death, as Mrs. Hillmer was not certain as to the exact date."

Somehow the few cinders attracted him. They had, perchance, witnessed a tragedy.

Suddenly he stopped smoking. He was so startled by something he had seen that the policeman must have noticed his agitation were not the detective at that instant intently screwing his eyes to peer behind the back of the elaborate cabinet.

On the hearth was a handsome Venetian fender. Into each end was loosely socketed a beautifully moulded piece of ironwork to hold the fire-irons. That on the left was whole, but from that on the right a small spike had been broken off.

By comparison with its fellow the missing portion was identical with the bit of iron found imbedded in the skull of the murdered woman. Of this damning fact Bruce had no manner of doubt, though the incriminatory article itself was then locked in a drawer in his own residence.

He did not move. He sat as one transfixed.

What a weapon for such a deed! Was ever more outlandish instrument used with murderous intent? The entire bracket could easily be detached from the fender, and would, no doubt, inflict a terrible blow. But why seize this clumsy device when it actually supported a heavy brass poker?

The thing savored of madness, of the wild vagary of a homicidal maniac. It was incomprehensible, strange beyond belief.

Yet as Bruce pictured the final scene in that tragedy, as he saw the ill-fated lady stagger helplessly to the ground before a treacherous and crushing stroke, a fierce light leaped into his face, and his lips set tight with unflinching purpose.

Had Mensmore been within reach at that moment he would assuredly have been lodged in a felon's cell forthwith. No excuse, no palliation, would be accepted. The man who could so foully slay a gentle, kindly, high-minded woman deserved the utmost rigor of the law, no matter what the circumstances that led to the commission of the crime.

It was not often that Bruce allowed impulse to master reason so utterly.

In strange altruistic mood he asked himself why he did not spring from his chair, and, tearing the bracket from its supports, exhibit it to his fellow-worker, while he gave, in a few passionate sentences, the information that would set the French police to scour the Mediterranean littoral until they found the *White Heather*. Of what matter to him was the suffering of a sister or sweetheart? Did the man who killed Lady Dyke reck of these things? Yes, he would do it—

But a cry of triumph from the detective arrested the fateful words even as they trembled on his lips. "Here's a find!" was the shout. "Thinking is all very well, Mr. Bruce, but hard work is better. What do you make of that?"

"That" was a letter, which, in the manner known to many a puzzled householder, had slipped down behind a drawer in the cabinet, to be crushed against the wardrobe at the back, and lie there forgotten and unnoticed.

Even in his perturbed state the barrister could not help glancing at the crumpled document, first noting the date, October 15th of the year just closed, with the superscription, "Mountain Butts, Wyoming." There was no envelope.

It was addressed to "Dear Bertie," and ran as follows:

"Your welcome note and its draft for fifty dollars came to hand last week. My sisters and I can never forget your generosity. We know you are hard up, and that you can ill spare these frequent gifts, or loans, as you are pleased to call them. You and I have been in many a tight place, old chap, and I never knew you to fail either with hand or heart. And when we drifted into this ranch, on my advice, and nearly starved to death, it was you who were bold enough to cut yourself adrift so that you might make something to keep the pot boiling.

"But the tide is turning. You know my failing; this time I will try not to be too sanguine. There have been big gold discoveries in this country. It is now firmly believed that all our land is auriferous, and the scoundrel who sold us this beggarly ranch has tried to upset our title. Thanks to your foresight, he was knocked out at the first round. So I may soon have big news for you. By Jove, won't it be a change if we both become rich! And won't we all have a time in Paris! However, I must not promise too much. I have been taught caution by repeated failures. Write by return, and say if this reaches you all right.

"Your faithful friend,
"SYDNEY H. CORBETT."

"What do you think of that?" cried the detective, when Bruce had slowly mastered the contents of the letter.

"Think! I am too dazed to think."

"We can now learn all about him from America."

"About whom?"

"About Corbett, of course."

"Then did Corbett travel by the same mail as this letter in order to murder Lady Dyke? It is dated October 15th, and she was killed November 6th. It takes twelve days, at the quickest, for a letter to come here from Wyoming. And Corbett, the writer of it, not the receiver, must have travelled in the same steamer, or its immediate successor."

Mr. White's face fell, but he stuck to his point:

"Anyhow, Corbett was here about that time. I have seen the secretary to the company that owns these flats. Corbett took the rooms for six months from September first. When asked for references he gave his sister's name, and as she banks with the National—and she has always paid her rent for five years—it was good enough. Still, I must confess that Corbett could hardly be in Wyoming in October if he lived here in September and in November."

The barrister answered between his set teeth: "Yes, it is rather puzzling."

"Perhaps the letter was left there as a plant."

"An elaborate one. It must have been conceived a month before the murder."

"But suppose it never came from Wyoming. We have no proof that it was written in America."

"We have proof of nothing at present."

"Well, Mr. Bruce, have you a theory? This is the place where you ought to shine, you know."

"I have no theory. I must think for hours, for days, before I see my way clear."

"Clear to what, sir."

"To telling you how, when, and where to arrest the murderer of Lady Dyke."

"So this find of mine is of great importance?"

"Undoubtedly. I remember its contents sufficiently, but you will let me see it again if necessary?"

"With pleasure, sir. And that reminds me. You never returned that small bit of iron to me. You recollect I lent it to you some time since."

"Perfectly. Come with me. I will model it in wax and give it to you."

"All right, sir; but as we are here I may as well continue my search. I may drop on something else of value."

Bruce resumed his seat, and did not stir until the detective had completely rummaged the cabinet. The reading of that queer epistle from Corbett to "Bertie"—from the real Simon Pure to the sham one—from one man to his double—had stopped him at the very threshold of disclosure.

The document impressed him as being genuine. If so, who on earth was Corbett, and why had Mensmore taken his name, if that was the solution of the tangle?

Whatever the explanation, he would not jump to a conclusion. The web had closed too securely round Mensmore to allow of escape. Hence, Bruce could bide his time. Another week might solve many elements in the case now indistinct and nebulous. He would wait.

The detective finally satisfied himself there was nothing else in the cabinet. He approached the fireplace, peered into every vase on the over-mantel, picked with his penknife at the back of the frame to feel for other letters, and in doing so several times kicked the fender.

The barrister vaguely wondered whether the man of method would note the missing portion of the iron "dog."

"Surely," he thought, "he will see it now," as Mr. White bent to examine the ashes, and actually took the poker from the very support itself in order to rake among the cinders.

The other even scrutinized the fire-irons, but the too obvious fact that, so to speak, stared him in the face, escaped notice. He was quite wrapped up in his theory that Lady Dyke had been killed at Putney, and not in Sloane Square.

At last he quitted the room, and walked off to the small apartments at the end of the main corridor.

Instantly Bruce sprang forward, fell on his knees, and intently examined the iron rest with a strong lens. It bore no unusual signs in the locality of the break. Taking some wax from his pocket, he took a slight impression of the fracture.

When Mr. White returned, he found the barrister sitting in his chair, still smoking, and with set face and fixed eyes.

Soon afterwards they quitted the flat, carefully leaving all things as they found them. They said little on their way to Victoria Street, for Bruce was trying to explain Mensmore's attitude at Monte Carlo, and the detective was considering the best use to which he could put that all-important letter.

Besides, Mr. White attributed his companion's silence to annoyance. Had not he, White, laid hands on the only direct piece of evidence yet discovered as to Corbett's identity, and this in defiance of Bruce's spoken philosophy? He could afford to be generous and not to worry his amateur colleague with questions.

Thus they reached the barrister's chambers. Bruce asked the other to sit down for a moment while he obtained a model of the small lump of iron. He took it into his bedroom, fitted in into the wax impression obtained at Raleigh Mansions, and noted that the two coincided perfectly.

He handed the bit of iron to White without comment.

The latter said: "It had better remain in my keeping now, sir, but if you want to see it again, of course I will be glad—"

"I shall never want it again," said Bruce, and his voice was harsh and cold, for he had seldom experienced such a strain as the last hours had given him. "It is an accursed thing. It has caused one death already, and may cause others."

"I sincerely hope it will cause a man to be hanged," cried the detective, "for this affair is the warmest I have ever tackled. However, I'll get him, as sure as his name's Corbett, if he has forty aliases and as many addresses."

Smith let Mr. White out. The latter, halting for a moment at the door, said quietly, "Is your name Corbett?"

"No, it ain't, any more than yours is Black. See?"

Each man thought he had had his joke, so they were better friends thenceforth, but Mr. White was thoughtful as he passed into the street.

"This is a funny business," he communed. "There isn't enough evidence against Corbett to hang a cat, yet I *think* he's the man. And Bruce is a queer chap. Was he cut up about me finding the letter, or has he got some notion in his head. He's as close as an oyster. I wonder if he *did* dine at Hampstead on the evening of the murder, as he said at the inquest? I must inquire into it."

CHAPTER XV

MRS. HILLMER HESITATES

"I wonder if I shall have such exciting times to-day as I had yesterday," said Bruce to himself, as he unfolded his *Times* next morning at breakfast.

Affairs had so jumbled themselves together in his brain the previous evening that he had abandoned all effort to elucidate them. He retired to rest earlier than usual, to sleep soundly, save for a vivid dream in which he was being tried for his life, the chief witnesses against him being Mrs. Hillmer, Phyllis Browne, and Jane Harding, the latter varying her evidence by entertaining the Court with a song and dance.

The weather, too, had improved. It was clear, frosty, and sunlit—one of those delightful days of winter that serve as cheerful remembrances during periods of seemingly interminable fog overhead and slush beneath.

During a quiet meal he read the news, and, with the invaluable morning smoke, settled himself cosily into an armchair to consider procedure.

In the first place he carefully weighed those utterances of Mensmore at Monte Carlo, which he could recall, and which seemed by the light of later knowledge, to bear upon the case.

Mensmore had alluded to "family troubles," to "worries," and "anxieties," that practically drove him from England.

Some of these, no doubt, referred to the Springbok speculation. Others, again, might have meant Mrs. Hillmer or some other presently unknown relative. But in Mensmore's manner there was nothing that savored of a greater secrecy than the natural reticence of a gentleman in discussing domestic affairs with a stranger.

This man had practically been snatched from death. At such a moment it was inconceivable that he could cloak the remorse of a murderer by the simulation of more honorable motives, in themselves sufficiently distressing to cause him deliberately to choose suicide as the best way of ending his difficulties.

The policeman had summarized the testimony against Corbett as insufficient to curtail the remarkable powers of endurance of a cat. But to Bruce the case against Mensmore, alias Corbett, stood in clearer perspective. Now that he calmly reasoned the matter he felt that the balance of probabilities swung away from the hypothesis that Mensmore was the actual slayer of Lady Dyke, and towards the theory that he was in some way bound up with her death, whether knowingly or unknowingly it was at present impossible to say.

The new terror to Bruce was Mr. White.

"Why, if that animated truncheon knew what I know of this business he would arrest Mensmore forthwith. If he did, what would result? A scandal, a thorough exposure, possibly the ruin of Mensmore's love-making if he be an innocent man. That must be stopped. But how, without forewarning Mensmore himself?—and he may be guilty. Chance may favor White, as it favored me, in disclosing the identity of the missing Corbett. And what of the *real* Corbett? What on earth has *he* got to do with it, and why has Mensmore taken his name? If ever I get to the bottom of this business I may well congratulate myself. The sole result of all my labor thus far may be summed up in a sentence—I have not yet come face to face with the man whom I can honestly suspect as Lady Dyke's murderer. Not much, my boy!"

Claude uttered the last sentence aloud, startling Smith, who was clearing the table.

"Beg pardon, sir," cried Smith.

"Oh, nothing. I was only expressing an opinion."

"I thought, perhaps, sir, you was thinkin' of Mr. White."

"What of him?"

"Your remark, sir, hexactly hexpresses my hopinion of 'im."

Smith was not a badly educated man, but the least excitement produced an appalling derangement of the letter "h" in his vocabulary.

"Mr. White is a sharp fellow in his own way, Smith."

"Maybe, but why should 'e come pokin' round 'ere pryin' into your little affairs-deecur?"

"My what?"

"Sorry, sir, but that's what a French maid I once knew called 'em. Flirtations, sir. Mashes."

"Smith, have you been drinking?"

"Me, sir?"

"Well, explain yourself. I never flirted with a woman in my life."

"That's what I told 'im, sir. 'My master's a regular saint,' says I, 'a sort of middle-aged ankyrite.' But Mr. White 'e wouldn't 'ave it at no price. 'Come now, Smith,' says 'e, 'your guv'nor's pretty deep. 'E's a toff, 'e is, an' knows lots of lydies—titled lydies.' 'Very like,' says I, 'but 'e doesn't mash 'em.' 'Then what price that lydy who called for 'im in a keb afore 'e went away? An' who's 'e gone to Monte Carlo with?' This was durin' your absence, sir."

"Go on, Smith. Anything else?"

"Well, sir, that rather flung me out of my stride, as the sayin' is, as I 'ad seen the lydy in question. An' Mr. White 'as a nasty way of putting you on your oath, so to speak. But I never owned up."

Claude laughed.

"Excellent. Mr. White has a keen nose for false scents. I have already told him to let my affairs alone. He means no harm."

But the reference to a "lydy in a keb" had suggested an immediate plan of action to the barrister. He would call to see Mrs. Hillmer. He wrote a note asking her if he might come to tea that afternoon, and sent it by a boy messenger.

In return he received this answer.

"Mrs. Hillmer will be at home at four o'clock if Mr. Bruce cares to call then."

"Whew!" he whistled. "What's in the wind there? This is an uncommonly stiff invitation. That rascal White has upset her, I'll be bound. I *must* choke him off somehow. Suppose he were to find that damaged bracket! He would have Mensmore under trial at the Old Bailey in double-quick time. After I leave Mrs. Hillmer I must visit No. 12 again, and carry off that pair of brackets before White discovers them, as he will haunt the place in future."

Bruce had a set of skeleton keys in his possession.

They were in his pocket when he approached Raleigh Mansions at the appointed hour.

The same trim maid opened the door for him and ushered him into the drawing-room. On the occasion of his first visit he was taken to the dining-room. It was a small matter, but Bruce paid heed to such.

Mrs. Hillmer appeared, very stately and undemonstrative. She greeted him coldly, seated herself at a distance, and said, in a cold, well-controlled voice:

"I did not expect the honor of another visit from you, Mr. Bruce."

"Why not?"

There was a fight brewing, and he would let the enemy open fire. The glitter in her eyes showed that the batteries were ready to be unmasked. He was not mistaken.

"Why not? Because I believed you to be a gentleman. Once you had stooped to sending your myrmidons to pester me I imagined that you would keep yourself in the background."

There was an indignant ring in her words as she concluded. When a woman is angry her own speech acts as a trumpet-call and fires her blood. Mrs. Hillmer began, as she intended, in icy disdain. She ended in tremulous anger.

"You allude to Mr. White?" said the barrister, looking steadily at her.

"Yes, that is the man. Some hireling from Scotland Yard. How *could* you so meanly induce my confidence at our first meeting? I have never been so deceived in a man in my life, and I have had a surfeit of bitter experience already."

"Brother and sister are alike. They have led queer lives," mused Bruce. Aloud he said:

"Your experience, Mrs. Hillmer, should at least lead you not to condemn any one unheard. May I explain that which is to you incomprehensible at this moment?—justly so, I admit."

"Explanations! I am a child in the hands of such as you. How can I hope to fathom your real intent? Presumably, if I accept your apologies now, it will be a prelude to further visits by impudent police officers."

"I am not here to apologize, Mrs. Hillmer."

"What then, pray?"

"To plead with you. For Heaven's sake do not distrust *me*. It may ruin those whom you hold dear. Listen to me first, and try to believe me afterwards."

He was so thoroughly in earnest, so impressive in manner, that she did not know what to make of him. In her despair, she adopted a woman's chief resource—her eyes filled with tears.

But he anticipated her.

"Now, Mrs. Hillmer," he cried, "let us act like sensible people. Compose yourself, order in some tea, and after an interlude I will tell you all about it. Candor is an indispensable element of confidence."

Mrs. Hillmer rose, made an effort to choke back her agitation, went out, and called to the maid for tea. She returned in a few moments. When they were alone Bruce said, with a smile:

"A little *poudre de ris* is an excellent corrective for signs of grief."

The lady blushed, and there was a perceptible return to her former pleasant manner.

"You are incorrigible, I fear," she cried.

"Not a bit. Impressionable, rather. Now, I am going to startle you considerably, so be prepared. And do not jump at conclusions. Though startling, my news is not alarming. All may yet end well."

Mrs. Hillmer was manifestly anxious, but she promised to try to understand him fully before she formed any judgment.

"Then," said he, "I can clear the air a good deal by a simple statement. Mr. White is no agent of mine, and I have seen your brother, Albert Mensmore, at Monte Carlo."

Mrs. Hillmer gave a little gasp of surprise. "You have seen Bertie?"

"Yes; your brother, is he not?"

"My half-brother, to be exact. My father was married twice. I—I am the elder of the two by four years."

"Apart from the compliment, you do not look it. But what you say explains the total absence of likeness between you."

"Possibly. People said we each resembled our mother. And Bertie, you know, has led a somewhat adventurous career. He roughed it a good deal in America. But what has all this got to do with detectives, and recent inquiries, and that sort of thing?"

"Much. The last time we met I told you that your brother was mixed up in some little affair with a lady."

Mrs. Hillmer laughed, a trifle constrainedly. "If you knew Bertie as well as I do, you would not harbor suspicions concerning him. He never had a love affair in his life. Indeed, he is something of a woman-hater."

"No doubt he was. But he has changed his opinions. He is in love, and is engaged to be married to a very charming girl. Thus far, his beliefs and his good fortune have pulled against each other."

"Bertie engaged to be married! Good gracious! Who is she? And how can he support a wife? He is poor, and in debt, and he won't even let me help him."

"I have stated the facts, nevertheless. The lady is a daughter of Sir William Browne, and they are now yachting with a large party in the Mediterranean."

"Are her people against the match? Is that why this Scotland Yard man—?"

"No. Mensmore is on board Sir William's yacht. But there is another lady, missing from her home for nearly three months, who is believed to be dead—murdered, the police say—and with whom your brother was in some indefinable way associated."

"Do they dare to say that Bertie killed her?" Mrs. Hillmer's color rose and her eyes flashed fire again.

"They say nothing. They are simply doing their duty in trying to discover the truth. And you may take it from me, as an undoubted fact, that the last place this lady visited before her death was one of the flats in these mansions. All present indications point to your brother's residence as being that place. Now, I pray you, be calm, and try to help me, for I have acted in this matter as your friend and as your brother's friend. At this very moment I am concealing his identity and his whereabouts from the police, who are searching for him under the assumed name of Corbett. If he is guilty of this crime, then I must hand him over to justice, for the murdered woman was a dear and good friend of mine. If he is innocent, as, indeed, I believe him to be, I will strive to help him and save his good name from the tarnish of being arrested on such an odious charge."

During this recital Mrs. Hillmer became deathly pale. Her agitation was the greater inasmuch as she forcibly controlled herself. But she could not remain seated. She sprang to the window and looked out, in the vain effort to seek inspiration from the gathering gloom of the street. Then she turned, and spoke very slowly:

"I think I understand. I must have faith in you, Mr. Bruce. Who—was—the lady?"

The barrister thought deeply before replying. He had previously decided upon this supreme step, but he hesitated now that it was imminent. There was no help for it.

"Her name," said he, "is one which is well known to the world. Lady Dyke, wife of Sir Charles Dyke, is missing from her home since the evening of November 6 last. She met with a violent death that night, and I—not the police—have good reason to believe that she was killed in your brother's residence."

Mrs. Hillmer flung herself on a lounge, buried her white face in her hands and moaned, in a perfect agony of terror:

"Oh, my God! What shall I do? What shall I do?"

This outburst astounded Bruce. He did not know what to make of it. His intelligence had certainly taken his hearer by surprise. What interpretation was he to place upon her words and her unrestrained actions?

"Now, Mrs. Hillmer," he began; but she broke in vehemently, running to him and clutching him by the arm:

"He is innocent, Mr. Bruce. He *must* be innocent. He could not lift his finger to any woman. You must save him—do you hear?—save him, or you will have his blood on your soul. It *was* true, then, that you came here to hunt for him. Save him, if you hope for mercy yourself when you are dying."

In her passion she shook him violently, and for an instant they looked intently at each other—the woman tensely piteous, entreating; the man amazed and questioning.

"Do you not see," he said at last, "that your vehemence reveals your thoughts? For anything you know to the contrary, your brother may have committed the crime. Nay, it requires but slight knowledge of human nature to read your suspicions lest it be true. At this moment I am convinced that you are, in your heart, less sceptical than I of his guilt."

Mrs. Hillmer flung herself again upon the lounge, silent, tearful, torn with violent emotion, which she vainly tried to suppress.

He tried to reason with her.

"It will, perhaps, serve to clear up a mystery that deepens each moment if you place your trust in me," he said. "Tell me fully and openly any cause you may have for fearing that your brother may be implicated in this terrible business. I ask you to adopt this course in all faith. I have seen your brother under most trying circumstances; I have been with him at an hour when it would be impossible for him to conceal his burden if the weight of Lady Dyke's death lay upon him. Yet I think him innocent. I think that chance has contributed to gather evidence against him. If I can learn even a portion of the truth it will enable me to quickly dispel the barrier of uncertainty that now hinders progress."

"What is it you want to know?"

Mrs. Hillmer's voice was hollow and broken. The barrister was shocked at the effect of his revelation, but he was forced to go on with the disagreeable task he had undertaken.

"Do you mean," he asked, "that you will answer my questions?"

"So far as I can."

"Would it not be better to tell me in your own words what you have to say?"

Mrs. Hillmer looked up, and the agony in her face filled him with keen pity.

"Oh, Heaven help me to do what is right!" she cried.

"Your prayer will surely be answered. I am certain of that. A great wrong has been committed by some one, and the innocent must not suffer to shield the guilty."

Mrs. Hillmer bowed her head and did not utter a word for some minutes. She appeared to be reasoning out some plan of action in a dazed fashion. When decision came she said in low tones:

"You must leave me now, Mr. Bruce. I must have time. When I am ready I shall send for you."

He knew instinctively that it was hopeless to plead with her. Frivolous, volatile women of her stamp often betray unusual strength of character in a supreme crisis.

"You are adopting an unwise course," he said sadly.

"Maybe. But I must be alone. I am not deceiving you. When I have determined something which is not now clear to me, I will send for you. It may be that I shall speak. It may be that I shall be silent. In either case I only can judge—and suffer."

"Tell me one thing at least, Mrs. Hillmer, before we part. Did you know of Lady Dyke's death before to-day?"

She came to him and looked him straight in the face, and said: "I did not. On my soul, I did not."

Then he passed into the hall; and even the shock of this painful interview did not prevent him from noting the flitting of a shadow past a distant doorway, as some one hurried into the interior of a room.

In their excitement they forgot that their voices might attract attention, and ladies' maids are proverbially inquisitive.

———

CHAPTER XVI

FOXEY

The keen, cold air of the streets soon restored the man to his habitual calm. He felt that a quiet stroll would do him good.

As he walked he pondered, and the more critically he examined Mrs. Hillmer's change of attitude the less he understood it.

"For some ridiculous reason," he communed, "the woman believes her brother guilty. Now I shall have endless trouble at getting at the truth. She will not be candid. She will only tell me that which she thinks will help him, and conceal that which she considers damaging. That is a woman's way, all the world over. And a desperately annoying way it is. Perhaps I was to blame in springing this business too hastily upon her. But there! I like Mrs. Hillmer, and I hate using her as one juggles with a self-conceited witness. In future I shall trouble her no more."

A casual glance into the interior of Sloane Square Station gave him a glimpse of the barrier, and he recognized the collector who had taken Lady Dyke's ticket on that fatal night when she quitted the Richmond train.

Rather as a relief than for other cause he entered into conversation with the official.

"Do you remember me?" he said.

"Can't say as I do, sir." The man examined his questioner with quick suspicion. The forgotten "season" dodge would not work with *him*.

"Maybe you remember these?" said Bruce, producing his cigar-case.

"Now, wot's the gyme?" said the collector to himself. But he smiled, and answered: "Do you mean by the look of 'em, sir?"

"Good!" laughed Claude. "Take three or four home with you. Meanwhile I am sure you remember me coming to see you last November concerning a lady who alighted here from Victoria one foggy evening and handed you a ticket to Richmond?"

"Of course I do, sir. And the cigars are *all* right. There was a lot of fuss about that lydy. Did she ever turn up?"

"Not exactly. That is to say, she died shortly after you saw her."

"No! Well, of all the rummy goes! She was a fine-looking woman, too, as well as I rec'llect. Looked fit for another fifty year. Wot 'appened to 'er."

"I don't know. I wish I did."

"An' 'ave you been on the 'unt ever since, guv'nor?"

"Yes, ever since."

"She's dead, you s'y?"

"Yes."

"But 'ow'd you know she's dead, if you 'ain't seen 'er since?"

"I have seen her. I saw her dead body at Putney."

"At Putney! Well, I'm blowed!"

A roar from beneath, the slamming of many doors, and the quick rush of a crowd up the steps, announced the arrival of a train. "Pardon, sir," said the man, "this is the 5.41 Mansion House. But don't go aw'y. There's somethin'—Tickets, *if* you please."

In a minute the collector had ended his task. While sorting his bundles of pasteboards he said:

"Nobody ever tell'd me that before. An' you ain't the only one on 'er track. Are you in the police?"

"No."

"I thought not. But some other chaps who kem 'ere was. None of 'em ever said the lydy was dead."

"Why; what matter?"

"Oh, nothin', but two 'eads is better'n one, if they're only sheep's 'eads."

"Undoubtedly. The rule is all the more reliable when one of them belongs to a shrewd chap like you."

The collector grinned. He understood that he was being flattered for a purpose, yet he liked it.

"That's one w'y of lookin' at it," he said, "but if this affair's pertickler, why, all I can s'y is it's worth somethin' to somebody."

"Certainly. Here's a sovereign for a start. If you can tell me anything really worth knowing I will add four more to it."

"Now, that's talkin'. I'm off duty at eight o'clock, an' I can't 'ave a chat now because I expect the inspector any minute."

"Suppose you call and see me in Victoria Street at nine?"

"Right you are, sir."

Bruce gave the man his address and recrossed the square. Few people were abroad, so he walked straight to the first door of Raleigh Mansions and made his way to the fourth floor.

Had he been a moment later he must have seen Mrs. Hillmer, closely wrapped up, leave her residence unattended. Her carriage was not in waiting. She walked to the cabstand in the square and called a hansom, driving back up Sloane Street.

Her actions indicated a desire to be unobserved even by her servants, as in the usual course of events the housemaid would have brought a cab to the door.

But the barrister, steadily climbing up the stairs, could not guess what was happening in the street. He soon opened Mensmore's door, and noted, as an idle fact, that the expected gust of cold air was absent.

There was no light on this landing, so he was in pitch darkness once he had passed the doorway. There was no need to strike a match, however, as he remembered the exact position of the electric switchboard—on the left beyond the dining-room door.

He stepped cautiously forward, and stretched forth his hand to grope for the lever. With a quick rush, some two or three assailants flung themselves upon him, and after a fierce, gasping struggle—for Bruce was a strong man—he was borne to the floor face downwards, with one arm beneath him and the other pinioned behind his back.

"Look sharp, Jim," shouted a breathless voice. "Turn on the light and close the door. We've got him safe enough."

They had. Two large hands were clutched round his neck, a knee was firmly embedded in the small of his back, another hand gripped his left wrist like a vice, while some one sat on his legs.

He could not have been collared more effectually by a Rugby International team.

The third man found the electric light and turned it on.

"Now, get up," said some one, "and don't give us any more trouble. It's no use."

The barrister, who had had his wind knocked out of him, rose to his knees. Then, as the light fell upon the horrified face of Mr. White, he vainly essayed to keep up the pretence of indignation. Once fairly on his feet, he nearly collapsed with laughter. He leaned against the wall, and, as his breath came again, he laughed until his sides ached.

Meanwhile the detective was crimson with rage and annoyance. His two assistants did not know what to make of the affair.

"What's wrong, Jim?" said one at last. "Isn't this Corbett?"

"No, of course it's not," was his angry growl.

"Then who the —— is it?"

"Oh, ask me another! How on earth could I guess, Mr. Bruce, that you'd come letting yourself in here with a latchkey?"

Claude was still holding his sore ribs and could not answer; but the policeman who had questioned White caught the name. He recognized it, and grinned at his companion.

"What did you want here, anyhow?" snarled the infuriated detective, as he realized that his great *coup* would be retailed with embellishments through every police station in the metropolis.

"I w-wanted you to ar-r-rest me, W-White," roared Claude. "I s-said you would, and you have."

"Confound it, how could you know I was here?"

"You were sure to wait here for a man who probably will not return for months."

"Was I, indeed? Well, you have yourself to blame if you are hurt. I hope my mates did not treat you too badly?"

"What?" cried the one who had not yet spoken. "He gave me such a punch on the bread-basket that I've only just recovered my speech."

"I think we're about quits," said the other, surveying a torn waistcoat and broken watch-chain.

"I shall be black and blue all over to-morrow," said Bruce; "but if you are satisfied I am. Come, Mr. White, bring your friends and we will open a bottle of wine. We all want it. Corbett won't be here to-night. Just now he is in Wyoming."

"How do you know?"

"By intuition. I am seldom mistaken."

"But why didn't you call out just now when you came in?"

"I hadn't a chance. You were on me like a thousand of bricks. I must confess that if Corbett were in my shoes he would be a doomed man."

White didn't know whether to believe Bruce or not. He was genuinely angry at the incident, but the barrister did not want to convert him into an enemy, and he vaguely felt that a catastrophe was imminent, and a false move by the police might do irretrievable mischief.

"Well, inspector," he said, "I must confess that this time you have got the better of me. I did not know you were here. I looked in for the purpose of quietly studying the ground, as it were, and I was never more taken by surprise in my life. Moreover, your plan was a very clever one, in view of the fact that Corbett might return at any moment."

The detective became more amiable at this praise from the famous amateur, for Bruce's achievements were well known to his two colleagues.

"I suppose you wondered what had happened," he said with a smile.

"I thought my last hour had come. I am only sorry that Corbett himself did not have the experience."

"Do you really believe he is in the States, sir?"

"I am sure of it."

"Then he must have returned there since he wrote that letter."

"That is the only solution of the difficulty."

"Hum. It's a pity."

"Why?"

"I would sooner prefer to arrest him on this side. To get him by extradition is a slow affair, and probably means a trip across the Atlantic."

Good-humor being now restored, the party quitted the flat and adjourned to a neighboring hotel, where the barrister started White on the full, true, and particular account of his pursuit and capture of the Winchmore Hill burglars, an exploit which was the pride of the detective's life.

At the end of a bottle of champagne and a cigar they all parted excellent friends, but Bruce did not attempt to revisit Raleigh Mansions that night.

Instead, he partook of a quiet meal at a restaurant, and hurried to his chambers to await the advent of the ticket-collector.

Punctual to the hour, this new witness arrived, and was admitted by Smith in obedience with previous instructions. The man was somewhat awed by the surroundings and the appearance of a servant in livery, but Bruce quickly put him at his ease.

"Come, sit near the fire. Do you drink whisky and soda? That box contains your favorite cigars. Now, tell me all you know about this business."

"I can't s'y as I know anythink about it, sir, but by puttin' two and two together it makes four sometimes—not always."

"Quite right. You're a philosopher. Let me hear the two two's. We will see about the addition afterwards."

"Well, sir, this yer lydy was a-missin' early in November. She tykes a ticket at Victoria Station on the District for Richmond; she gives it up to me at Sloane Square, arsks a newsboy the w'y to Raleigh Mansions, for 'e tell'd me so after you'd bin to see me, an' from what you s'y, 'as bin swallered up ever since."

"The Lord Chief couldn't state the case more simply."

"That's the first two. Now, for the second two, an' you won't forgit as I knew nothink about the lydy bein' dead, or I should 'ave opened my mouth long afore this."

"Go on. No one can blame you."

"There's an old chap—Foxey they calls 'im, but I don't know 'is right nyme—who drives a four-wheeler around Chelsea, an' 'e 'ad tyken a fare from the Square to the City. It might be four o'clock or it might be five, but 'e was on 'is w'y back from Cornhill when a gent, a tall, good-looking gent, a youngish, military chap, 'ails 'im and says: 'Cabby, drive me to Sloane Square. There's no 'urry, but tyke care, because it's foggy.' Old Foxey nearly jumped out of 'is skin at this bit of good luck. 'E was pretty full then, for 'e's a regular beer-barrel, 'e is, but 'e made up 'is mind to 'ave a fair old skinful that night. Well, Foxey drives 'im all right to the Square. The gent gives 'im five bob and says: 'Wite 'ere for me, cabby. You can drive me 'ome in about an hour's time.' This was at 5.30. Foxey drew up near the stytion, tells me all about it, an' stan's me two beers, 'e was that pleased with 'isself. 'E goes to give 'is 'oss the nose-bag, in comes the Richmond train, and out pops the lydy with the Richmond ticket. D'ye follow me?"

"Every word."

"An' you see now 'ow it is I can fix the d'y?"

"Perfectly."

"Well, I sees no more of Foxey. I missed 'im about the Square, so one d'y I axes at the rank,—'Where's Foxey?' An' where d'ye think 'e was?"

"I can not tell."

"In quod."

"In jail. Why?"

"That's hit. That's number two of the twos. Pardon me, but I'm gettin' a bit mixed. Well, it seems that that very night, comin' back from Putney as drunk as a lord, old Foxey runs over a barrer. 'E an' the coster 'as a fight. The police come, and Foxey dots one bobby in the blinkers and another on the boko. You wouldn't think it was in 'im. 'E must 'ave bin paralytic."

"So he was locked up?"

"Locked up! 'E was dragged there by the 'eels. Next mornin' 'e comes before the beak. 'We was all drunk together, your wurshup,' 'e says. 'I took a fare from the City to Sloane Square, an' 'e left me for more'n an hour. 'E comes back excited like—bin boozin' 'ard, I suppose—brings my keb up to a 'ouse, carries in a lydy who was that 'toxicated she couldn't stand, an' tells me to drive to Putney. We gits there, an' I says 'you've nearly killed my 'oss, guv'nor.' With that 'e tips me a fiver—a five-pun note, your wurshup.' 'What has that got to do with the charge?' says the beak. 'Wot?' says Foxey. 'If a chap give you a fiver for drivin' 'im to Putney wouldn't you get drunk?' With that the magistrate gives 'im three months for assaulting the police, and fines 'im the balance of the fiver for bein' drunk in charge of a 'oss and keb."

The ticket collector took a long drink after this recital.

"I hope you will not follow Foxey's example," said Bruce, rising.

"'Ow do you mean, sir?"

"Because I am going to keep my word. Here are the four sovereigns I owe you. In your case your two and two have made five."

"Thank you, sir. You're a brick. No fear of me meltin' this little lot. The missus will be on 'em like a bird w'en I tell her." And the man spat upon the coins with evident relish as he handled them.

"One word more," said Bruce. "Where was this man tried?"

"At the West London Police Court."

"You can get me his real name and post it to me?"

"Sure, sir. Anyway, I'll try."

"I am greatly obliged to you."

"An' 'as my yarn bin of any use to you, sir?"

"The greatest. It has solved a puzzle. However, I will see you again. Good-bye. Don't forget to write."

"Cornhill is the direct line from Leadenhall Street," mused Claude, when he was alone. "Any one coming to Sloane Square from Dodge & Co.'s office would pass through it. Upon my word, things look very black against Mensmore. Yet I cannot believe it."

CHAPTER XVII

A POSSIBLE EXPLANATION

Bruce now had several lines of inquiry open.

Apart from the main and vital question as to the exact method of Lady Dyke's death, and the identity of the person responsible for it, a number of important matters required attention.

Why had Jane Harding quitted her situation so suddenly?

Whence did she obtain the money that enabled her to blossom forth as Marie le Marchant?

Who was Sydney H. Corbett?

Why did Mensmore adopt a false name; and, in any case, why adopt the name of Corbett?

Why did Mrs. Hillmer exhibit such sudden terror lest her brother might be guilty?

Whom did Mrs. Hillmer marry? Was her husband alive or dead?

Was the man who conveyed Lady Dyke's body from Raleigh Mansions to Putney responsible also for her death?

Finally, why did he select that particular portion of the Thames banks for the bestowal of his terrible burden?

Many other minor features suggested themselves for careful attention, but the barrister knew that if he elucidated some of the major questions the rest would answer themselves.

The last query promised to yield a good crop of information should it be satisfactorily dealt with. Turning to his notes, he found that the former owner of the Putney house was a tutor or preparatory schoolmaster, named the Rev. Septimus Childe.

Could it be that this was the school in which both Sir Charles Dyke and Mensmore were fellow-students? If so, Bruce failed to see why he should not forthwith place the whole of the facts in his possession at the service of the police, and allow the law to take its course.

On this supposition, the case against Mensmore was very black; not, indeed, incapable of explanation—for circumstantial evidence occasionally plays strange pranks with logic—but of such a grave nature that no private individual would be justified in keeping his knowledge to himself.

The deduction was intensely disagreeable; but Bruce resolved to coerce his thoughts, and do that which was right, irrespective of consequences.

He did not possess a Clergy List. No letter came from Mrs. Hillmer, so he walked across the Park to his club in Pall Mall to consult the appropriately bound black and white volume which gives reference to the many degrees of the Church of England.

Septimus Childe was a distinctive, though simple, name. And it was not there. There was not a Childe with a final "e" in the whole book. Without that important letter, as his informant might be mistaken, there were several. Close scrutiny of each man's designation and duties convinced him that though any of these might be one of the particular Childe's children, none answered to the description of the gentleman he sought.

Of course, he could always apply to Sir Charles Dyke, but he dreaded approaching the grief-stricken baronet on this matter. Now there was no help for it. The barrister was beginning to feel impatient at the constant difficulties which barred progress in each direction. After all, it was a small thing merely to ask his friend if he ever knew a reverend gentleman named Childe.

Bruce was sure that Sir Charles would not be acquainted with Mr. Childe, and also with the fact that the Putney house had served as his school, for it would be strange beyond credence if it were so that he had not mentioned it.

The weather was still clear and cold, and a wintry sun made walking pleasant. Claude, on quitting his club, set out again on foot. He crossed St. James's Square, Jermyn Street, and Piccadilly, and made his way to Oxford Street up New Bond Street.

Not often did he frequent these fashionable thoroughfares, and he had an excellent reason. When walking, he was given to abstraction, and seldom saw his acquaintances if he encountered them in unusual quarters. He would thus cut dead a woman at whose house he had dined the previous evening, or, when he was in practice at the Bar, fail to notice the salutation of his own leader.

To Claude himself this short-coming was intolerable; consciousness of it when in the West made him the most alert man in the crowd to note anybody whom he knew, except on the rare occasions when he forgot his failing.

This morning Bond Street was pleasantly full. People were beginning to return to town. Parliament re-assembled in a few days, and he passed many who were on his visiting list.

Outside a well-known costumer's he saw a brougham, into which a lady had just been assisted by the commissionaire.

It is no uncommon thing to recognize an acquaintance by the color of his horse, or the peculiar cut of the coachman's whiskers. This time Bruce knew the driver as well as the equipage, but the lady was not Mrs. Hillmer.

Instantly he was at the door, with his hat lifted; he assumed an expression of polite regret as he saw Dobson, the maid, in her mistress's place.

"Sorry," he said, "I knew the carriage, and thought that Mrs. Hillmer was inside. She is well, I trust."

"Not very, sir," answered the maid with an angry pout.

"Indeed, what is the matter?"

"Madame is going away, and has put us all on board wages."

Dobson had some of the privileges of a companion, and resented this relegation to the servants' hall.

"Going away?" cried Bruce. "A sudden departure, eh?"

The girl was arranging some parcels on the seat in front of her. She was not disinclined for a conversation with this good-looking gentleman, so she smiled archly, as she said: "Didn't you know, sir? I thought you would know all about it."

What he might have ascertained by a longer chat the barrister could not tell, for an interruption occurred. The coachman was more loyal to his mistress than the maid.

"Beg pardon, sir," he cried, "but the missus told us to hurry"; and he whipped his steed into the passing stream of carriages.

"More complications," murmured Claude. "Mrs. Hillmer contemplates a bolt. Shall I pay her another visit and surprise her? No, confound it, I will not. Let her go, and let things take their course."

Not in the most amiable frame of mind at this discovery, he pursued his walk to Portman Square.

Sir Charles Dyke was at home. He always was, now.

"For goodness' sake, Mr. Bruce," whispered Thompson in the hall, "try to persuade Sir Charles to quit smokin', and readin', and thinkin'. He sits all day in the library and 'ardly has anything to eat."

Claude reproached himself for having neglected his resolution to stir his friend into something like animation. He was wondering what he should do in the matter, when the baronet rose at his entrance, saying, with a weary smile:

"Well, old fellow, what news?"

The other suddenly decided to throw all questioning to the winds for the moment. "I have come to bring you out. I won't hear of a refusal. Let us walk to the club and have lunch and a game of billiards."

Sir Charles protested. He had slept badly and was tired.

"All the more reason that you should sleep well to-night. Come, now, be advised. You will allow yourself to become a hopeless invalid if you go on in this way."

Dyke unwillingly consented, and they left the house. The older man brightened up considerably amidst the bustle of the streets. His color returned, he talked with some degree of cheerfulness, and even laughed as he said:

"I never understood you were a doctor, Claude, in addition to your other varied acquirements. For the first time since—since November last, I feel hungry."

"Why don't you take my advice, and go away for some shooting? It is not too late, even now, to go after a hare."

"I will think of it. I wonder who we shall meet at the club."

"Lots of fellows, no doubt. And, by the way, you must be prepared for one little difficulty. Suppose they ask about your wife?"

The baronet's momentary gaiety vanished. He stopped short, and clutched Bruce's arm. "Don't you see," he almost moaned, "that this is the reason I have remained indoors for so long? What shall I say?"

"You must make the best of it. Say, off-handedly, you don't know where she is—either with relations or in Italy. Anything will do, and it will create a false impression."

"I am sick of false impressions. I cannot do it."

"You must."

The stronger will prevailed, and they entered the doors of the Imperial, where, of course, Dyke was hailed at once by a dozen men.

"Hallo, Charlie! Been seedy?"

"Good gracious, Dyke! have you had influenza? I've missed you for months, now I come to think of it."

"I haven't seen your wife for quite a time. How is she?"

In the multitude of questions there was safety.

Sir Charles answered vaguely, and a chance arrival created a diversion by announcing that the favorite had broken down in his preparation for the Grand National.

Later in the afternoon, the two found themselves ensconced in a quiet corner of the smoking-room. Bruce seized the opportunity.

"You told me," he said, "that Mensmore and you were at school together?"

"Did I?" said the baronet.

"Yes; don't you remember?"

"I get mixed up in thinking about things. But it is all right. We were."

"Whereabouts?"

"Oh, a private establishment kept by an old chap called Septimus Childe,—Lucky Number was our nickname for him."

Bruce betrayed no surprise at this startlingly simple statement. He said casually:

"I mean where was the school situated?"

"At Brighton in my time. But afterwards he shifted to some place near London—something to do with examinations, I fancy."

"But don't you know where?"

"How should I? I was at Sandhurst then. I believe the old boy is dead. Why do you ask?"

"Oh, it has something to do with the inquiry. I won't trouble you now with the details."

"Go on, I can stand it."

"But where is the good in paining you needlessly?"

"That stage has passed, old chap. My wife's memory has almost become a dream to me."

"Well, it is an extraordinary thing, but that place where—that house at Putney, you know, must have been the new school of the Rev. Septimus Childe."

"How did you learn that?"

"I have known it for months, ever since the inquest."

"And you did not tell me?"

"True, but at the time it seemed of no consequence. Now that Mensmore turns out to be a pupil of his, and probably passed the remainder of his early school days at that very establishment, the incident assumes a degree of importance."

Sir Charles looked earnestly at his friend as he put his next question: "Tell me, Claude, do you seriously believe that Mensmore had anything to do with my wife's death?"

"I cannot honestly give you a satisfactory answer."

"But what do you think?"

"If you press me I will try to put my opinion into words. Mensmore was in some mysterious way associated with the crime; but the degree of association, and whether conscious or unconscious, I do not know."

"What do you mean by 'conscious or unconscious'?"

"I am sure that Lady Dyke met her death in his residence; but it is impossible to say now if he was aware of her presence. He was in London at the time, that is quite certain."

"Do the police know all this?"

"No."

"I am glad of it. Mensmore did not kill my wife. The suggestion is absurd—wildly absurd."

"Things look black against him, nevertheless."

"I tell you it is nonsense. You are on the wrong track, Bruce. What possible reason could he have had to decoy my wife to his flat and there murder her?"

"None, perhaps."

"Then why do you hesitate to agree with me?"

"Because there is a woman in the case."

"Another woman?"

"Yes; Mensmore's sister, or half-sister, to be exact. She also lives in Raleigh Mansions."

"Indeed. So all kinds of things have been going on without my knowledge. Yet you promised faithfully to keep me informed of every incident that transpired."

"I am sorry, Dyke; but you were so upset—"

"Upset, man. Don't you realize that this affair is all I have to think about in the world?"

The baronet was so disturbed that Claude at once made up his mind to tell him as little as possible in the future. These constant possibilities of rupture between them must be avoided at all hazard.

To change the conversation he said: "Never mind; this time you must pardon my inadvertence. How do your wife's people bear the continued mystery of her disappearance?"

"At first they were awfully cut up. But lately they have been reconciled to her death, which they say must have resulted from accident, and that her identity must have been mixed up with that of some other person. Such things do happen, you know. Anyway, her sister has gone into mourning for her. You didn't hear, I suppose, that I have made my little nephew my heir?"

"Was that step necessary at your time of life?"

"I shall never marry again, Bruce."

"Well, let us drop the subject. You have done right as regards the boy under present circumstances; but, as a man of the world, I only point out that it is an unwise thing to bring up a youngster in expectation of something which chance might determine differently."

"Chance! There is no chance! My wife cannot return from the grave!"

"True. You have done right, no doubt. But the suddenness of the thing caused me to speak unwittingly."

They were silent for a little while, when Sir Charles returned to the subject nearest his heart.

"Has your search developed in other directions?"

Bruce fenced with the query. "To be candid," he said, "I am now most busily engaged in the not very difficult task of throwing dust in the eyes of the police. My motives are hardly definite to myself, but I do not want this unfortunate man, Mensmore, to be arrested until I have personally become convinced of his guilt."

"You are right. Your instinct seldom fails you. I question if he ever, to his own knowledge, saw my wife."

"Ah! You see you have hit upon the difficulty. Show me her reason for making that secret journey, and I will tell you how she met her death."

His concluding words sank to a murmur. An old friend of Dyke's had entered the room and came toward them.

A few minutes later Bruce quitted the Imperial and drove to his chambers, where he found a note from the ticket collector stating that Foxey's name was William Marsh.

The day was still young, and the barrister paid a visit to the West London Police Court, where the records soon revealed the conviction of the cab-driver and the period of his sentence.

"Let me see," said the resident inspector, "his time at Holloway is up on February 6. That is a Monday, and as Sunday doesn't count, he will be liberated on the 4th, about 8 A.M. That is the habit, sir, in the matter of short sentences. If you want to see him when he leaves the jail you can either wait at the gates or at the nearest public-house, where the prisoners go for their first drink. They seldom or never miss."

Bruce thanked the official and returned home.

He was on the point of going out to drive, when he received a letter from Sir Charles Dyke. It ran:

"*My Dear Claude,*—Today's experiences have taught me to take the inevitable step of announcing my wife's death. Hence, I have forwarded the enclosed notice to an advertisement agency, with instructions to insert it in the principal papers. I have also decided to follow your advice and leave town for a few days. I am going to Wensley, my place in Yorkshire, should you happen to want me.

"Yours,
"CHARLES DYKE."

The notice read:

"DYKE.—On November 6, Alice, wife of Sir Charles Dyke, Bart., suddenly, at London."

Next morning it figured in the obituary columns of many newspapers. Bruce, though taken back by the suddenness of his friend's resolve, saw no reason to endeavor to dissuade him. In the words of the letter, it was "the inevitable step."

CHAPTER XVIII

WHAT HAPPENED ON THE RIVIERA

The *White Heather* swung quietly at her moorings in the harbor of Genoa the Superb. The lively company on board, tired after a day's sight-seeing, had left the marble streets and palace cafés to the Genoese, and sought the pleasant seclusion of the yacht's airy promenade deck.

"Dinner on board, followed by a dance," said Phyllis, as arbiter of the procedure. A few hasty invitations sent out to British residents in Genoa met with general acceptance, and the lull between afternoon tea and the more formal meal was a grateful interlude.

Genoa is so shut in by its amphitheatre of hills that unless a gale blows from the west its bay is unruffled, and its atmosphere oppressively hot during the day, even in the winter months.

Sir William Browne's excursion had proved so attractive to those invited that the *White Heather* was taken farther along the coast than was originally intended. When all the best known resorts of the Riviera itself were exploited, some one, probably prompted thereto by Phyllis or Mensmore, suggested a run to Genoa.

They had been in the port three days, and on the morrow would hand the yacht over to the owner's agents, those on board separating on their different routes. The Brownes went to Florence and Rome, and Mensmore was pretending to hold out against a pressing request to accompany them, cordially given by his prospective father-in-law.

This afternoon Phyllis and he were leaning over the taffrail and discussing the point.

The young lady was slightly inclined to be angry. Her eyes roamed over the magnificent panorama of church-crowned hills and verdant valleys, with the white city in front and the picturesque quays looking as though they had been specially decked for a painting by Clara Montalba. But Phyllis paid heed to none of these things. She wanted her lover to come with her, and not to fly away to smoke-covered London.

"Business!" she cried, "it is always business that men think of. Of course I know that affairs must be attended to, but now that everything is settled and we are quite happy, it is too bad of you to run away immediately."

"But, dearest—"

"There! Take your hand off my arm. You are not going to coax me into agreement. Just because you receive a horrid letter this morning you go and upset all the arrangements."

"Phyllis, listen to me. I—"

"You *shan't* go. I think it is mean of you to insist upon it when I am so urgent."

"I am not insisting. You might at least help me to settle matters; otherwise they will get terribly mixed."

"And you *will* stay?"

"What else can I do when you ask me?"

"Oh, you darling!"

This little quarrel was very delightful, and made them feel ever so much more in love than before; but it did not help Mensmore out of his difficulty.

"Let us see what Corbett really says," he remarked, ruefully taking a letter from his pocket.

"Am I to look, too?"

"Of course. I have no secrets from you, little woman."

Phyllis nestled up close to him. This time she did not object to his hand resting on her shoulder, and together they read the following letter:

"*My Dear Bertie*,—At last I am able to write you definitely. The prospectors have struck it rich on our property, and I have sold two claims outright for $50,000. With this nest-egg I am taking the girls to New York, and shall then start by the *Teutonic* for your side of the pond. I am due in Liverpool on February 4, so look out for me.

"Yours ever,
"SYDNEY H. CORBETT."

Both gazed thoughtfully at the document for a few moments before Phyllis said:

"Does that mean we shall be rich, Bertie?"

Her companion emphasized the gratification of the plural pronoun by a squeeze.

"I hope so, sweet."

"That will be very nice, won't it? I will marry you even if you have to take a place in father's office; but it will be so much better if we haven't to explain to him that we are poor after all."

Mensmore laughed. "It is not so bad as that in any case," he said. "This Springbok Mine speculation will probably turn out well, but I look to Wyoming to yield the best and most permanent results."

"Why is Mr. Corbett coming to London?"

"Because it is only in London that capital can be obtained for large undertakings, and if the Wyoming Goldfield is really a valuable one we may be able to realize some portion of our interests for a considerable sum. Anyhow, he wants to consult me."

"Do you both own the ranch?"

"Yes; it was a joint transaction, but I found the money."

"And why did you come away?"

"Well, we made very little out of it, Phil. As Corbett has two sisters, I thought it best to leave what there was for him. He was absurdly grateful about what he called my generosity in the matter, but now that the land has proved valuable, of course all that nonsense is at an end, and we go half-shares in the deal."

"Two sisters! They pretty?"

"What! Jealous already! They are very nice, but much older than their brother, and he is my senior by two years."

Miss Browne was graciously pleased to accept this explanation. She knitted her smooth brow into a reflective frown as she said:

"Mr. Corbett arrives on the 4th. It is now January 30th. You really ought to go home, Bertie."

"Now my dear, sensible little woman is talking like her own self."

"I see I must give you permission. But I did hope we would see Florence together."

"So we shall. I'll tell you what I can do. I shall write to Corbett to-day, care of the steamer at Liverpool, tell him to go to my flat, and stay there a few days until I arrive, and go home myself at the end of next week. He is sure to spend some time seeing the sights before tackling business, and he can do that as well without me as if I were there. A line to my old housekeeper, who has a spare key, will make the place habitable for him. Happy thought, I'll do it."

"And another happy thought! I'll come and watch you do it."

She did not notice that Mensmore's face clouded at this otherwise pleasant intimation. Nevertheless, he raced off with her to the saloon and seated himself at the writing-table. But before he placed pen to paper, Phyllis bending over him meanwhile, he suddenly exclaimed, in a tone of annoyance:

"Now, what a bore this is. I don't know how to address the letter to make sure of reaching him at once, and it is very important that it should not miss him."

"Father will know. Let us ask him."

"No," said Mensmore judicially, "I will row across the harbor to the Florio-Rubattino office, find out the exact thing, and send off the letter. Back in half-an-hour. Be good!"

And before Phyllis could argue the matter he was at the gangway shouting for a boat.

She blew a kiss to him as he shot over the narrow strip of water inside the mole, and little realized that Mensmore was saying to himself:

"That was a narrow squeak. Never again, as long as I live, will I take another man's name. It causes no end of bother, and at the most unexpected moments."

He did not trouble the Florio-Rubattino people, as he well knew that a letter addressed to the White Star offices would insure any communication reaching his friend.

The context of the missive, as finally indited at the post-office, explains his hesitancy to write it in the presence of his *fiancée*.

"*My dear Sydney,*—Your good news is more than surprising. Although I believe you, I cannot yet grasp its full significance. However, let us leave explanations until we meet. I am fixed here for a few days more, as I have just become engaged to the sweetest girl in the world, but will return home at the end of next week. Meanwhile I want you to take up your residence at my flat, No. 12 Raleigh Mansions, Sloane Square, where my housekeeper has instructions to receive you. Do not be surprised if you find the name of Corbett familiar there. Indeed, I took the place in your name in August last. However, all explanations when we meet.

"Yours ever,
"BERTIE MENSMORE."

This, with a note to the housekeeper, Mrs. Robinson, and another to the hall-porter of the Universities Club, lest by any chance the Liverpool letter missed his friend, completed his task.

He laughed as he hurried from the post-office to the harbor.

"By Jove!" he said to himself, "won't old Robinson be surprised when she gets my letter telling her that another Mr. Corbett is coming from America, and that my name, concealed for family reasons, is Mensmore. I guess that Sydney will feel a bit mixed up, too, until I tell him the whole yarn."

No wonder his housekeeper would fail to understand him.

Others, whose influence on his fortunes he little suspected, were already puzzled by the circumstances. Bruce, for instance, and White would be very glad if some occult power enabled them to read the seemingly trivial letters posted that day in Genoa.

Every person known to the reader, and not the least the visitor from the United States, was on the eve of a mad whirl of events, the outcome of which no man could prophesy. As yet, one man only, Claude Bruce, had the slightest suspicion that affairs were approaching a crisis.

When Mensmore reached the *White Heather* he found Lady Browne and Phyllis dressed for a drive before dinner. Sir William seized the opportunity to cross-examine his daughter's suitor as to his means. Phyllis was an only child, and her father did not propose that she should live in penury, whatever the financial position of her husband might be. He liked Mensmore, and had ascertained by private inquiries that his social position was good.

"His father was a Major-General," said his informant, "who lost his savings by speculation, and was unable to maintain his son in a crack cavalry corps, so the youngster resigned and went to America to try to better himself. There was a daughter, too, by the first wife, a very charming woman, who, when the crash came, was supposed to have gone on the stage. But I have never heard of her since."

So far, the credentials were not bad; but Sir William thought it his duty to ascertain definite particulars.

Mensmore was quite candid with him.

"I have been somewhat of a rolling stone," he said, "but I am glad to believe that people have never had cause to think ill of me. At times, my affairs have been at a desperate stage, but I hope such periods have passed forever. I have already spoken to you about the Springbok Mine—"

The old gentleman nodded.

"Well, this morning I have received very satisfactory news from America," and he handed over Corbett's letter for perusal.

"Yes," agreed Sir William, "these things promise well. We will look into them when we reach England. Meanwhile, I give my provisional sanction to my daughter's engagement. She is a good girl, Mensmore. She will be a true and excellent wife. I think you are worthy of her, and I hope that whatever clouds may have darkened your life will now pass away. You two ought to be happy."

"We will, sir," said Mensmore fervently.

"By the way, where is your sister? Is she in England or abroad?"

Mensmore had been expecting this question. He was prepared for it.

"Mrs. Hillmer is my half-sister," he explained. "I have not seen much of her since—since an unhappy marriage she contracted some years ago."

"Indeed. Is her husband alive?"

"I can hardly tell you. I believe so. But she does not live with him. She is well provided for, but it was partly on account of this matter that I came to the Riviera for the winter. To tell the truth, I quarrelled with her about it."

"Ah, well. Her troubles need not affect Phyllis and you, except to give you warning. And take my advice. Never interfere between husband and wife. However good your motive, ill is sure to come of it."

In the growing dusk Sir William Browne did not note his companion's embarrassment in discussing this topic. Mensmore was essentially an honorable man, and he detested the necessity which forced him to permit false inferences to be drawn from his words. Yet there was no help for it. He was compelled to suffer for the faults of another.

It was relief when the dressing-bell for dinner allowed him to escape to his cabin.

There was quite a large gathering for dinner. Places like Genoa contain a number of highly interesting personages if the visitor discovers them. The British race produces a richer variety of human flotsam and jetsam than any other. These derelicts come to anchor in out-of-the-way parts of the earth. They seem to have been everywhere and have done everything, while the whole world is an open book to them.

Thus there was no lack of variety in the conversation, and, as usual in such assemblies, it dealt more with persons than with incidents.

Phyllis had arranged the guests, so it may be taken for granted that her lover was near her—in fact, he sat exactly opposite. The lady he took in to dinner was the wife of an English doctor, and the British consul at the port was Miss Browne's table companion.

The consul was a chatty man, who kept himself well informed concerning society events.

"By the way," he said to Phyllis, "did you ever meet Lady Dyke?"

"No, her name is not familiar to me."

"Do you mean the wife of Sir Charles Dyke?" said Mensmore; and the sudden interest he evinced caused Phyllis to glance at him wonderingly.

"Yes, that is she."

"I know Sir Charles well. What is there new about his wife?"

"She is dead."

"Good Heavens! Dead! When, and how?"

Mensmore was so obviously agitated that others present noticed it, and Phyllis marvelled much that in all their confidence the name of Dyke had never escaped his lips.

The consul, too, was a little nonplussed by the sensation caused by his words.

"I fear," he said, "that I have blurted out the fact rather unguardedly. The Dykes are friends of yours?"

"No, no, not in that sense. Sir Charles I have known for many years. But are you sure his wife is dead?"

"My authority is an announcement in the *Times* to hand by to-day's post. I should not have mentioned it were not her ladyship so well known in society, and the affair is peculiar, to say the least."

"Peculiar—how?"

In his all-absorbing interest in the consul's statement, Mensmore paid no heed to the curious looks directed at him; he had become very pale, and was more excited in manner than the circumstances appeared to warrant.

"In this sense: The paper is the issue of January 28, yet the notice says that Lady Dyke died on November 6. This is odd, is it not? A woman of her position could hardly have quitted life so quietly that no one would trouble to publish the fact until nearly three months after the event."

"It is extraordinary—inexplicable!"

"Did you know Lady Dyke personally, Bertie?" put in Phyllis timorously.

The question restored Mensmore to some sense of his surroundings.

"I have never even seen her," he said, trying desperately to be commonplace; "but her husband is an old schoolfellow of mine, and I have heard much of both of them since their marriage. I am quite shocked by the news."

"I can only repeat my regret for having spoken of it so carelessly," said the polite consul.

"Oh, I am glad to know of it since it has happened. Poor Lady Dyke! How strange that she should die!"

Phyllis had the tact to change the conversation, and Mensmore gradually recovered his self-possession. A woman's eyes are keener than a man often gives her credit for; and Phyllis saw quite plainly that after the first effect of the news had passed it, in some indefinable way, seemed to have a good effect on her lover. But if a woman's intuition is seldom at fault her reasoning faculties are narrow.

Trying to arrive at a solution of the mystery attending Mensmore's behavior, Phyllis suddenly became hot all over.

She felt furiously and inordinately jealous of a woman she did not know, and who was admittedly dead before Mensmore and she herself had met.

Hence her nose went high in the air when Bertie claimed her for the first dance.

"Who is this Lady Dyke in whom you are so deeply interested?" she said, drawing him beneath a sheltering awning.

"As I said," replied Mensmore, "she is the wife of an old acquaintance of mine."

"But you must have been very fond of her to feel so keenly when you heard of her death?"

"Fond of her! I have never, to my knowledge, laid eyes on her."

"Oh!" And the tone was somewhat mollified. "Then why did you look so worried during dinner?"

"Simply because I know Sir Charles."

"What a dear, sympathetic little boy you are! When I die, Bertie, I suppose you will drop down stiff from grief at once."

"Don't talk nonsense. We are missing all this delightful music."

And they whirled away down the snowy deck, forgetful of all things save one, that they were in love.

Now, what a pity it was that Bruce was not on board the *White Heather* that night. Many complications, and not a little misery, would have been avoided thereby.

CHAPTER XIX

WHERE MRS. HILLMER WENT

Sir Charles Dyke, in sending off the hurried announcement of his wife's death, forgot the "society" papers.

Such a promising topic did not come in their way every week, and they made the most of it. Where did Lady Dyke die? Under what circumstances did she die? They rolled the morsel under their tongue in every conceivable manner.

Details were not forthcoming.

"Our representative called at Wensley House, Portman Square, but was informed that Sir Charles was in Yorkshire." Inquiry by a local reporter from Sir Charles in person elicited no information. "Lady Dyke is dead," wrote this enterprising journalist; "of that there can be no manner of doubt, but her husband states that for family reasons he is unable to supply the public with the precise facts concerning his wife's demise."

This ill-advised authentic statement only fanned the flame. An evening journal got hold of the proceedings at the Putney Coroner's Court which inquired into the death of a woman found in the Thames, and, with a portentous display of headlines, published an interview with the doctor giving particulars of the iron spike found imbedded in the skull.

The paper was also able to state "on the best authority" that at this inquest Sir Charles Dyke and the missing lady's personal maid were called in to identify the body, but failed.

A first-class sensation was in full swing and threatened to reach the question stage in the House of Commons when Bruce took hold of affairs.

He went to Sir Charles Dyke's solicitors, and induced them to send out the following authoritative communication to the press:

"Much unnecessary pain is being caused to Sir Charles Dyke and to the relatives of his late wife by the comments which have appeared in many newspapers regarding Lady Dyke's death. Her ladyship left her home on November 6th to pay a visit to her sister at Richmond, and since that date has not been seen or heard of. There was no possible reason for her disappearance. After a long and agonizing search, her husband and relatives have come to the conclusion that she met with some accident on the date named, with the result that her identity was not established, and she was probably buried from some hospital or other institution long before her friends seriously entertained the thought that she was dead. Every such case of accidental death followed by the interment of unknown persons by the authorities, occurring on or about November 6th, has since been rigidly investigated, but no definite trace has been found of the missing lady. Sir Charles Dyke determined to take the public step of announcing his wife's death in the hope that any hitherto undiscovered clue might thereby come to light. But there are no grounds to suppose that any other explanation of the occurrence than that given will be forthcoming. The investigation has been in the hands of Scotland Yard throughout, so no good purpose can be served by further discussion in the press of what is now, and threatens to remain, a mystery rendered more complex by the simplicity of its leading features."

Several newspapers, of course, pointed out that they were helping forward the inquiry by noising it abroad, but thenceforth the paragraphs ceased, being eclipsed in interest by the revelations of a great divorce case in which there were no less than six titled co-respondents.

One man was much puzzled by the original obituary notice and the semi-official statement supplied by the solicitors.

Mr. White did not know what to make of them. He guessed that Bruce had inspired that "explanation," and he read the concluding sentence many times.

"It threatens to remain a mystery, does it not?" he murmured. "Just wait, Mr. Bruce, until I lay my hands on Corbett. Clever as you are, I think I will show you that Scotland Yard can occasionally get the better of your theories. Anyhow, Corbett will have to be very explicit about his movements before I am satisfied that he knows nothing about this business."

He had written to the Chief of Police at Cheyenne, and something definite would soon come to hand.

Nevertheless, he felt somewhat shaken in his diagnosis of the crime. Wyoming was a long way from London, and the letter from Corbett, which he had in his possession, did not exactly confirm his suspicion that this man was concerned in the murder of Lady Dyke.

He quickly became aware of Mrs. Hillmer's departure, and at once jumped to the conclusion that she had recently left England for the United States. A close scrutiny of the passenger lists at Liverpool and Southampton did not help him much, and he ultimately resolved to call on Bruce, in the hope that a chance exclamation might reveal the barrister's opinion of the situation.

Claude was not at a loss to account for Mr. White's presence.

"I expected you," he said.

"Really now, may I ask why, sir?"

"Because you have missed Mrs. Hillmer, and you want me to help you find where she has gone, and why."

The detective smiled.

"I won't say that you are wrong, sir," he cried. "In these affairs it is always well to keep an eye on the woman, you know."

"When did Mrs. Hillmer leave Raleigh Mansions?"

"On the 30th."

"It is now February 3. Four days ago, eh?"

"That is the time. She might have left by the American line from Southampton or the Cunard from Liverpool on Wednesday, but she did not, and no one answering to her description is booked by the White Star to-morrow."

"Southampton! Liverpool! Do you think she has gone to America?"

"Where else? She's in league with Corbett, somehow, of that I am certain, and I think that the Monte Carlo address was a mere blind—a clever one, too, as it even deceived you, Mr. Bruce."

"Yes. It did deceive me."

"Then why are you so surprised at the suggestion that the lady should attempt to cross the Atlantic?"

"Because I have not your rapid perception of the points of the case."

"That's your way of pulling my leg, Mr. Bruce."

The barrister smiled.

Mrs. Hillmer, of course, had gone to Monte Carlo. Once there she would have little difficulty in tracing the *White Heather*, and overtaking Mensmore.

She would warn him of the police pursuit, and there would be a scene between them.

How would it result? Would Mensmore, guilty, seek safety in flight? Would he, innocent, return to London and demand to be confronted with his accusers?

For the life of him, Bruce could not say positively. Yet he felt the situation was too delicate to be dealt with by Mr. White's bludgeon methods, and he forebore to speak.

The detective interpreted his silence as an admission of inability to find a satisfactory explanation of Mrs. Hillmer's absence.

He went on:

"Corbett is not at Monte Carlo."

"So I imagined."

"Well, it is a fact. The police have made constant inquiries for him at the Hotel du Cercle and elsewhere. Not the slightest trace of him can be found."

"I was there myself, you know."

"Yes, sir. I have not forgotten that. But it shows what a clever rascal the fellow is in concealing his identity. However, he could never have counted on my discovering that letter of his. Even if he is not in America we shall have some reliable data to go upon in answer to my queries."

"There I fully agree with you. You will have done a great deal if you thoroughly clear up the mystery regarding Corbett. May I ask you to let me know the result?"

"With pleasure, sir. And now, can I request a favor in return?"

"Certainly."

"Tell me, then, what is, in your opinion, the best way to find Mrs. Hillmer."

Bruce did not expect to be thus openly challenged on the matter. It was one thing to withhold his own theories and discoveries from this representative of the majesty of the law, but quite another to refuse to help a detective with whom he was nominally working.

Besides, Mrs. Hillmer had four days' start. It would take some time—possibly a telegram would not be sufficiently explicit—to obtain the desired assistance from the Continental police. Yes—in this instance, Mensmore must take his chances.

"If I were you," said Bruce, slowly weighing his words, "I would inquire at the Continental booking-offices at Victoria and Charing Cross, and from the guards in charge of the morning mail trains on the 30th. In fact, it would be quite safe if you were to wire the authorities at Monte Carlo, asking if Mrs. Hillmer is not now at the Hotel du Cercle."

The detective started as though he had been shot.

"What!" he cried, "you think she is there all the time?"

"I think she has been there since Wednesday morning."

"That is what I mean. Why did you not tell me sooner?"

"Because you never asked me. And now, Mr. White, one word of advice. Go slow."

"It's all jolly fine telling me to go slow when I have no reason to go fast. The case even against Corbett is shadowy enough at present."

"Exactly. Wait until you can grasp a substance."

"I will, sir," said White, jamming his hat on; "but when I lay my hands on Corbett I will grasp him hard enough."

It took the policeman all that day to satisfy himself that Mrs. Hillmer had really booked for the Riviera by the Club train from Charing Cross on the preceding Monday.

Just as he verified the fact, came a reply from the Monte Carlo police:

"Mrs. Hillmer arrived at the Hotel du Cercle on Wednesday. Left for Italy same afternoon. Shall we endeavor to trace her?"

"Oh, bother," he growled. "Corbett may be in Jerusalem by this time. And here have I been fussing about Wyoming or some other potato-patch in the Far West."

However, he wired again to Monte Carlo:

"Yes. Locate Mrs. Hillmer, if possible. I will then telegraph instructions to local police."

When this message was despatched he felt easier in his mind.

The chase was at least getting warm.

"I cannot arrest him yet," he reflected; "but if I once get fairly on his track, I will not lose sight of him again if I can help it. I suppose it will mean a trip to Italy for me. I must lay the evidence before the Treasury to see if a warrant is justified."

Two days passed without incident.

Late on Sunday evening, February 5, a Continental telegram was handed to him at Scotland Yard:

"Mrs. Hillmer's present address, Hotel Imperiale, Florence."

He promptly wired the Chief of Police at Florence:

"Keep Mrs. Hillmer, English visitor, Hotel Imperiale, under surveillance. Also watch her associates, particularly Englishman named Corbett, if there. Letter follows."

"That's a good stroke of business," said he, when the message was sent. "Now we shan't be long!"

It was in contented mood that he lit a cigar in his office, before walking home for dinner, but a messenger with the badge of the Commercial Cable Company in Northumberland Avenue bustled past him.

"Who's the cable for, boy?" said the detective.

"White, Scotland Yard," was the answer.

"That's me."

He tore open the envelope, and found that the contents were coded, but he caught the word "Corbett" amidst the unintelligible jumble.

With some excitement he rushed into the office to find the A B C Code, and after some confusion in deciphering the words, this was what he read:

"Regret delay in replying to your communication. Corbett left New York in *White Star* steamer due Liverpool, February 4."

"February 4? Why, that's yesterday. Good gracious, he's here all the time. Well, of all the—"

But exclamations were useless. Calling another plain-clothes man to accompany him, he drove off in mad haste to Sloane Square.

About an hour later Bruce received a typewritten slip gummed on to a telegraph form. It was from Florence, and ran as follows:

"My brother wildly excited regarding allegations. We start for London to-night. Meanwhile fearful complications expected. Mr. Corbett, of Wyoming, my brother's friend, is probably occupying his flat, and may be arrested. We both trust you to save him. Wire us at Modane or Gare du Nord.

"GWENDOLINE HILLMER."

So Bruce also raced off in a hansom towards Sloane Square.

CHAPTER XX

MR. SYDNEY H. CORBETT

The detective glanced up at Bruce's chambers while passing through Victoria Street.

"I wonder what he would think if he knew what we are after," he said to his colleague, one of the two who accompanied him when the barrister was arrested by mistake.

"What *are* we after?" said the policeman.

"This time we are going to nail the right Corbett," was the confident answer.

"Will we cart him off?"

"Well, now, that depends. I think I am quite right in collaring him unless he explains to my satisfaction, which is hardly likely."

"The charge is one of murder, isn't it?"

"Yes."

"Who did he kill?"

"Well, up to now it hasn't come out, for the sake of the family. But if Corbett is here you will know soon enough."

"It's a funny way to go to work."

"Commissioner's orders, my boy. I am not to reveal the la— the name until it cannot be helped. However, as I have said so much, I don't mind telling you it's a woman, and a big one too."

"Big! Fat, do you mean?"

"No. A woman of high position."

"Phew! A regular society scandal, I suppose?"

"That's about the size of it."

On arrival at Sloane Square they quickly ascended to No. 12 Raleigh Mansions.

A stout, elderly woman answered their knock, and a glance at her face revealed the map of Ireland, although her name was Saxon Robinson.

"Mr. Corbett in?" inquired White.

"Faix, he's not."

"Then where is he?"

"I don't know, misther, an' if I did I wouldn't be afther telling when axed in an oncivil manner."

"All right, Mrs. ——"

"Robinson's my name, if that's anny use to ye."

"Very well, Mrs. Robinson. We wish to have a word with Mr. Corbett, and we will be much obliged if you can tell us when he is likely to return, if he is in London."

"Arrah, it's meself is mixed intirely about him. Sure *this* Mr. Corbett is in London right enough, and is comin' in to dinner in half-an-hour, so by yer lave I'll jist go on wid me wurruk."

"May we come in and wait for him?"

Mrs. Robinson surveyed them suspiciously, but seemingly decided in their favor.

"Stip in here, gintlemen both," she said, and conducted them to the sitting-room.

A fire now burned brightly in the grate wherein Bruce had made his pregnant discovery. The damaged bracket still stared at White, so to speak, but he saw it not.

Mrs. Robinson bustled away to the kitchen, and the two officers sat silently waiting developments. Suddenly a thought occurred to White, and he went into the passage.

"Mrs. Robinson," he said, "what did you mean by referring to *this* Mr. Corbett?"

A quick step came bounding up the stairs, and a key rattled in the lock.

"You'd betther ax him yerself," responded the housekeeper pithily, and the door opened to admit a handsome, well-knit man, tall and straight, with the clearly cut features of the true Westerner, and the easy carriage of one accustomed to the freedom of the prairie.

He was quietly dressed. The only sign that he was not a Londoner was given by his wide-awake felt hat, the last token of environment relinquished by a wandering citizen from the region of the Rockies. In the semi-darkness of the interior he could but dimly discern the form of the detective behind the ready-tongued housekeeper.

"There's two gintlemen to see ye, Misther Corbett," said she.

"Well, now, that's curious," he answered cheerfully. "I can only see one of you, but I'm glad to have you call, stranger, anyway. Come right in. Are you sent by my friend to kinder cheer me up? I find this big city of yours a powerful kind of tonic after Wyoming. Come right in."

Mr. White was as greatly nonplussed by the newcomer's attitude as by his flow of language.

Within the drawing-room Corbett caught sight of the second detective. "Hello! Here's the other one. Ve-ry glad to meet you both. Now, if you'll just tell me your names we'll get along straight away, as I guess you know mine all right."

The man was genuinely pleased by this unexpected visit. He smilingly pushed towards them a box of cigars, green ones, and helped himself to a weed.

"My name," said the detective, "is Inspector White, of Scotland Yard, and my friend here accompanies me officially."

"And hasn't he got a name?"

"Yes; but it doesn't matter."

"Well, if it doesn't matter, we won't quarrel. I guess you've got a message of some sort for me, else you wouldn't trouble to climb these stairs. Why don't you have el-e-vators in these big buildings?"

"As I said," began Mr. White, "we are from Scotland Yard."

"That's so. I've got that fixed O.K. Your name is I. White, from Scotland Yard. I don't know where Scotland Yard is, but we'll worry along without the geography of it."

"I am in the police. My title is Inspector. It is not my Christian name. Scotland Yard is the headquarters of the London police."

The American's eyes opened wide in wonder at this announcement, and a perplexing thought seemed to occur to him. But he said quietly:

"I'll figure it out better when you tell me why you've been good enough to call. And suppose we all sit down. I'm not used to stone pavements. I'm tired."

"Your name is Sydney H. Corbett?" said the detective severely, though he took a chair.

"So my people always told me."

"And you have occupied these chambers since August last?"

"Have I?"

"So I am informed."

"Get along with your story."

"You have just returned to England from Wyoming. The New York police cabled me that you arrived in Liverpool yesterday."

"Did they now? That was real cute of 'em."

"I want to ask you, in the first instance, the exact date of your departure from this country."

Before replying to the detective Corbett looked at him fixedly, as though he was trying to read what was passing in his mind.

At last he said with a smile:

"Say, what are you after, Mr. White of Scotland Yard? What's the game? Who's been fooling you?"

"That is not the way to talk to me, sir. Answer my question fully and properly, or it may be worse for you."

"Jehosh! Have you come to wipe the floor with me?"

"Are you going to reply to me or not?"

"I'm not going to speak square to any man who comes along and puts a thing like you do."

"Very well. I can get my information by other means. You leave me no alternative—"

Mr. White had half risen and was about to add, "but to arrest you," when, with a rapidity known only to those accustomed to "draw" from boyhood, Corbett whipped a revolver from a hip pocket and covered the bridge of White's nose with the muzzle.

"Just you sit still, right there, Mr. White of Scotland Yard, or I will let daylight through you and your nameless friend if he interferes. You'd better believe me. By gad! I won't speak twice."

Neither White nor his companion were cowards. But they were quite helpless. They had not grappled with the circumstances with sufficient alertness, and they were utterly at this man's mercy. They were away from the door, and a table separated them from Corbett, while there was that in his eye which told them he would shoot if either of them moved. They both sprang to their feet, and glared at him impotently.

"Now, gentlemen," said Corbett, with the utmost coolness, "let me persuade you to sit down again and go on with your story, which interests me."

White was scarlet with wrath and annoyance.

"Let me tell you—" he roared.

"Sit down!"

"Make the best of it, Jim," murmured the other policeman; and the queer gathering resumed their seats.

"That's better," said Corbett genially. "Now, we'll have a nice little chat. Am I correct in supposing that you were about to march me off to jail just now, when I spoilt the proposition?"

"There's no use in resisting," growled White. "You cannot escape. If you have an atom of sense left you will come with us quietly, as it's all up with you."

"It looks like it," said Corbett, with a grim smile. "But if it's so bad a case as all that, there's no desperate hurry, is there?"

"You're only making matters more difficult for yourself."

"Maybe. But as I happen to be a citizen of the United States, I allow that I can't be whipped off to prison just because a fool like you thinks it's good for me. I've been a law-abiding man all my life, and I've lived in places where each man made his own law. If you can show good cause for your action, I'll stand the racket. At present I regard you as a blamed idiot."

The situation overcame the detective. He could only mutter:

"Time will show who's the idiot."

"I'm getting hungry, Mr. White of Scotland Yard, and I've a kind of notion that the old lady is ready with the eatables. Will you be good enough to say what you're after?"

"I came here to ask you to account for your movements, and, failing a satisfactory explanation, to arrest you."

"On what charge?"

"For being concerned in the murder of Lady Dyke, on or about November 6 last."

"Lady Dyke?"

"Yes."

"Arrest *me?*"

"Yes."

"I placed you right away. You are a blamed idiot, Mr. White of Scotland Yard."

This repetition of his name and address goaded the detective almost beyond endurance.

"Now you know the charge," he shouted, "are you coming with us quietly, or—"

"Or what?"

The revolver still hovered across the table.

"Are we going to sit here all night?"

It was a weak conclusion, but to suggest an attack was sheer madness under the conditions.

"I guess not," was the calm answer. "I want my dinner, and I mean to have it."

"Very well. Eat your dinner and have done with it."

"That's better. You and your friend shall join me. We'll have a nice little talk and straighten out matters, which have got kinder mixed."

This was too much for White's associate. He burst out laughing.

"I allowed there was a joke in the deal, somewhere," went on Corbett, "but I haven't quite got the hang of it yet. Now, Mr. White of Scotland Yard, are you going to act like a reasonable man, or must I keep your nose in line with the barrel?"

White was saved from deciding which horn of the dilemma he would land on, for a sharp rat-tat at the door induced silence, and a moment later Bruce's voice was heard inquiring:

"Is Mr. Corbett in?"

"Faix, there may be a half-a-dozen of him in by this time," cried Mrs. Robinson. "I dunno where I am, at all, at all. The gintlemen are in the parlor, sir."

And Bruce entered.

In order to enfilade the new-comer scientifically, Corbett backed to the corner. Claude glanced at the three, saw the revolver, and said with a comical air of relief:

"Thank goodness, nothing has happened. Put away your pistol, Mr. Corbett; you will not need it."

Although the barrister's manner differed considerably from the brusque methods adopted by Mr. White, the American remained on his guard. He said stiffly:

"You all seem to know me fairly well; but if you had the advantage of closer acquaintance, you would allow that I am not the man to be rushed on a confidence trick. If somebody doesn't explain quick I will lose my temper, and there will be trouble."

"I sympathize with you!" cried Bruce. "But the first thing you must learn in this country is to keep dry cigars for your visitors. Our respective tastes differ in that respect."

"I guess I'll cotton to you, stranger; but I'm tired holding this pistol."

"Put it away, then. I tell you it is not wanted. White, listen to me. You have hit upon the wrong man."

"Wrong man!" cried the detective, feeling more confident in the barrister's presence. "Why, I've had a cable about him from New York."

"Possibly; but you're mistaken, nevertheless. Mr. Corbett has not been within five thousand miles of England for years, possibly not in his life."

"Bully for you, stranger!" broke in Corbett.

"Then who is Mr. Sydney H. Corbett whom you believe, as well as I, to be the murderer of Lady Dyke?"

"Steady, White. The last time I saw you I appealed to you to go slow. The man whom you want, simply because he happens to be the real occupant of these rooms, is at present travelling to London as fast he can from Florence, and his sister, Mrs. Hillmer, is with him."

"Florence! Mrs. Hillmer!" gasped the policeman. "I've just arranged to have her watched there."

"Your arrangements, though admirable, are somewhat late in the day."

"Then what is her brother's name?"

"Albert Mensmore. For some reason, hidden at this moment, he lived here under the name of the gentleman who has, I see, been giving you a practical lesson in the art of not jumping at conclusions."

"Have you known this long?"

"For some weeks."

"Then why didn't you tell me?"

"Because I have no definite reason for connecting Mensmore with Lady Dyke's death. If I had, his action in returning to London the moment he hears of the charge would shake my belief."

"Who told him?"

"Mrs. Hillmer."

"Oh, this business is quite beyond me. I can't fathom it a little bit."

And White sank dejectedly to his chair again.

"I don't know what you're talking about, gentlemen," said Corbett, pocketing his revolver; "but it dawns upon me that I shan't be required to shoot anybody or sleep in jail to-night."

"Why didn't you answer my questions properly, and save all this nonsense?"

"I'll tell you why, sir. The name of a friend of mine has been mentioned. Albert Mensmore has been more than a brother to me. I allowed you meant mischief to him, as you thought you were talking to him all the time. I don't know much about you, but I hope that your first action would not be to give away your chum if he is in trouble."

The detective did not answer, though his look of astonishment at Corbett's declaration of motive was eloquent enough.

"Before we quit this business," went on the American, "let me say one thing. Any man who tells you that Albert Mensmore murdered a woman is telling you a lie. I don't know anything about this Lady Dyke, or how she may have died, but I do know my friend. He's good in a tight place, but, to think of him killing a woman—Jehosh, it's sickening."

Mrs. Robinson burst in, with face aflame.

"Is this palaverin' to go on all night?" she demanded angrily. "Here's the dinner sphilin', after all me worry and bother, with the head of me vexed to know who is the masther and who ishn't."

"All right, mother," laughed Corbett. "Bring in the whole caboodle."

"Mr. Corbett," said Bruce, "I hope you will come and have lunch with me to-morrow, at this address," handing him a card. "I want to have a long talk with you. Mr. White, if you come with me I will explain a good deal to you of which you are now in ignorance."

"Surely, Mr. Corbett will answer a few questions first," said the detective.

"Don't you think you have troubled him sufficiently for this evening? Besides, he can tell us nothing. All the explanation is really due to him, and I propose to give it to him to-morrow. Come, White, this time I promise you that a considerable portion of your inquiry shall be cleared up, and I do not speak without foundation, as you have often learned hitherto."

So the mysterious Sydney H. Corbett was left in undisturbed possession of his flat and his dinner, while the trio passed out into the quietude of the streets.

CHAPTER XXI

HOW LADY DYKE LEFT RALEIGH MANSIONS

Mr. White was actually inclined to preserve silence while they walked to Victoria Street. The events of the preceding hour had not exactly conduced to the maintenance, in the eyes of his brother officer, of that pre-eminent sagacity which he invariably claimed.

His companion rubbed in this phase of the matter by saying: "I should think, Jim, you will give Raleigh Mansions wide berth for some time to come, after making two bad breaks there."

But it was no part of Bruce's scheme that the detective should be rendered desperate by repeated failures. "It is not Mr. White's fault," he said, "that these errors have occurred. They are rather the result of his pertinacity in leaving no clue unsolved which promises to lead to success. When this case ends, if ever it does end, I feel sure he will admit that he has never before encountered so much difficulty in unravelling the most complex problems within his experience."

"That is so," chimed in the senior detective. "The thing that beats me in this affair is the want of a beginning, so to speak. One would imagine it the work of a lunatic if Lady Dyke herself had not contributed so curiously to the mystery of her disappearance."

"There you are, White; that is the true scent. Find the motive and we find the murderer, if Lady Dyke was wilfully put to death."

"*If* she was, Mr. Bruce? Have you any doubt about it?"

"There cannot be certainty when we are groping in the dark. But the gloom is passing; we are on the eve of a discovery."

At Bruce's residence White's colleague left him. Soon the barrister and the policeman were sitting snugly before a good fire.

There Claude took him step by step through each branch of his inquiry as it is known to the reader.

He omitted nothing. The discovery of Jane Harding and of Mensmore, the latter's transactions with Dodge & Co., his dramatic *coup* at Monte Carlo and its attendant love episode—all these were exhaustively described. He enlarged upon Mrs. Hillmer's anxiety when the tragedy became known to her, and did not forget Sir Charles Dyke's amazement at the suggestion that his old playmate might prove to be responsible for the death of his wife.

He produced the waxen moulds of the piece of iron found on the body at Putney, and the ornamental scroll from which it had been taken.

At this bit of evidence Mr. White's complacency forsook him. Thus far he had experienced a feeling of resentment against Bruce for having concealed from him so much that was material to their investigation.

But when he realized that a powerful link in the chain of events had all along been placidly resting before his eyes his distress was evident, and the barrister came to his rescue.

"You are not to blame, White," he said, "for having failed to note many things which I have now told you. You are the slave of a system. Your method works admirably for the detection of commonplace crime, but as soon as the higher region of romance is reached it is as much out of place as a steam-roller in a lady's boudoir. Look at the remarkable series of crimes the English police have failed to solve of late, merely because some *bizarre* element had intruded itself at the outset. Have you ever read any of the works of Edgar Allan Poe?"

The detective answered in the affirmative. "The Murders of the Rue Morgue" and "The Mystery of Marie Roget" were familiar to him.

"Well," went on Bruce, "there you have the accurate samples of my meaning. Poe would not have been puzzled for an hour by the vagaries of Jack the Ripper. He would have said at once—most certainly after the third or fourth in the series of murders—'This is the work of an athletic lunatic, with a morbid love of anatomy and a morbid hatred of a certain class of women. Seek for him among young men who have pestered doctors with outrageous theories, and who possess weak-minded or imbecile relatives.' Then, again, take the murder on the South-Western Railway. Do you think Poe would have gone questioning bar-tenders or inquiring into abortive love affairs? Not he! Jealous swains do not carry pestles about with them to slay their sweethearts, nor do they choose a four-minutes' interval between suburban stations for frenzied avowals of their passion. Here you have the clear trail of a clever lunatic, dropping from the skies, as it were, and disappearing in the same erratic manner. That is why I tell you most emphatically that neither you nor I have yet the remotest conception as to who really killed Lady Dyke."

"Surely things look black now against this Mensmore?"

"Do they? How would it have fared with an acquaintance of one of the unfortunate women killed by Jack the Ripper had the police found him in the locality with fresh blood-stains on his clothes? What would have resulted from the discovery of a chemist's mortar among the possessions of one of Elizabeth Camp's male friends? Come now, be honest, and tell me."

But Mr. White could only smoke in silence.

"Therefore," continued Bruce, "let us ask ourselves why, and how, it was possible for Mensmore to commit the crime. Personally, notwithstanding all that we apparently know against him circumstantially, I should hardly believe Mensmore if he confessed himself to be the murderer!"

"Now, why on earth do you say that, Mr. Bruce?"

"Because Mensmore is normal and this crime abnormal. Because the man who would blow out his brains on account of losses at pigeon-shooting never had brains enough to dispose of the body in such fashion. Because Mensmore, having temporarily changed his name for some trivial reason, would never resume it with equal triviality with this shadow upon his life."

"Then why have you told me all these things that tell so heavily against him?"

"In order that, this time at least, you may feel that the production of a pair of handcuffs does not satisfactorily settle the entire business."

"I promise there shall be no more arrests until this affair is much more decided than it is at present."

"Good. I shall make a detective of you after my own heart in time."

"Yet I cannot help being surprised at the very strange fact that his own sister should seem to suspect him!"

"Ah! Now you have struck the true line. Why did she have that fear? There I am with you entirely. Let us ascertain that and I promise you an important development. Mrs. Hillmer and Mensmore are both concerned in the disappearance of Lady Dyke, yet neither knew that she had disappeared, and both are deeply upset by it, for Mrs. Hillmer flies off to warn her brother, and the brother posts back to London the moment it comes to his ears through her. There, you see, we have a key which may unlock many doors. For Heaven's sake let it not be battered out of shape the instant it reaches our hands."

But Mr. White was quite humble. "As I have told you," he said, "I have done with the battering process."

"I am sure of it. And now listen to the most remarkable fact that has yet come to light. Lady Dyke's body was taken from Raleigh Mansions to Putney in a four-wheeler. The cabman was forthwith locked up by the police and clapped into prison for three months. He was released yesterday, and will be here within the next quarter of an hour."

The detective's hair nearly rose on end at this statement.

"Look here, Mr. Bruce!" he cried, "have you any more startlers up your sleeve, or is that the finish?"

"That is the last shot in my locker."

"I'm jolly glad! I half expected the next thing you would say was that you did the job yourself."

"It wouldn't be the first time you thought that; eh, my friend?"

White positively blushed.

"Oh! that's chaff," he said. "But why the dickens did the police lock up this cabman—the only witness we could lay our hands upon? Why, I myself questioned every cabman in the vicinity several times."

"Because he got drunk on the proceeds of the journey, and subsequently thought he was Phaeton driving the chariot of the sun. But, there, he will tell you himself. I met him yesterday morning outside Holloway Jail, and persuaded him to come here to-night, provided he has not gone on the spree again with disastrous results."

The entrance of Smith—obviously relieved to see his master and the "tec" on such good terms—to announce the arrival of "Mr. William Marsh," settled any doubts as to the cabman's intentions, and his appearance established the fact of his sobriety. Three months "hard" had made the cab-driver a new man.

Recognition was mutual between him and Mr. White.

"Hello, Foxey," cried the latter. "It's you, is it?"

"Me it is, guv'nor; but I didn't know there was to be a 'cop' here"—this with a suspicious glance at Bruce and a backward movement towards the door.

"Do not be alarmed," said the barrister; "this gentleman's presence implies no trouble for you. We want you to help us, and if you do so willingly I will make up that lost fiver you received for driving two people to Putney the night you were arrested."

The poor old cabman became very confused on hearing this staggering remark. Up to that moment he regarded Bruce as the agent for a charitable association, and there was no harm, he told his "missus," in trying to "knock him for a bit."

He stood nervously fumbling with his hat, but did not answer. White knew how to deal with him.

"Sit down, Foxey, and have a drink. You need one to cheer you up. Answer this gentleman's questions. He means you no harm."

"Honor bright?"

"Honor bright."

"Well, I don't mind if I do. No soda, thank you, sir. Just a small drop of water. Ah, that's better stuff 'n they keep in Holloway."

Thus fortified, Marsh had no hesitation in telling them what he knew. Substantially, his story was identical with the version given to Bruce by the ticket collector.

"Can you describe the gentleman?" said the barrister.

"No, sir. He was just like any other swell. Tall and well-dressed, and talked in the 'aw-'aw style. It might ha' been yerself for all I could tell."

"Do you think it was I?"

Foxey scratched his head.

"No, p'r'aps it wasn't, now I come to rec'llect. He 'ad a moustache, and you 'aven't. Beggin' yer pardon, sir, but you 'ave a bit of the cut of a parson or a hactor, an' this chap wasn't neither—just an every-day sort of toff."

"Could you swear to him if you saw him?"

"That I couldn't, sir. I am a rare 'and at langwidge, but I couldn't manage that."

"Why?"

"Because that night, sir, I were as full as a tick when I started. Lord love you, it must 'ave poured out of me afterwards when I started fightin' coppers. Mr. White, 'e knows, I ain't no fightin' man as a rule."

"And the *lady*? Did you see her?"

"No, sir. Leastways, I seed a bundle which I took to be a lydy, but her face was covered up with a shawl, and she was lyin' 'eavy in 'is arms as though she was mortal bad. He tell'd me she was sick."

"Did he? Anything else?"

"No, sir."

"Are you sure it was a shawl?"

A vacuous smile spread over Foxey's countenance as he answered, "I ain't sure of anythink that 'appened that night."

"But were you not surprised when a man hired your cab under such peculiar circumstances, and paid you such a high fare?"

"We four-wheelers are surprised at nothink, sir. You don't know all wot goes on in kebs. Why, once crossin' Waterloo Bridge—"

"Never mind Waterloo Bridge, Foxey," put in the detective. "Keep your wits fixed on as much as you can remember of November 6."

"Where did he tell you to drive to?" went on Bruce.

"Just Putney. I was to drive my'ardest. I recollect wantin' to pull up at the Three Bells, but 'e put 'is 'ead out an' said, 'Go on, driver. I am awfully late already.' So on I went."

"Where did you stop?"

"I don't know no more than the child unborn. By that time the drink was yeastin' up in me. The fare kept me on the road 'e wanted by shoutin'. When we pulled up, 'e carries 'er into a lane. There was a big 'ouse there. I know that all right. After a bit 'e comes back and tips me a fiver. With that I whips up the old 'oss and gets back to the Three Bells. You know the rest, as the girl said when she axed the Bench to—"

"Yes, we know the rest," interrupted Bruce, "but I fear you are not able to help us much."

"This isn't a five-pun' job, eh, guv'nor?" said Foxey anxiously.

"Hardly at present. We shall see. Can you say exactly where you drew up your cab when the lady was carried into it?"

"Sure as death," replied the cabman, in the hope that his information might yet be valuable. "It was outside Raleigh Mansions, Sloane Square."

"We know that—"

"It seems to me, sir, as ye know as much about the business as I do," broke in Marsh.

"Were you in the Square or in Sloane Street?"

"In Sloane Street, of course. Right away from the Square."

"Not so very far away, surely."

Foxey was doubtful. His memory was hazy, and he feared lest he should be mistaken. "No, no," he said quickly, "not far, but still well in the street."

"Were there many people about?"

"You could 'ardly tell, sir; it was that foggy and nasty. If the lydy 'ad bin dead nobody would 'ave noticed 'er that night."

"Did any one besides yourself see the gentleman carrying the lady into the cab?"

"I think not. I don't remember anybody passin' at the time."

"Did the gentleman keep your cab waiting long at the kerb before he brought the lady out?"

"It might 'a' bin a minute or two?"

"No longer?"

"Well, sir, it's 'ard for me to say, especially after bein' away for a change of 'ealth, so to speak."

"Did not the lady speak or move in any manner?"

"Not so far as I know, sir."

"And do you mean to tell me that, although you had been drinking, you were not astonished at the whole business?"

"I never axes my fares any questions 'cept when they says 'By the hour.' Then I wants to know a bit."

"Yes; but this carrying of a lady out of a house in such fashion—did not this strike you as strange?"

"Strange, bless your 'eart, sir. You ought to see me cartin' 'em off from the Daffodil Club after a big night—three and four in one keb, all blind, paralytic."

"No doubt; but this was not the Daffodil Club at daybreak. It was a respectable neighborhood at seven o'clock, or thereabouts, on a winter's evening."

"It ain't my fault," said Foxey doggedly. "Wot was wrong with the lydy? Was it a habduction?"

"The lady was dead—murdered, we believe."

The cabman's face grew livid with anxiety.

"Oh, crikey, Mr. White," he cried, addressing the detective, "I knew nothink about it."

"No one says you did, Foxey," was the reply. "Don't be frightened. We just want you to help us as far as you can, and not to get skeered and lose your wits."

Thus reassured, Marsh mopped his head and said solemnly:

"I will do wot lies in my power, gentlemen both, but I wish I 'adn't bin so blamed drunk that night."

"You say you would not recognize your fare if you saw him," continued Bruce. "Could you tell us, if you were shown a certain person, that he was *not* the man? You might not be sure of the right man, but you might be sure regarding the wrong one."

"Yes, sir. It wasn't you, and it wasn't Mr. White, and it wasn't a lot of other people I know. I think if I saw the man who really got into my keb, I would be able to swear that 'e was like him, at any rate."

"All right. That will do for the present. Leave us your address, so that we may find you again if necessary. Here is a sovereign for you."

When Marsh had gone, Bruce turned to the detective.

"Well," he said, "if Mensmore were here now, I suppose you would want to lock him up."

"No," admitted White sadly; "the more I learn about this affair the more mixed it becomes. Still, I don't deny but I shall be glad to have Mensmore's explanation of his movements at that time. And so will you, Mr. Bruce."

CHAPTER XXII

A WILFUL MURDER

Bruce sent a telegram to Mrs. Hillmer at Paris. "Matters satisfactorily arranged pending your arrival," he wired, and early on Monday morning he received a reply:

"Due Charing Cross 7.30 P.M. Will drive straight to your chambers with my brother.

"GWENDOLINE HILLMER."

He forwarded the message with a note to the detective, asking him to be present.

About one o'clock Corbett turned up.

"Guess I slept well last night after the excitement," he said, with a pleasant smile. "You seemed to skeer those chaps more with a few words, Mr. Bruce, than I did with a revolver."

"The English police are not so much afraid of revolvers as they are of making mistakes," was the answer.

"Now, is that so? On our side they wouldn't have stopped to argy. Both of 'em would have drawn on me at once."

"Then I am glad, for everybody's sake, Mr. Corbett, that the affair happened in London."

"Why, sure. But tell me. Has my friend Mensmore been getting himself into trouble?"

"Not so much as it looks. Others appear to have involved him without his knowledge, and he has lent color to the accusations by involuntary actions of a suspicious nature."

"Well, if it is permissible, I should like to hear the straight story."

Under the circumstances, Bruce thought that this stranger from America had a right to know why he was in danger of being arrested during his first twenty-four hours' residence in the country, so he gave him a succinct narrative of the *prima facie* case against Mensmore.

Corbett listened in silence to the recital. When it ended he said:

"Mr. Bruce, my friend was incapable of murdering any woman. He was equally incapable of conducting any discreditable *liaison* with any woman. I have known him for years, and a straighter, truer, more honorable man I never met. I don't know what his reason was for assuming my name, which he undoubtedly did, as the agent called this morning, and I find the flat is taken in my name."

"What did you say?"

"Oh, just that Mensmore had acted for me. The man seemed a bit puzzled, but he didn't kick when I offered to pay up the rent owing since Christmas, and another quarter in advance."

"I don't suppose he did. The rent was due, then?"

"Yes. It seems that Mensmore, writing in my name, sent a letter from Monte Carlo a month ago, saying he would return about this time and settle up."

"Thus proving his intention all along to come back to London. It is a queer muddle, Mr. Corbett, is it not?"

"Very; but you will pardon me, as an outsider, saying one thing—you all appear to have overlooked a clear trail."

"And what is that?"

"What about Mrs. Hillmer? Who is she? Who are her friends? Who maintains her in such style? Bertie was with me four years and never mentioned her name. She could not have been rich by inheritance, as it was on account of their father going broke that Mensmore had to leave the Army and come to the States. It strikes me, Mr. Bruce, that the woman knows more about this affair than the man."

"You may be right. But do not forget the absolute proofs we possess that the crime occurred in Mensmore's chambers, and the extraordinary coincidence that he left England immediately afterwards."

"I am not forgetting anything. Those facts tell both ways. Just because he quitted the country at the time somebody may have tried to throw the blame on him."

The theory was plausible, though Bruce could not accept it. Nevertheless, after Corbett had taken his departure he could not help thinking about his references to Mrs. Hillmer. That there was force in them he could not deny, and with the admission came the unpleasant thought that perhaps he, Bruce, was in some sense responsible for the neglect to clear up her antecedents.

However, a few hours might explain much.

With unwonted impatience the barrister awaited the coming of night. He tried every expedient to kill time, and found each operation tedious.

He dined early, and as half-past seven came and passed he wondered why the detective did not appear.

But his doubts on this point did not last long.

"White is looking at Charing Cross to make sure of their arrival," he said to himself.

At ten minutes to eight the detective came in hurriedly.

"They will be here directly," he announced. "A servant has taken their luggage to Mrs. Hillmer's place, and they are evidently driving straight here after taking some refreshment at the station."

"Have you no faith in human nature, Mr. White? Could you not trust their words?"

"Well, sir, my experience of human nature is that you can very seldom trust anybody's word."

At last Smith announced Mrs. Hillmer and Mr. Mensmore.

When they entered Bruce was for the moment at a loss to know exactly how to receive them.

But Mrs. Hillmer settled the matter by greeting him with a quiet "Good-evening," and seating herself. Mensmore stood near the door, very pale and stern-looking.

"It appears, Mr. Bruce," he said, "that we met in Monte Carlo under false pretences. You were, it seems, a detective on the track of a murderer, and you were good enough to believe that I was the person you sought. It would have saved some misconception on my part had you explained our *rôles* earlier. However, I am here, to meet the charge."

Claude was not unprepared for this attitude on Mensmore's part. But he was determined that it should not continue if he could help it.

"When we parted at Monte Carlo, Mensmore," he said, "we parted as friends."

"Yes."

"Then tell me what has happened since to cause this obvious change in your opinion of me?"

"Is it not true that you suspect me of murdering Lady Dyke?"

"No."

"But why has my sister been told that I ran serious risk of being apprehended on that account?"

"Because we certainly did suspect a mysterious personage who called himself Sydney H. Corbett, and whose behavior was so unaccountable that the authorities required a reasonable explanation of it."

"Do I understand, Bruce, that we meet with no more suspicion between us than when we last saw each other?"

"Most certainly."

"Then I ask your pardon for my manner and words. I have suffered keenly during the last three days from this cruel thought. Let us shake hands on it."

As their hands met they both heard Mrs. Hillmer stifle a sob. Mensmore turned to her.

"Now, Gwen," he said, "don't be foolish. We will soon clear up this miserable business. So far as we are concerned, all we need to do is to tell the truth and fear nobody."

"That's it," said White. "If you adopt that course the matter will soon be ended."

Mensmore turned to the speaker. He guessed his identity, but Bruce introduced the detective by name.

"Well," said Mensmore, "I have come here to answer questions. What is it you want to know?"

Mr. White glanced at the barrister, and the other explained.

"I have, as you may already realize, taken more than a passive interest in this inquiry, so the questioning largely devolves on me. First, tell me why you adopted the name of Corbett?"

"Simply enough, though stupid, I now admit. When I returned from the States I was very hard up, but managed to pick up a subsistence by writing for the sporting press, and occasionally backing horses. But I knew this could not last, so I tried to secure some financial interests in the City. In doing so I made the acquaintance of a man named Dodge, and committed myself to the underwriting of a new venture named the Springbok Mine. This fell through at the time, and with this collapse came other demands. I hate being worried by creditors, so when my sister offered to take and furnish a flat for me, near her own, I thought I would live quietly for a time and conceal my name so as to have peace there at any rate. Therefore, I assumed the name of a friend in America, little thinking that I should land both him and myself into such trouble by doing it. That is the explanation. By the way, what has happened to Corbett?"

"He is all right. He expects to see you to-night. You know Sir Charles Dyke, do you not?"

"Yes."

"Intimately?"

"Well, no, not exactly. He and I were at school together at Brighton, at Childe's place."

"At Brighton?"

"Yes. I was a little chap when Dyke was a senior. After he left, the headmaster changed the school to a place called Seton Lodge, at Putney, on account of cramming operations for Army exams."

"Then you were at Putney?"

"Yes, for two years."

"And Dyke was not?"

"No; that I am sure of."

"Have you and Sir Charles been friendly since?"

Mensmore's face hardened somewhat as he answered, "I have seen very little of him, and hardly ever spoken to him."

"Why? Did you quarrel?"

"N-no, but we just did not happen to meet. Bear in mind, I was in business some years ago, and I am not yet thirty."

"Did you know his wife?"

"I have never, to my knowledge, seen her."

"How, then, can you account for the fact that she visited your flat at Raleigh Mansions on November 6."

"I say that such a statement is mere nonsense."

"But if it can be proved?"

"It cannot."

"I assure you, on my honor, that it can."

"But look here, Bruce. Why should she come to see me? I question greatly if she knew of my existence."

"Nevertheless, it is the fact."

"I can only tell you it is not. I left London on November 8, and on the two previous evenings I dined alone. Mrs. Robinson, my housekeeper, can tell you that not another soul entered my flat for a week prior to my departure, except my sister and—and—I had forgotten—some workmen."

"Some workmen?"

"Yes; some fellows from a furniture warehouse."

"What were they doing?"

"Well, don't you see, I told you I was not well off, and my sister furnished my flat for me, in August last that was, but the drawing-room was left bare for a time. Just before I left for France she decided to refurnish her drawing-room, and she gave me the whole fit-out. The things were brought in by the men who brought her purchases."

At this astounding revelation Bruce and the detective were utterly taken aback. It was with difficulty that the barrister enunciated his next words clearly.

"Can you tell me with absolute certainty the date of this change of the furniture?"

"Oh yes. It was the day before I started for the Riviera; that must have been November 7."

"Are you positive of this?"

"Undoubtedly. Is it a matter of importance? Gwen, you know all about it. Besides, the bills for your new furniture will show the exact date of delivery, and it was the same day."

Mrs. Hillmer's face was hidden by her veil, but she nodded silently.

Three people in the room knew the significance of Mensmore's straightforward words; he alone was unaware of the direction towards which the investigation now tended.

"Let us analyze the matter carefully," said Bruce, who had recovered his self-possession, though he was almost terrified at the possibilities of the situation. "Did the whole of the contents of your drawing-room come from your sister's flat?"

"Every stick. There was nothing there before but the bare boards."

"Do you remember a handsome ornamental fender being among these articles?"

"Perfectly. My housekeeper said the men broke it during the transit. They denied this, and looked for the piece chipped off, but could not find it. She told me about it that night."

"Did you mention it to Mrs. Hillmer?"

"No. To tell the honest truth, Gwen and I had quarrelled a couple of days before. That is to say, we disagreed seriously about a certain matter, and it was this which led to my making off to Monte Carlo. Therefore it was hardly likely I should mention such a trivial matter to her."

"May I ask what you quarrelled about?"

"I have told her since that it ought to be made known, but she has implored me not to reveal it, so I cannot. But she will tell you herself that we agreed I should be at liberty to make this guarded explanation."

Bruce and the detective exchanged glances of wondering comprehension.

"I do not think we need question Mr. Mensmore further," said the barrister to White.

"No," was the reply. "The matter is clear enough. Mrs. Hillmer must tell us how that furniture came to be transferred from her premises on the morning of the 7th."

"If she chooses."

The barrister's tone was sad, and its ominous significance was not lost on his hearers.

Mrs. Hillmer raised her veil. Her face was deathly pale and tense in its fixed agony. But in her eyes was a light which gave a curious aspect of resolve to her otherwise painful aspect of utter grief.

"I do not choose," she said quietly, looking, not at Bruce or the detective, but at her brother.

For a little while no one spoke. Mensmore at last broke out eagerly:

"Don't act absurdly, Gwen. I cannot even guess where all this talk about the furniture is leading us, but I do know that you are as innocent of any complicity in Lady Dyke's death as I am, so it is better for you to help forward the inquiry than to retard it."

"I am not innocent," said Mrs. Hillmer, her words falling with painful distinctness upon the ears of the three men. "Heaven help me! I am responsible for it!"

Her brother started to his feet, and caught her by the shoulder.

"What folly is this," he cried. "Do you know what you are saying?"

"Fully. My words are like sledge-hammers. I will forever feel their weight. I tell you I am responsible for the death of Lady Dyke."

"Then how did she die, Mrs. Hillmer?" said Bruce, whose glance sought to read her soul.

"I do not know. I do not want to know. It matters little to me."

"In other words, you are assuming a responsibility you should not bear. You were not even aware of this poor lady's death until I told you. Why should you seek to avert suspicion from others merely because Lady Dyke is shown to have met her death in your apartments?"

"But how is it shown?" interrupted Mensmore vehemently. He was more disturbed by his sister's unaccountable attitude than he had ever been by the serious charge against himself.

"Easily enough," said White, feeling that he ought to have some share in the conversation. "A piece of the damaged fender placed in your rooms, Mr. Mensmore, was found in the murdered lady's head."

"Was it?" he cried. "Then, by Heaven, I refuse to see my sister sacrificed for anybody's sake. She has borne too long the whole burden of misery and degradation. I tell you, Gwen, that if you do not save yourself I will save you against your will. That furniture came to my room because—"

"Bertie, I beseech you, for the sake of the woman you love, to spare me."

Mrs. Hillmer flung herself on her knees before him and caught hold of his hands, while she burst into a storm of tears.

Mensmore was unnerved. He turned to Bruce, and said:

"Help me in this miserable business, old chap. I don't know what to say or do; my sister had no more connection with Lady Dyke's death than I had. This statement on her part is mere hysteria, arising from other circumstances altogether."

"That I feel acutely," said the barrister. "Yet some one killed her, and, whatever the pain that may be caused, and whoever may suffer, I am determined that the truth shall come out."

"I tell you," wailed Mrs. Hillmer between her sobs, "that I must bear all the blame. Why do you hesitate? She was killed in my house, and I confess my guilt."

"This *is* rum business," growled Mr. White aloud, half unconsciously.

At that moment the door opened unexpectedly, and Smith entered.

Before Bruce had time to vociferate an order to his astounded servitor the man stuttered an excuse:

"Beg pardon, sir," he said, "but Sir Charles Dyke has called, and wants to know if you will be disengaged soon."

CHAPTER XXIII

THE LETTER

Quick on the heels of the footman's stammered explanation came the voice of Sir Charles himself:

"Sorry to disturb you, Bruce, if you are busy, but I must see you for a moment on a matter of the utmost importance."

There was that in his utterance which betokened great excitement. He was not visible to the occupants of the room. During the audible silence that followed his words, they could hear him stamping about the passage, impatiently awaiting Bruce's presence.

Mrs. Hillmer quietly collapsed on the floor. She had fainted.

The barrister rushed out, calling for Mrs. Smith, and responding to Sir Charles Dyke's proffered statement as to the reason for his presence by the startling cry:

"Wait a bit, Dyke. There's a lady in a faint inside. We must attend to her at once."

Mrs. Smith, fortunately, was at hand, and with the help of her ministrations, Mrs. Hillmer gradually regained her senses.

After a whispered colloquy with White, the barrister said to Mensmore:

"You must remove your sister to her residence as quickly as possible. She is far too highly strung to bear any further questioning to-night. Perhaps to-morrow, when you and she have discussed matters fully together, you may be able to send for us and clear up this wretched business."

For answer Mensmore silently pressed his hand. With the help of the housekeeper he led his sister from the room, passing Sir Charles Dyke in the hall. The baronet politely turned aside, and Mensmore did not look at him, being far too engrossed with his sister to pay heed to aught else at the moment. As for Mrs. Hillmer, she was in such a state of collapse as to be practically unconscious of her surroundings.

She managed to murmur at the door:

"Where are you taking me to, Bertie?"

"Home, dear."

"Home? Oh, thank Heaven!"

They all heard her, and even the detective was constrained to say:

"Poor thing, she needn't have been afraid. She is suffering for some one else."

Sir Charles Dyke grasped Bruce's arm.

"What on earth is going on?" he said.

"Merely a foolish woman worrying herself about others," replied Bruce grimly.

"But those people were my old friends, Mensmore and his sister?"

"Yes."

"What are they doing here?"

"Mensmore has been brought back to London by Mrs. Hillmer to face the allegations made against him with regard to your wife's disappearance. They came here by their own appointment, and—"

"Did I not tell you that this charge against Mensmore was wild folly on the face of it?"

"So it seems, when we have just discovered that your wife was killed in his sister's house, and Mrs. Hillmer persists in declaring that she was responsible for the crime."

"Look here, Bruce. Don't lose your head like everybody else mixed up in this wretched business. My wife is not dead."

"What!" The cry was a double one, for both Bruce and White gave simultaneous utterance to their amazement.

"It is true. She is alive all the time. I have had a letter from her."

"A letter. Surely, Dyke—"

"I am neither mad nor drunk. The letter reached me by this morning's post. I came here with it as fast as I could travel. I have been in the train all day, and am nearly fainting from hunger."

"Where is it?" cried White. "Is it genuine?"

"I could swear to her writing amidst a thousand letters. Here it is. I have brought some old correspondence of hers for the purpose of comparison, as I could hardly believe my eyes when I first received it."

Bruce was so dumfounded by this remarkable development that he could but mutely take the document produced by the baronet and read it.

He himself recognized Lady Dyke's handwriting, which he had often seen— a clear, bold, well-defined script, more like the caligraphy of a banker than of a fashionable lady.

The letter was dated February 1, bore no other superscription, and read as follows:

"*My Dear Charles*,—I have just seen in the newspapers the announcement of my death, and the theories set on foot to account for my disappearance on November 6. This seems to convey to me the strange fact that you have not received the explanation I sent you of my reasons for leaving London so suddenly. Otherwise you must have kept your own counsel very closely. However, I do not now desire to reopen the question of motive; let it suffice to say that no one save myself was responsible for my disappearance, and that neither you nor any one acquainted with me will ever see me again. Do not search for me; it will be time wasted. If you have legal proof of my death and wish to marry again, be satisfied. Tear up this letter and forget it. I am dead—to you and to the world. You can neither refuse to accept the genuineness of this letter nor trace me by reason of it, as I have taken such precautions that the latter course will be impossible. Let me repeat—forget me.

"ALICE."

The barrister carefully refolded the sheet after scrutinizing the water-mark against the light, and noting that the paper was British made; he then examined the envelope. The obliterating postmark was "London, February 4, 9 P.M., West Strand." The office of delivery was "Wensley, February 6."

"Posted at the West Strand Post-Office on Saturday," he said. "Detained in London all Sunday, and delivered to you this morning in the North."

"Exactly."

"It was written three days earlier, if the date be accurate. So the writer is somewhere in Europe."

"That's how I take it," said Sir Charles.

"Unless the whole thing is a fraud."

"How can it be a fraud? I am sure as to the handwriting. Why, even yourself, Bruce, must have a good recollection of my wife's style."

"Undoubtedly. No man born could swear that this was not Lady Dyke's production."

"Well, what are we to do?"

"And what did Mrs. Hillmer mean by kicking up that fuss when we spoke to her?" interpolated White. "I'll take my oath that some one was killed in her house, else how comes it that a woman found in the Thames at Putney is carrying about in her head some of Mrs. Hillmer's ironwork? I wish she hadn't fainted just now. Why, she said herself that she was the cause of Lady Dyke's death, and here is Lady Dyke writing to say she is alive. This business is beyond me, but Mrs. Hillmer has got to explain a good deal yet before I am done with her."

The detective's wrath at this check in the hunt after a criminal did not appeal to the baronet.

"You can please yourself, Mr. White, of course," he said coldly; "but so far as I am concerned, I will respect my wife's wishes, and let the matter rest where it is."

"My dear fellow," said the barrister, "such a course is impossible. Assuming that her ladyship is really alive, why did she leave you?"

"How can I tell? She herself refuses to give a reason. She apparently stated one in a letter which never reached me, as you know. She has selfishly caused me a world of suffering and misery for three long months. I refuse to be plagued in the matter further."

Sir Charles was excited and angry. He was in bitter revolt against circumstances.

"Do you intend to show this letter to Lady Dyke's relatives?" asked Bruce, at a loss for the time to discuss the situation coherently.

"I do not know. What would you advise? I trust fully to your judgment. But is it not better to obey her wishes?—to forget, as she puts it?"

"We must decide nothing hastily. I am perplexed beyond endurance by this business. There is so much that is wildly impossible in its irreconcilable features. I must have time. Will you give me a copy of the letter?"

"Certainly, keep it yourself. We have all seen it."

"Thank you." Bruce placed the envelope and its contents in his pocket-book. Then, turning to the detective, he said:

"Now, Mr. White, do me a favor. Do not worry Mrs. Hillmer until you hear from me."

"By all means, Mr. Bruce. But am I to report to the Commissioner that Lady Dyke has been found, or has, at any rate, explained that she is not dead?"

"There is no immediate necessity why a report of any kind should be made."

"None."

"Then leave matters where they are at present."

"But why," put in Sir Charles. "Is it not better to end all inquiries, at least so far as my wife is concerned? It is her desire, and, I may add, my own, now that I know something of her fate."

"Of course, if you wish it, Dyke, I have no valid objection."

"Oh, no, no. Do not look at it in that way. I leave the ultimate decision entirely to you."

"In that case, I recommend complete silence in all quarters at present."

The detective left them, and as he passed out into Victoria Street his philosophy could find but one comprehensive dictum. "This *is* a rum go," he muttered, unconsciously plagiarizing himself on many previous occasions.

The baronet sat down, and meditatively chewed the handle of his umbrella.

"What is this nonsense Mensmore's sister talked about being responsible for my wife's death?" he said.

"I do not pretend to understand," answered Bruce. "Little more than a week ago she learned for the first time of your wife's supposed murder. Of that I am quite positive. She feared that her brother was implicated, and, without trusting me with the reasons for her belief, took the measures she thought best to safeguard him."

"Took measures! What?" Sir Charles jerked the words out impetuously.

"She followed him to the South of France, and found him in Florence. What she said I cannot guess, but the result was their visit here to-night. During our interview it came out, quite by accident, that some furniture was taken from her place to her brother's on the morning of November 7, thus shifting the venue of Lady Dyke's death—or imaginary death I must now say—from No. 12 Raleigh Mansions to No. 61. This discovery was as startling to Mrs. Hillmer as to us, for she forthwith protested that the whole affair arose from her fault, and practically asked the detective to arrest her on the definite charge of murder."

"Pooh! The mania of an hysterical woman!"

"Possibly!"

"Why 'possibly'? No one was murdered in her abode. Do you for a moment believe the monstrous insinuation?"

"No, not in that sense. But her brother was about to make some revelation regarding a third person when she appealed to him not to speak. What would have happened finally I do not know. At that critical moment my servant announced your arrival."

"But what can Mrs. Hillmer have to conceal? She and her brother have been lost to Society since long before my marriage. Neither of them, so far as I know, has ever set eyes on my wife during the last seven years."

"Yet Mrs. Hillmer *must* have had some powerful motive in acting as she did."

"Is it not more than likely that she had a bad attack of nerves?"

"A woman who merely yields to nervous prostration behaves foolishly. This woman gave way to emotion, it is true, but it was strength, not weakness, that sustained her."

"What do you mean?"

"There is but one force that sustains in such a crisis—the power of love. Mrs. Hillmer was not flying from consequences. She met them half-way in the spirit of a martyr."

"'Pon my honor, Bruce, I am beginning to think that this wretched business is affecting your usually clear brain. You are accepting fancies as facts."

"Maybe. I confess I am unable to form a logical conclusion to-night."

"Why not abandon the whole muddle to time? There is no solution of a difficulty like the almanac. Let us both go off somewhere."

"What, and leave Mrs. Hillmer to die of sheer pain of mind? Let this unfortunate fellow, Mensmore, suffer no one knows what consequences from the events of to-day? It is out of the question."

"Very well, I leave it to you. Every one seems to forget that it is I who suffer most." The baronet stood up and dejectedly gazed into the fire.

"I, at least, can feel for you, Dyke," said Bruce sympathetically, "but you must admit that things cannot be allowed to remain in their present whirlpool."

"So be it. Let them go on to their bitter end. If my wife was tired of my society she might at least have got rid of me in an easier manner."

With this trite reflection Sir Charles quitted his friend's house.

Bruce sat motionless for a long time. Then, as his mind became calmer, he lit a cigar, took out the doubly mysterious letter, and examined it in every possible way, critically and microscopically.

There could be no doubt that it was a genuine production. The condition of the ink bore out the correctness of the date, and the fact that the note paper and envelope were not of Continental style was not very material.

It did not appear to have been enclosed in another envelope, as the writer implied, for the purpose of being re-posted in London. Rather did the slightly frayed edges give rise to the assumption that it had been carried in some one's pocket before postage. But this theory was vague and undemonstrable.

The handwriting was Lady Dyke's; the style, allowing for the strange conditions under which it was written, was hers; yet Bruce did not believe in it.

Nothing could shake his faith in the one solid, concrete certainty that stood out from a maze of contradictions and mystery—Lady Dyke was dead, and buried in a pauper's grave at Putney.

At last, wearied with thought and theorizing, he went to bed; but Smith sat up late to regale his partner with the full, true, and particular narrative of the "lydy a-cryin' on her knees, and the strange gent lookin' as though he would like to murder Mr. White."

CHAPTER XXIV

THE HANDWRITING

Like most men, Claude took a different view of events in the morning to that which he entertained over night.

Yesterday, the surprises of the hour were concrete embodiments, each distinct and emphatic. To-day they were merged in the general mass of contradictory details that made up this most bewildering inquiry.

That matters could not be allowed to rest in their present state was clear; that they would, in the natural course of things, reveal themselves more definitely, even if unaided, was also patent.

Mrs. Hillmer's partial admissions, her brother's evident knowledge of some salient features of the puzzle, that utterly strange letter in the admitted handwriting of Lady Dyke herself, and bearing the prosaic testimony of dates stamped by the Post-office—these sensational elements, when brought into juxtaposition, could not avoid reaction into clearer phases.

Long experience in criminal investigation told him that, under certain circumstances, the best course of all was one of inactivity.

On the basis of the accepted truism in the affairs of many people that "letters left unanswered answer themselves," the barrister knew that there must be an outcome from the queer medley of occurrences at his residence on the Monday evening.

Reviewing the history of the past three months several odd features stood out from the general jumble.

In the first place, he wondered why he had failed to deduce any pertinent fact from the manner in which Mrs. Hillmer's dining-room was furnished on the occasion of his first visit to Raleigh Mansions.

He distinctly remembered noting his reception in an unusual room littered with unusual articles, when the luxurious and well-appointed suite of apartments was considered as a whole. It was suggested to him at the time that the drawing-room, which he saw during his second visit, was dismantled earlier, but he did not connect this trivial incident with the feature in Mensmore's flat that he noted immediately—namely, the discrepancies between the arrangement of the sitting-room and the other chambers in the place.

These things were immaterial now, but he indexed them as a guide for future use.

Lady Dyke's motive for that secret visit to Raleigh Mansions—that was the key to the mystery. But how to discover it? Who was her confidant? To whom could he turn for possible enlightenment? It was useless to broach the matter again to her husband. The baronet and his wife had been friends sharing the same *ménage* rather than husband and wife. Her relatives had already been appealed to in vain. They knew nothing of the slightest value in this search for truth.

In this train of thought the name of Jane Harding cropped up. She was the personal maid of the deceased lady. She had sharp eyes and quick wits. Her queer antics shortly after the inquest were not forgotten. Here at least was a possibility of light if the girl would speak.

If she refused what could be her motive?

Anyhow it was worth while to make a fresh effort. Early in the afternoon he called at the stage-door of the Jollity Theatre.

"Is Miss Marie le Marchant still employed here?" he asked the attendant.

"I dunno," was the careless answer.

"Well, think hard," said the barrister, laying a half-crown on the battered blotting-pad which is an indispensable part of the furniture in the letter bureau of a theatre.

"Yes, sir, I believe she is, but she has been away on a week's leave."

"Indeed. Has she returned?"

"I was off last night, sir, but if you will pardon me a moment I'll inquire from the man who took my place."

The stage-doorkeeper disappeared into the dark interior, to return quickly with the information that Miss le Marchant had appeared as usual on Monday night.

"She was away most part of last week, sir," added the man, "and I believe it wasn't a holiday, as she was a-sort of flurried about it as if some one was ill."

"Thank you. Do you know where she lives?"

A momentary hesitation was soon softened by another half-crown.

"It's against the rules, sir. If you were to find yourself near Jubilee Buildings, Bloomsbury, you would not be far out."

The information was sound. Miss Marie le Marchant's name was painted outside a second-floor flat.

Bruce knocked, and the door was opened by an elderly woman whom he had no difficulty in recognizing.

"Is your daughter in, Mrs. Harding?" he said.

For a moment she could not speak for surprise.

"Well, I never," she cried, "but London is a funny place. Do you know me, sir?"

"Any one would recognize you from your daughter, if they did not take you for her elder sister," he said. Bruce's smile was irresistible.

"My daughter is not in just now, sir," replied Mrs. Harding, "but I expect her in to tea almost immediately."

"Then may I come in and await her arrival?"

"Certainly, sir."

Once inside the flat, he was impressed by the pretentious but fairly comfortable nature of its appointments; the ex-lady's maid's legacy must have been a nice one to enable her to live in such style, as the poor pittance of a coryphée would barely pay the rent and taxes. Moreover, the presence of her mother in the establishment was a distinct factor in her favor.

Mrs. Harding had brought the visitor to the tiny sitting-room. She seated herself near the window and resumed some sewing.

"Have you been long in town, Mrs. Harding?" he said, by way of being civil.

"In London, do you mean, sir? About two months. Ever since my daughter got along so well in her new profession. She's a good girl, is my daughter."

"Miss Harding is doing well on the stage, then?"

"Oh yes, sir. Why, she's been earning £6 a week, and last week she was sent for on a special engagement, which paid her so well that she's going to buy me a new dress out of the money."

"Really," said the barrister, "you ought to be proud of her."

"I am," admitted the admiring mother. "I only wish her brother, who went off and 'listed for a sojer, had turned out half as well."

Mrs. Harding nodded towards a photograph of a cavalry soldier in uniform on the mantelshelf, and Bruce rose to examine it, inwardly marvelling at the intelligence he had just received. Was it reasonable that the girl could be the recipient of a legacy without the knowledge of her mother? In any case, why did she conceal the real nature of her earnings? The story about "£6 a week" was a myth.

Near to the portrait of the gallant huzzar was a large plaque presentment of Miss Marie herself, in all the glory of tights, wig, and make-up. Across it was written, in the best theatrical style, "Ever yours sincerely, Marie le Marchant." And no sooner had Bruce caught sight of the words than he almost shouted aloud in his amazement.

The handwriting was identical with that of Lady Dyke.

Gulping down his surprise, he devoured the signature with his eyes. The resemblance was truly remarkable. What on earth could be the explanation of this phenomenon.

"Your daughter is a remarkably nice writer, Mrs. Harding," he said, turning the photograph towards her.

"Yes," said the complacent mother, "she taught herself when—before she went on the stage. She was always a clever girl, and when she grew up she improved herself. I wasn't able to afford her much schooling when she was young."

"I have seldom seen a nicer hand," he went on. "Have you any other specimens of her writing? I should like to see them if they are not private."

The smooth surface of the photograph might perhaps lend a deceptive fluency to the pen. He wanted to make quite sure that he was not mistaken.

"Oh yes. She's just copying out the part of Ophelia in *Hamlet*. And she acts it beautiful."

Mrs. Harding handed over a large MS. book, and there, written on the first page, was the name of the luckless woman whose fatal passion has moved millions to tears.

He admired Miss Marie le Marchant's efforts in the matter of self-culture, but he was determined, once for all, to wrest from her some explanation of her actions.

The rattle of a key in the outer door caused him to throw aside the coveted "part," and the young lady herself entered. A few weeks of stage experience had given her a more stylish appearance. There was a "professional" touch in the arrangement of her hat and the droop of her skirt.

She knew him instantly, and listened with evident anger to her mother's explanation that "this gentleman has just called to see you, dear."

"All right, mother," she cried. "I see it is Mr. Bruce. Will you get tea ready while I talk with him? I shall be ready in two minutes." This with a defiant look at the visitor.

When Mrs. Harding quitted the room her daughter said in the crisp accents of ill-temper:

"What do you want with me, now?"

"I want to ask why you dared to write a letter to Sir Charles Dyke in the name of your dead mistress."

The answer was so direct, the tone so menacing, its assumption of absolute and unquestioned knowledge so complete, that for a moment Marie le Marchant's assurance failed her.

She stood like one petrified, with eyes dilated and breast heaving. At last she managed to ejaculate:

"I—I—why do you ask me that question?"

"Because I must have the truth from you this time. You are playing a very dangerous game."

That he was right he was sure now beyond doubt. It was impossible for the girl to deny it with those piercing eyes fixed on her, and seeming to read the secrets of her heart.

Yet she was plucky enough. Although she was confused and on the point of bursting into tears, she snapped viciously:

"I will tell you nothing. Go away."

"You are obstinate, I know," said Bruce, "but I must warn you that you are juggling with edged tools. You should not imagine that you can trifle with murder. What is your motive for deliberately trying to conceal Lady Dyke's death? If you do not answer me you may be asked the question in a court of law."

"You have no right to come here annoying me!" she retorted.

"I am not here to annoy you. I come, rather, as a friend, to appeal to you not to incur the grave risk of keeping from the authorities information which they ought to possess."

"What information?"

"The reasons which led you to leave Sir Charles Dyke's house so suddenly, the source from which you obtain your money, paid to you, doubtless, to secure your silence, the motive which impelled you to use your ability to imitate her ladyship's handwriting in order to spread the false news that she is alive. This is the information needed, and your wilful refusal to give it constitutes a grave indictment."

"I don't care *that* for you, Mr. Bruce," replied the girl, her face set now in a scarlet temper, while she snapped her fingers to emphasize the words. "You can do and say what you like, I will tell you nothing."

"You cannot deny you wrote that letter to Sir Charles Dyke last Saturday?"

"I am waiting for my tea. Sorry I can't ask you to join me."

"Your flippancy will not avail you. See, here is the letter itself—your own production—written on paper of which you have a quantity in this very room."

The shot was a bold one, and it very nearly hit the mark. She was staggered, almost subdued by this melodramatic production of the original, and his clever guess at the existence of similar notepaper in the house.

But her dogged temperament saved her. Jane Harding was British, notwithstanding her penchant for a French-sounding name, and she would have died sooner than beat a retreat.

"I will thank you to leave me alone, Mr. Bruce," she said.

There was nothing for it but to retire as gracefully as possible, but the barrister was more than satisfied with the result of his visit. He had now established beyond a shadow of doubt that for some reason which he could not fathom the ex-lady's maid not only knew of her mistress's death, but wished to conceal it.

This desire, too, had the essential feature of every other branch of the inquiry; it grew to maturity long after the day when Lady Dyke was actually killed. What did it all mean?

From Bloomsbury he strolled west to Portman Square, and found Sir Charles on the point of going for a drive in the Park.

He briefly told him his discovery.

The baronet at first was sceptical. "Do you mean to say, Claude," he cried, fretfully, "that I do not know my wife's writing when I see it?"

"You may think you do, but when another person can imitate it exactly, of course, you may be deceived. Besides, if this girl, as is probable, was helped in her education by your wife, what is more likely than that Jane Harding should seek to copy that which she would consider the ideal of excellence. Don't harbor any delusions in the matter, Dyke. The letter you received on Monday morning was written by Jane Harding. I am sure of that from her manner no less than from the accidental resemblance of the two styles of handwriting. What I could not find out was her motive for the deceit."

"It is a queer business altogether," said Sir Charles wearily; "I wish it were ended."

CHAPTER XXV

MISS PHYLLIS BROWNE INTERVENES

Bruce was quite positive in his belief that Jane Harding was the paid agent of some person who wished to conceal the facts concerning Lady Dyke's death.

Her unexpected appearance in the field at this late hour, no less than the bold *rôle* she adopted, proved this conclusively. But in England there was no torture-chamber to which she might be led and gradually dismembered until she confessed the truth.

So long as she adhered to the policy of pert denial she was quite safe. The law could not touch her, for the chief witness against her, Sir Charles Dyke, was obviously more than half-inclined to admit the genuineness of the letter, even in opposition to the superior judgment of his friend.

Yet it was a matter which Bruce considered ought to be made known to the police, so he sent for Mr. White and told him of the strange result of his interview with Miss Marie le Marchant.

"Dash everything!" cried the detective, when he heard the news. "I made a note sometime ago that that girl ought to be watched, but I clean forgot all about it."

"Remember," said Bruce, "that my discovery was the result of pure accident. My object in visiting her was to endeavor to induce her confidence with regard to Lady Dyke's former life and habits. Indeed, I handled the business very badly."

"I don't see that, sir. You got hold of a very remarkable fact, and thus prevented the success of a bold move by some one which, in my case at any rate, nearly choked me off the inquiry."

"True. Thus far, chance favored me. But I ought to have been content with the assumption. There was no need to frighten her by pressing it home."

"Oh, from that point of view—" began the detective.

But Bruce was merely thinking aloud—rough-shaping his ideas as they grouped themselves in his brain.

"Perhaps I am wrong there too," he went on. "If this girl is working to instructions she would have refused to help me in any way, and she already knows that I am on the trail. There is one highly satisfactory feature in the Jane Harding adventure, Mr. White."

"And what is that?"

"The person, or persons, responsible for Lady Dyke's death know that the matter has not been dropped. They are inclined to think that the circle is narrowing. In some of our casts, Mr. White, we must have come so unpleasantly close to them, that they deemed it advisable to throw us off the scent by a bold effort."

"No doubt you are right, sir, but I wish to goodness I knew when we were 'warm,' as I am becoming tired of the business. Every new development deepens the mystery."

The detective's face was as downcast as his words.

"Surely not! The more pieces of the puzzle we have to handle the less difficult should be the final task of putting them together."

"Not when every piece is a fresh puzzle in itself."

"Why, what has disconcerted you to-day?"

"Mrs. Hillmer."

"What of her?"

"I have had another talk with the maid,—her companion, you know,—a girl named Dobson. It struck me that it was advisable to know more about Mrs. Hillmer than we do at present."

Bruce made no comment, but he could not help reflecting that Corbett, the stranger from Wyoming, had entertained the same view.

"Well," continued the detective, "I went about the affair as quietly as possible, but the maid, though willing, could not tell me much. Mrs. Hillmer, she thinks, married very young, and was badly treated by her husband. Finally, there was a rumpus, and she went on the stage, while Hillmer drank himself to death. He died a year ago, and they had been separated nearly five years. He was fairly well-to-do, but he squandered all his money in dissipation and never gave her a cent. Three years last Michaelmas she set up her present establishment at Raleigh Mansions, and there she has been ever since."

"Then where does the money come from? It must cost her at least £2,000 a year to live."

"That's just what the maid can't tell me. Her mistress led a very secluded life, and was never what you could call fast, though a very pretty woman. During this time she had only one visitor—a gentleman."

"Ah!"

"It sounds promising, but it ends in smoke, so far as I can see."

"Why?"

"This gentleman was a Colonel Montgomery—an old friend—though he wasn't much turned thirty, the maid says. He interested himself a lot in Mrs. Hillmer's affairs, looked after some investments for her, and was on very good terms with her, and nobody could whisper a word against the character of either of them. He was never there except in the afternoon. On very rare occasions he took Mrs. Hillmer, whose maid always accompanied them, to Epping Forest, or up the river, or on some such journey."

"Go on!"

"I'm sorry, sir, but the chase is over. He's dead."

"Dead?"

"Yes. The maid doesn't know how, or when, exactly, but one day she found her mistress crying, and when she asked her what was the matter, Mrs. Hillmer said, 'I've lost my friend.' The maid said, 'Surely not Colonel Montgomery, madam?' and she replied, 'Yes.' She quite took on about it."

"Had the maid no idea as to the date of this interesting occurrence?"

"Only a vague one. Sometime in the autumn or before Christmas. By Jove, yes; it escaped me at the time, but she said that soon after the Colonel's death another gentleman called and took her mistress out to dinner. I was so busy thinking about the colonel that I slipped the significance of that statement. It must have been you, Mr. Bruce."

"So it seems."

The barrister's active brain was already assimilating this new information. If a woman like Mrs. Hillmer had lost a dear and valuable friend—one who practically formed the horizon of her life—she would certainly have worn mourning for him. It was a singular coincidence that Mrs. Hillmer "lost" Colonel Montgomery about the same time that Lady Dyke disappeared. Detective and maid alike had drawn a false inference from Mrs. Hillmer's words.

"We must find Colonel Montgomery," he said, after a slight pause.

"Find him!"

"Yes."

"I hope neither of us is going his way for some time to come, Mr. Bruce," laughed the policeman.

"White, I shall never cure you from jumping at conclusions. Upon your present evidence Colonel Montgomery is no more dead than you are."

"But the maid said—"

"I don't care if fifty maids said. There are many more ways of 'losing' a friend than by death. Pass me the Army List, on that bookshelf behind you there."

A brief reference to the index, and Bruce said:

"I thought so. There is no *Colonel* Montgomery. There are several captains and lieutenants, and a Major-General who has commanded a small island in the Pacific for the last five years, but not a single colonel. White, you have blundered into eminence in your profession."

"I'm glad to hear it, even as you put it, Mr. Bruce. But I don't see—"

"I know you don't. If you did, a popular novelist would write your life and style you the English Lecocq. Mrs. Hillmer 'lost' the gallant colonel at the same time that the world 'lost' Lady Dyke. Find the first, and I am much mistaken if we do not learn all about the second."

"Now I wonder if you are right."

The detective's eyes sparkled with animation. It was the first real clue he had hit upon, and Bruce's method of complimenting him on the fact did not disconcert him.

"Of course I am right. You have done so well with the maid that I leave her in your hands. Try the coachman and the cook. But keep me informed of your progress."

White rushed off elated. So persistent was he in striving to elucidate this new problem that he paid no heed during some days to the side-light furnished by Jane Harding and her exceedingly curious powers as a letter-writer.

Bruce purposely left the inquiry to the policeman.

He realized intuitively that the disappearance of Lady Dyke would soon be explained, but he shrank from subjecting Mrs. Hillmer to further questioning.

His abstinence was rewarded later in the week, for Mensmore came to see him. The young man wore an expression of settled melancholy which surprised the barrister greatly.

"Have you prevailed on your sister to take us into her confidence?" he said, when Mensmore was ensconced in a chair in his cosy sitting-room.

"No. She is more fixed than ever in her resolve to take the whole blame on herself."

"Surely this mistaken idea can be shaken?"

"I fear not."

"And you also share it?"

"I do. Bear with us, Bruce. This is a terrible business. It has broken me up utterly."

"Nonsense. You are in no way concerned save to shield your sister, and no one credits her wild statements regarding her complicity in this crime."

"Look here, my dear fellow, I have come to ask you if this investigation cannot be allowed to rest. It means a lot of misery that you cannot foretell or prevent. Knowing what I do, I cannot believe that Lady Dyke was murdered."

"Knowing what I do, I cannot accept any other conclusion. A worthy and estimable lady leaves her home suddenly, without the slightest imaginary cause, and she is found in the Thames with a piece of iron driven into her brain, while the medical evidence is clear that death was not due to drowning. What other inference can be drawn than that she was foully done to death?"

"Heaven help me, I cannot tell. Yet I appeal to you to let matters rest where they are if it is possible."

"It is not possible. I cannot control the police. I am merely a private agent acting on my own responsibility and on behalf of Lady Dyke's relatives."

"Don't misunderstand me, Bruce. I am not asking this thing on account of my sister or myself."

"On whose account, then?"

Mensmore did not answer for a moment. He looked mournfully into the fire for inspiration.

"Perhaps I had better tell you," he said, "that I have broken off my engagement with Miss Browne."

The other jumped from his chair.

"What the dickens do you mean?" he cried.

"Exactly what I have said. When we met on Monday night, I did not mention that Sir William and Lady Browne and their daughter travelled back to England with us. On Tuesday I saw Phyllis. In view of the shadow thrown on me by this frightful charge I thought it my duty to release her from any ties. If my sister has to figure in a court of law as a principal, or accomplice, in a murder case—and possibly myself with her—I could not consent to associate my poor Phyllis's name with mine. So I took the plunge."

"You are a beastly idiot," shouted Bruce. "If I had the power I would give you six months' hard labor this moment. Who ever threatened to put you or your sister in the dock?"

"You have done your best that way, you know."

"I?—I have shielded you throughout!"

"I feel that. But your admission shows that I am right. Shielded us from what? From arrest by the police, of course."

"But why take this precipitate action? What has Lady Dyke's death to do with your marriage to Miss Browne?"

"That's it, Bruce. I cannot explain. I must endure silently."

"Did you give her any reason for your absurd resolution?"

"Yes. I could have no secrets from her."

"Did you inflict all this wretched story on a woman you loved and hoped to marry?"

"You may be as bitter as you like. That is my idea of square dealing, at any rate. What other pretext could I invite for—for giving her up?"

Mensmore found it hard to utter the words. In his heart Bruce pitied him, though he raged at this lamentable issue of the only bright passage in the whole story of death and intrigue.

"And what did Miss Browne say?"

"Oh, she just pooh-poohed the affair, and pretended to laugh at me, though she was crying all the time."

"A nice kettle of fish you have made of it," growled the barrister. "You help your sister in her folly of silence and then proceed to give effect to it by ruining your own happiness and that of your affianced wife. Have you seen Miss Browne since?"

"No."

His visitor was so utterly disconsolate that Bruce was at a loss to know how to deal with him. He felt that if Mensmore would but speak regarding Mrs. Hillmer's strange delusion, and the cause of it, all these difficulties and disasters would disappear. He resolved to try a direct attack.

"Have you ever heard of a Colonel Montgomery?" he said suddenly, bending his searching gaze on the other's downcast face.

The effect was electrical. Mensmore was so taken back that he was spellbound. He looked at Claude, the picture of astonishment, before he stammered:

"I—you—who told you about him?"

"He was your sister's friend, adviser, and confidant," was the stern reply. "He it is who, in some mysterious way, is bound up with Lady Dyke's disappearance."

Mensmore rose excitedly.

"I cannot discuss the matter with you," he cried. "I have given my sacred promise, and no matter what the cost may be I will not break my word."

"I do not press you. But may I see Mrs. Hillmer again? When she is calmer I might reason with her."

The other placed his hand on Bruce's shoulder, and his voice was very impressive, though shaken by strong emotion:

"Believe me," he said, "it is better that you should not see her. It will be useless. She is leaving London, not to avoid consequences, but to get away from painful memories. Her departure will be quite open, and her place of residence known to any one who cares to inquire. One thing she is immovable in. She will never reveal to a living soul what she knows of Lady Dyke's death. She would rather suffer any punishment at the hands of the law."

"Don't you understand that this man, Montgomery, is now known to the police. Sooner or later he will be found and asked to explain any connection he may have had with the crime. Why not accomplish quietly that which will perforce be done through the uncompromising channels of Scotland Yard?"

"Your reasoning appears to be good, but—"

"But folly must prevail?"

"Put it that way if you like."

"So this wretched imbroglio may cost you the love of a charming and devoted girl?"

"Heaven help me, it may—probably will."

"I swear to you," cried the barrister, who was unusually excited, "that I will tear the heart out of this mystery before the week expires."

Mensmore bowed silently and would have left the room, but Smith entered. In their distraction they had not heard the bell ring. Smith handed a card to his master. Instantly Bruce controlled himself. His admiration for the dramatic sequence of events overcame his eagerness as an actor. It was with an appreciative smile that he said, without the slightest reference to Mensmore:

"Show the lady in."

Mensmore was passing out, but the sight of the visitor drove him back as though he had been struck. It was Phyllis Browne.

Her recognition of him was a bright smile. She advanced to Bruce, saying pleasantly:

"I am glad to meet you, though the manner of my call is somewhat unconventional. I heard much of you from Bertie in the Riviera, and more since my return to town."

He suitably expressed his delight at this apparition. Mensmore, not knowing what to do, stood awkwardly at the other end of the room.

Neither of the others paid the least heed to him.

"Of course I had a definite object in coming to see you, Mr. Bruce," went on the young lady. "I have been coolly told that, because somebody killed somebody else some months ago, a young gentlemen who asked me to be his wife, is not only not going to marry me but intends to spend the rest of his life in Central Africa or China—anywhere in fact but where I may be."

"A most unwise resolve," said the barrister.

"So I thought. You appear to hold the key to the situation; and, as it is an easy matter to trace you through the Directory, here I am. My people think I am skating at St. James's."

"Well, Miss Browne," said Claude, "I am neither judge nor jury nor counsel for the prosecution, but there is the culprit. I hand him over to you."

"Yes; but that goose didn't kill anybody, did he?"

"No."

"And I am sure his sister did not; from what little I saw of her she would not hurt a fly."

"Quite true."

"Then why don't you find the man who caused all the mischief—and—and—lock him up at least, so that he cannot go on injuring people?"

Miss Phyllis was very brave and self-confident at the outset. Now she was on the verge of tears, for Mensmore's saddened face and depressed manner unnerved her more than his passionate words at their last interview.

"You ask me a straight question," replied Bruce, though his eyes were fixed on Mensmore, "and I will give you a straight answer. I *will* find the man who killed Lady Dyke. As you say, it is time his capacity for doing injury to others should be limited. Before many days have passed Mr. Mensmore will come to you and beg your pardon for his hasty and quite unwarranted resolve."

"Do you hear that, Bertie?" cried the girl. "Didn't I tell you so?"

Mensmore came forward to her side of the table.

"I need not wait, Phil, dear," he said simply. "I ask your pardon now. This business is in the hands of Providence. I was foolish to think that anything I could do would stave off the inevitable."

"And if you have—to go—to China—you w-will take me with you?"

Bruce looked out of the window, whistled, and said loudly, addressing a beautiful lady in short skirts who figured in a poster across the way:

"Let me ring for some tea. All this talk makes one dry."

CHAPTER XXVI

LADY HELEN MONTGOMERY'S SON

When the young people had gone—Mensmore ill at ease, though tremuously happy that Phyllis had so demonstrated her trust in him, Phyllis herself radiantly confident in the barrister's powers to set everything right—Bruce devoted himself to the task of determining a new line for his energies.

The first step was self-evident. He must ascertain if the Dykes knew a Colonel Montgomery.

IIe drove to the Club frequented by Sir Charles, but the baronet was not there, so he went to Wensley House.

Sir Charles was at home, in his accustomed nook by the library fire. He looked ill and low-spirited. The temporary animation he had displayed during the past few weeks was gone. If anything, he was more listless than at any time since his wife's death.

"Well, Claude," he said wearily, "anything to report?"

"Yes, a good deal."

"What is it?"

"I want to ask you something. Did you ever know a Colonel Montgomery, or was your wife acquainted with any one of that name to your knowledge?"

"I do not think she was. Had she ever met such a man I should probably have heard of him. Who was he?"

The baronet's low state rendered his words careless and indefinite, but his friend did not wish to bother him unduly.

"The police have discovered," he said, "that Mrs. Hillmer formed a close intimacy with some one whom she designated by that name and rank, though I have failed to trace any British officer who answers to his description. He disappeared, or died, as some people put it, about the same time as your wife."

"Is it not known what became of him, then?"

"No."

"Won't Mrs. Hillmer tell you?"

"She absolutely refuses to give any help, whatever."

"On what ground?"

"That is best known to herself. My theory is that a man she loves is implicated in the affair, and she is prepared to go to any lengths to shield him."

"Ah!"

Sir Charles bent over and poked the fire viciously. Then he murmured: "Women are queer creatures, Bruce. We men never understand them until too late. My wife and I did not to all appearance care a jot for one another while she lived. Yet I now realize that she loved me, and I would give the little remaining span of existence, dear as life is, to see her once more."

This was a morbid subject; the younger man tried to switch him off it.

"It is almost clear to me," he said, "that Colonel Montgomery's name was assumed. Few people realize the use of the *alias* made in modern life. I have a notion that the custom among otherwise honorable people has arisen from the publicity given to the fact that Royal and other distinguished personages frequently choose to conceal their identity under less known territorial titles."

"The idea is ingenious. We are all slaves to fashion."

"However that may be, it should not be a difficult task to lay hands on the gentleman should he be still living."

"Suppose you succeed. How can you connect him with my wife's death?"

"At this moment I am unable to say. But the cabman might be of some use."

"The cabman. What cabman?"

"Did I omit that? I ought to have told you that I have found the driver of the four-wheeler in which your poor wife was taken, dead or insensible, from Sloane Square to Putney."

"What an extraordinary thing!"

"What is?"

"That you should have forgotten to inform me of such a striking fact."

"Not so. Now that I recollect, I have not had the opportunity. It was impossible to discuss anything else but that forged letter on the last two occasions we met, and it was only a few hours prior to your visit on Monday that I got the cabman's story fully. By the way, do you now see any reason why Jane Harding should have tried to deceive you in such a manner?"

The barrister perceived that Sir Charles was nervous and irritable, so he deemed it a needless strain to enlarge on the history of his discovery of Foxey.

"I am tired of letters, and plots, and mysteries. My life is resolving into one huge note of interrogation. Soon the great question of eternity will dominate all others."

Dyke's mood unfitted him for sustained conversation. Bruce could but pity him, and hope that time would calm his fevered brain, and soothe the unrest that shed this gloom over him.

"Really," said Claude, after a long interval, during which both men sought inspiration from the dancing flames in the fireplace, "really this is too bad of you, Dyke. You showed a marked improvement for a little space, and now you are letting yourself slip back into a state of lonely and unoccupied moping again."

"My thoughts find me both occupation and company," was the despondent reply.

"There is nothing for it," continued Bruce cheerfully, "but a tour round the world. You must start immediately. A complete change of scene and surroundings will soon pull you back to a normal state of mind and health."

"I have been thinking of a long journey for some time past."

The barrister glanced sharply at his friend. The *double entente* was not lost on him. Dyke was in a depressed and nervous condition. The uncertainty regarding his wife's fate was harassing him unduly and it was with a twinge of conscience that Bruce reflected upon his own eagerness to pursue a quest which, by very reason of its indefiniteness, attracted him as an intellectual pursuit.

"Look here," he cried, on the spur of the moment, "I have long desired to see the Canadian Pacific route. Will you arrange to start West with me a fortnight hence? We can return when the spirit moves us."

"We will see. We will see. To-day I feel unable to decide anything."

"Yes, I know, but the mere fact that you take the resolution will serve to reanimate you."

"It is very good of you, Claude, to trouble so about me. Had you asked me earlier I might have gone straight away. But let it rest for a little while. When I have recovered my spirits somewhat I will come to you to ask you to sail next day, or something of the sort."

Beyond this, the other could not move him.

There was one link in the chain of evidence that would be irrefragable if discovered. Was this "Colonel Montgomery" in any way connected with the house at Putney where the murderer had disposed of the body? If this could be established, the unknown visitor to Raleigh Mansions would experience a good deal of difficulty in clearing himself of suspicion. Bruce was certain that, once the "Colonel" was traced, much would come to light explanatory of Mrs. Hillmer's, and her brother's, dread lest his identity should be discovered.

An inquiry addressed to the house agents to whom possible tenants were referred elicited the information that the present owner, a lady, was prepared to let the house annually or on a lease. They enclosed an order to view, which Bruce retained in case he should happen to need it.

A second letter gave him the address of the lady's solicitors, Messrs. Small & Sharp, Lincoln's Inn.

He called on them as a possible tenant, with a desire to purchase the property outright if his proposal could be entertained.

Mr. Sharp, the partner who dealt with the estate, became very suave when the suggestion reached his ears.

"You will understand, Mr. Bruce, that your request requires some consideration. The rent my client asks is comparatively low, because the house is old-fashioned, but the splendid riparian position of the property, a free-hold acre on the banks of the Thames at Putney, gives it a highly increased future value. Any figure you may have based on a rental calculation would therefore—"

"Not meet the case at all," said the barrister, repressing a smile at the familiar opening move in the game of bargaining.

"Precisely."

"May I ask who the present owner is?"

"Certainly, the lady's name is Small. In fact, she is my partner's wife. Her father, the late Rev. Septimus Childe, purchased the estate some years ago, largely because the house suited his requirements as the head of a successful private school."

"Has the estate changed hands frequently then?"

"Oh, dear, no. Indeed, it is well understood that the Rev. Mr. Childe acquired it more as a friendly transaction than otherwise. The estate is a portion of the separate estate of the late Lady Helen Montgomery, who married Sir William Dyke, father of the present baronet, who perhaps—good gracious, my dear sir, what is the matter?"

Had Bruce been a woman he must have fainted.

As it was, the shock of the intelligence nearly paralyzed him. Sir Charles Dyke!—Montgomery!—The house at Putney the property of his mother! What new terror did not this frightful combination suggest?

Why did his friend conceal from him these most important facts? Why did he pretend ignorance not only of the locality but of his mother's maiden name? Like lightning the remembrance flashed through Bruce's troubled brain that he had only heard of the earlier Lady Dyke as a daughter of the Earl of Tilbury. A suspicion—profoundly horrible, yet convincing—was slowly mastering him, and every second brought further proof not only of its reasonableness, but of its ghastly and inflexible certainty.

Again the lawyer's voice reached his ears, dully and thin, as though it penetrated through a wall.

"Surely, you feel ill? Let me get you some brandy."

"No—no," murmured the barrister. "It is but a momentary faintness. I—I think I will go out into the fresh air. Are you—quite sure—that Mr. Childe bought the property from Lady Helen Montgomery's trustees?"

"Quite sure. If you wait even a few moments I will show you the title-deeds."

"No, thank you. I will call again. Pray excuse me."

Somehow Bruce crossed the quiet square of the Inn, and plunged into the turmoil of the street. Amid the bustle of Holborn he had a curious sensation of safety. The fiend so suddenly installed in his consciousness was less busy here suggesting strange and maddening thoughts.

Why—why—why—fifty questions beat incessantly against the barrier of agonized negation he strove to set up, but the noise of traffic made the attack confused. Each incautious bump against a passer-by silenced a demand, each heavy crunch of a 'bus on the gravel-strewed roadway temporarily silenced a doubt.

He was so unmanned that he felt almost on the verge of tears. He absolutely dared not attempt to reason out the fearful alternative which had so fiercely thrust itself upon him.

At last he became vaguely aware that people were staring at him. Fearful lest some acquaintance should recognize and accost him he hailed a hansom and drove to Victoria Street.

All the way the heavy beat of the horse's feet served to distract his thoughts. He forced himself to count the quick paces, and tried hard to accommodate the numerals of two or more syllables to the rapidity of the animal's trot. He failed in this, but in the failure found relief.

Nevertheless, though the horse was willing and the driver eager to oblige a fare who gave a "good" address, the time seemed interminable until the cab stopped in front of his door.

Once arrived there, he slowly ascended the stairs to his own flat, told Smith to pay the cabman half-a-crown and to admit no one, and threw himself into a chair.

At last he was face to face with the troublous demon who possessed him in Lincoln's Inn, struggled with him through the crowd, and travelled with him in the hansom. Phyllis Browne should have her answer sooner than he had expected.

The man who murdered Lady Dyke was her own husband.

"Oh, heavens!" moaned Bruce, as he swayed restlessly to and fro in his chair, "is it possible?"

He sat there for hours. Smith entered, turned on the lights and suggested tea, but received an impatient dismissal.

After another long interval Smith appeared again, to announce that Mr. White had called.

"Did you not say I was out?" said Claude, his hollow tones and haggard air startling his faithful servitor considerably.

"Yes, sir—oh yes, sir. But that's no use with Mr. White. 'E said as 'ow 'e were sure you were in."

"Ask him to oblige me by coming again—to-morrow. I am very ill. I really cannot see him."

Smith left the room only to return and say: "Mr. White says, sir, 'is business is of the *hutmost* himportance. 'E can't leave it; and 'e says you will be very sorry afterwards if you don't see 'im now."

"Oh, so be it," cried Bruce, turning to a spirit-stand to seek sustenance in a stiff glass of brandy. "Send him in."

Quite awed by circumstances, Smith admitted the detective and closed the door upon the two men, who stood looking at each other without a word of greeting or explanation.

CHAPTER XXVII

MR. WHITE'S METHOD

The policeman spoke first. "Has Jane Harding been here, then?" he said.

His words conveyed no meaning to his hearer.

They were so incongruous, so ridiculously unreasoning, that Bruce laughed hysterically.

"You must have seen her," cried the detective excitedly. "I know you have learned the truth, and in no other way that I can imagine could it have reached you."

"Learnt what truth?"

"That Sir Charles Dyke himself is at the bottom of all this business."

"Indeed. How have you blundered upon that solution?"

"Mr. Bruce, this time I am right, and you know it. It was Sir Charles Dyke who killed his wife. Nobody else had anything else to do with it, so far as I can guess. But if you haven't seen Jane Harding, I wonder how you found out."

"You are speaking in riddles. Pray explain yourself."

"If Sir Charles Dyke had not been out of town, the riddle would have been answered by this time in the easiest way, as I should have locked him up."

"Excellent. You remain faithful to tradition."

"Mr. Bruce, please don't try to humbug me, for the sake of your friend. I am quite in earnest. I have come to you for advice. Sir Charles Dyke is guilty enough."

"And what do you want me to do?"

"To help me to adopt the proper course. The whole thing seems so astounding that I can hardly trust my own senses. I spoke hastily just now. I would not have touched Sir Charles before consulting you. I was never in such a mixed-up condition in my life."

Whatever the source of his information, the detective had evidently arrived at the same conclusion as Bruce himself. There was nothing for it but to endeavor to reason out the situation calmly and follow the best method of dealing with it suggested by their joint intelligence. Claude motioned the detective to a chair, imposed silence by a look, and summoned Smith. He was faint from want of food. With returning equanimity he resolved first to restore his strength, as he would need all his powers to wrestle with events before he slept that night.

Mr. White, nothing loth, joined him in a simple meal, and by tacit consent no reference was made to the one engrossing topic in their thoughts until the table was cleared.

"And now, Mr. White," demanded the barrister, "what have you found out?"

"During the last two days," he replied, "I have been unsuccessfully trying to trace Colonel Montgomery. No matter what I did I failed. I got hold of several of Mrs. Hillmer's tradespeople, but she always paid her bills with her own cheques, and none of them had ever heard of a Colonel Montgomery. That furniture business puzzled me a lot—the change of the drawing-room set from one flat to another on November 7, I mean. So I discovered the address of the people who supplied the new articles to Mrs. Hillmer—"

"How?"

"Through the maid, Dobson. Mrs. Hillmer has given her notice to leave, and the girl is furious about it, as she appears to have had a very easy place there. I think it came to Mrs. Hillmer's ears that she talked to me."

"I see. Proceed."

"Here I hit upon a slight clue. It was a gentleman who ordered the new furniture, and directed the transfer of the articles replaced from No. 61 to No. 12 Raleigh Mansions. He did this early in the morning of November 7, and the foreman in charge of the job remembered that there was some bother about it, as neither Mrs. Hillmer nor Mr. Corbett, as Mensmore used to be called, knew anything about it. But the gentleman came the same morning and explained matters. It struck the foreman as funny that there should be such a fearful hurry about refurnishing a drawing-room, for the gentleman did not care what the cost was so long as the job was carried out at express speed. Another odd thing was that Mrs. Hillmer paid for the articles, though she had not ordered them nor did she appear to want them. The man was quite sure that Mensmore's first knowledge of the affair came with the arrival of the first batch of articles from Mrs. Hillmer's flat, but he could only describe the mysterious agent as being a regular swell. He afterwards identified a portrait of Sir Charles Dyke as being exactly like the man he had seen, if not the man himself."

"How did you come to have a portrait of Sir Charles in your possession?"

"That appears later," said the detective, full of professional pride at the undoubtedly smart manner in which he had manipulated his facts once they were placed in order before him.

"Of course," he went on, "I jumped at the conclusion that the stranger was this Colonel Montgomery. Then, while closely questioning the maid about the events of November 7, she suddenly remembered that she lost an old skirt and coat about that time. They had vanished from her room, and she had never laid eyes on them since. This set me thinking. I confronted her with the clothes worn by Lady Dyke when she was found in the river, and I'm jiggered if Dobson didn't recognize them at once as being her missing property. Now, wasn't that a rum go?"

"It certainly was," said Bruce, who was piecing together the story of the murder in his mind as each additional detail came to light.

"Naturally I thought harder than ever after that. It then occurred to me that Jane Harding must have had some powerful reasons for so suddenly shutting up about the identification of her mistress's underclothing. She was right enough, as we know, in regard to the skirt and coat, but she admitted to me that the linen on the dead body was just the same as Lady Dyke's. Curiously enough, it was not marked by initials, crest, or laundry-mark, and I ascertained months ago that owing to some fad of her ladyship's, all the family washing was done on the estate in Yorkshire. This explained the absence of the otherwise inevitable laundry-mark."

"Thus far you are coherence itself."

"Well," said Mr. White complacently, "I was a long time getting to work, Mr. Bruce, and had it not been for your help I should probably never have got at the truth, but I flatter myself that, once on the right track, I seldom leave it. However, as I was saying, I felt that Jane Harding knew a good deal more than she would tell, except under pressure, so I decided to put that pressure on."

"In what way?"

"I frightened her. Played off on her a bit of the stage business she is so fond of. This afternoon I placed a pair of handcuffs in my pocket and went to her place at Bloomsbury, having previously prepared a bogus warrant for her arrest on a charge of complicity in the murder of Lady Dyke."

"It was a dangerous game!"

"Very. If it had gone wrong and reached the ears of the Commissioner or got into the papers, I should have been reduced or dismissed. But what is a policeman to do in such cases? I was losing my temper over this infernal inquiry and never obtaining any real light, though always coming across startling developments. It had to end somehow, and I took the chance. The make-believe warrant and the production of handcuffs for a woman—they are never used, you know, in reality—have often been trump-cards for us when everything else failed."

"This time, then, the 'properties' made up the 'show,' as Miss Harding would put it?"

"They did, and no mistake. I gave her no time to think or act. I found her sitting with her mother, admiring a new carpet she had just laid down. I said, 'Is your name Jane Harding, now engaged at the Jollity Theatre, under the alias of Marie le Marchant, but formerly a maid in the service of Lady Dyke?' She grew very white, and said 'Yes,' while her mother clutched hold of her, terrified. Then I whipped out the warrant and the cuffs. My, but you should have heard them squeal when the bracelets clinked together. 'What has my child done?' screamed the mother. 'Perhaps nothing, madam,' I answered; 'but she is guilty in the eyes of the law just the same if she persists in screening the guilty parties.' Jane Harding was trembling and blubbering, but she said, 'It is very hard on me. I have done nothing.' I trembled myself then, as I feared that she might offer to come with me to the police station, in which case I should have been dished. But the mother fixed the affair splendidly. 'I am sure my daughter will not conceal anything,' she said, 'and it is a shame to disgrace her in this way without telling what it is you want to know.' I took the cue in an instant. 'I am empowered,' I said, 'to suspend this warrant, and perhaps do away with it altogether, if she answers my questions fully and truthfully.' 'Why, of course she will,' said the mother, and the girl, though desperately upset, whimpered her agreement. With that I got the whole story."

"Sir Charles Dyke inspired her actions, I suppose."

"From the very beginning almost. At first Jane Harding herself believed, when she gave evidence at the inquest, that the body she saw was not that of Lady Dyke; but afterwards she changed her opinion, especially when she recalled the exact pattern and materials of the underclothing. Then my inquiries put her on the scent. Being rather a sharp girl, she jumped to the conclusion that Sir Charles knew more about the matter than he professed. In any case, her place was gone, and she would soon be dismissed, so she resolved on a plan even bolder than mine in threatening to lock her up. She watched her opportunity, found Sir Charles alone one day, and told him that from certain things within her knowledge, she thought it her duty to go to the police-station. He was startled, she could see, and asked her to explain herself. She said that her mistress had been killed, and she might be able to put the police on the right track. He hesitated, not knowing what to say; so she hinted that it would mean a lot of trouble for her, and she would prefer, if she had £500, to go to America, and let the matter drop altogether. He told her that he did not desire to have Lady Dyke's name brought into public notoriety. Sooner than to allow such a thing to occur he would give her the money. An hour later he handed her fifty ten-pound notes."

"What a wretched mistake," cried Bruce involuntarily. This unmasking of his unfortunate friend's duplicity was the most painful feature of all to him.

"Perhaps it was," replied the detective, "but the thing is not yet quite clear to me. That is why I am here. But to continue. The girl admitted that she lost her head a bit. Instead of leaving the house openly, without attracting comment, she simply bolted, thus giving rise to the second sensational element attending Lady Dyke's disappearance. But she resolved to be faithful to her promise. When you found her she held her tongue, and even wrote to Sir Charles to assure him that she had not spoken a word to a soul. He sent for her, and pitched into her about not going to America, but took her address in case he wished to see her again."

"He recognized her letter-writing powers, no doubt."

"Evidently. She was surprised last Thursday week to receive a telegram asking her to meet him at York Station. When she arrived there he asked her to write the letter he handed to you and to post it in London on Saturday evening. He explained that his action was due to his keen anxiety to shield his wife's name, and that this letter would settle the affair altogether. As he handed her another bundle of notes, and promised to settle £100 a year on her for life, she was willing enough to help him. During your interview with her you guessed the reason why she wrote Lady Dyke's hand so perfectly. She had copied it for three years."

"All this must have astonished you considerably?"

"Mr. Bruce, astonished isn't the word. I was flabbergasted! Once she started talking I let her alone, only rattling the handcuffs when she seemed inclined to stop. But all the time I felt as if the top of my head had been blown off."

"I imagine she had not much more to tell you?"

"She pitched into you as the cause of all the mischief, and went so far as to say that she was sure it was not Sir Charles who killed Lady Dyke, but you yourself."

Bruce winced at Jane Harding's logic. Were he able to retrieve the past three months the mystery of Lady Dyke's death would have remained a mystery forever.

"Now about the photograph," said the detective. "After I had left Jane Harding with a solemn warning to speak to no one until I saw her again, I made a round of the fashionable photographers and soon obtained an excellent likeness of Sir Charles. I showed it to Dobson, and she said: 'That is Colonel Montgomery.' I showed it to the foreman of the furniture warehouse, and he said: 'That is the image of the man who ordered Mrs. Hillmer's suite.' Now, what on earth is the upshot of this business to be? I called at Wensley House, but was told Sir Charles was not in town. Had he been in, I would not have seen him until I had discussed matters with you."

"That is very good of you, Mr. White. May I ask your reason for showing him this consideration?"

The policeman, who was very earnest and very excited, banged his hand on the table as he cried:

"Don't you see what all this amounts to? I have no option but to arrest Sir Charles Dyke for the murder of his wife."

"That is a sad conclusion."

"And do you believe he killed her?"

"Strange as it may seem to you, I do not."

"And I'm jiggered if I do either."

"I—I am greatly obliged to you, White."

Claude bent his head almost to his knees, and for some minutes there was complete silence. When he again looked at the detective there were tears in his eyes.

"What can we do to unravel this tangled skein without creating untold mischief?" he murmured.

"It beats me, sir," was the perplexed answer. "But when I came in I imagined that Jane Harding or some one had been to see you. Surely, you had learned something of all this before my arrival?"

"Yes, indeed. I had reached your goal, but by a different route. Unfortunately, my discovery only goes to confirm yours."

Bruce then told him of his visit to the lawyer's office, and its result. Mr. White listened to the recital with knitted brows.

"It is very clear," he said, when the barrister had ended, "that Lady Dyke was killed in Mrs. Hillmer's flat, that Sir Charles knew of her death, that he himself conveyed the body to the river bank at Putney, and that ever since he has tried to throw dust in our eyes and prevent any knowledge of the true state of affairs reaching us."

"Your summary cannot be disputed in the least particular."

"Well, Mr. Bruce, we must do *something*. If you don't like to interfere, then *I* must."

"There is but one person in the world who can enlighten us as to the facts. That person obviously is Sir Charles Dyke himself."

"Unquestionably."

Bruce looked at his watch. It was 10.30 P.M. He rose.

"Let us go to him," he said.

"But he is not in London."

"He is. I expect you will find that he gave orders for no one to be admitted, and told the servants to say he had left town to make the denial more emphatic."

"It will be a terrible business, I fear, Mr. Bruce."

"I dread it—on my soul I do. But I cannot shirk this final attempt to save my friend. My presence may tend to help forward a final and full explanation. No matter what the pain to myself, I must be present. Come, it is late already!"

CHAPTER XXVIII

SIR CHARLES DYKE'S JOURNEY

The streets were comparatively deserted as they drove quickly up Whitehall and crossed the south side of Trafalgar Square. It is a common belief, even among Londoners themselves, that the traffic is dense in the main thoroughfares at all hours of the night until twelve o'clock has long past.

But to the experienced eye there is a marked hiatus between half-past nine and eleven o'clock. At such a time Charing Cross is negotiable, Piccadilly Circus loses much of its terror, and a hansom may turn out of Regent Street into Oxford Street without the fare being impelled to clutch convulsively at the brass window-slide in a make-believe effort to save the vehicle from being crushed like a walnut shell between two heavy 'buses.

Such considerations did not appeal to the barrister and his companion on this occasion.

For some inexplicable cause they both felt that they were in a desperate hurry.

A momentary stoppage at the turn into Orchard Street caused each man to swear, quite unconsciously. Now that the supreme moment in this most painful investigation was at hand they resented the slightest delay. Though they were barely fifteen minutes in the cab, it seemed an hour before they alighted at Wensley House, Portman Square.

In response to an imperative ring a footman appeared. Instead of answering the barrister's question as to whether Sir Charles was at home or not, he said: "You are Mr. Bruce, sir, aren't you?"

"Yes."

"Sir Charles is at home, but he retired to his room before dinner. He is not well, and he may have gone to bed, but he said that if you came you were to be admitted. I will ask Mr. Thompson."

"Better send Thompson to me," said Bruce decisively; and in a minute the old butler stood before him.

"I hear that Sir Charles has retired for the night," said Claude.

Thompson had caught sight of the detective standing on the steps. A few hours earlier he had himself told him that the baronet was out of town. It was an awkward dilemma, and he coughed doubtingly while he racked his brains for a judicious answer.

But Bruce grasped his difficulty. "It is all right, Thompson. Mr. White quite understands the position. Do you think Sir Charles is in bed?"

"I will go and see, sir. He was very anxious that you should be sent upstairs if you called. But that was when he was in the library."

Bruce and the detective entered the hall, the butler closed the door behind them, and then solemnly ascended the stairs to Sir Charles Dyke's bedroom, which was situated on the first floor along a corridor towards the back of the house.

They distinctly heard the polite knock at the door and Thompson's query, "Are you asleep, Sir Charles?"

After a pause, there was another knock, and the same question in a slightly louder key.

Then the butler returned, saying as he came down the stairs:

"Sir Charles seems to be sound asleep, sir."

Bruce and the detective exchanged glances. The barrister was disappointed, almost perturbed, but he said:

"In that case we will not disturb him. Sir Charles does not often retire so early."

"No, sir. I have never known him to go to his room so early before. He told me not to serve dinner, as he wasn't well. He would not let me get anything for him. He just took some wine, and I have not seen him since."

"Since when?"

"About 7.30, sir."

Bruce turned to depart, but Thompson, with the privilege of an old servant when talking to one whom he knew to be on familiar terms with his master, whispered:

"That there blessed maid turned up again this afternoon, sir."

The barrister started violently.

"Not Jane Harding, surely?"

"Yes, sir. She came at four o'clock and asked for Sir Charles, as bold as brass."

"Did he see her?"

"Oh yes, sir."

"Do you hear that, White?"

The detective nodded.

"She must have reached the house about half-an-hour before me," he said, addressing the butler.

"That's about right, sir."

"But I understood," went on Bruce, "that Sir Charles was not at home to ordinary callers?"

Thompson shuffled about somewhat uneasily. He wished now he had held his tongue.

"I had my orders, sir," he murmured, in extenuation of his apparently diverse actions.

"Tell me what your orders were," persisted Bruce.

The man hesitated, not wishful to offend his master's friend, but too well trained to reveal the explicit instructions given him by Sir Charles Dyke.

"Do not be afraid. I will explain everything to Sir Charles personally. We cannot best judge what to do—whether to wake him or not—unless we know the position," went on the barrister.

Thus absolved from blame, Thompson took from his waistcoat pocket a folded sheet of notepaper.

"I don't pretend to understand the reason, sir," he said, "but Sir Charles wrote this himself, and told me to be careful to obey him exactly."

The barrister eagerly grasped the note and read:

"If Mr. Bruce, Jane Harding, or Mrs. Hillmer should call, admit any of them immediately. To all others say that I have left town—some days ago, should they ask you.

"C. D."

White, round-eyed and bullet-headed, gazed with goggle orbs over Bruce's shoulder.

"That settles it, Mr. Bruce," he said. "We *must* see him."

"Thompson," said Bruce, "does Sir Charles usually lock his door?"

"Never, sir."

"Very well. Knock again, and then try the door. We will go with you."

Something in the barrister's manner rather than his words sent a cold shiver down the old butler's spine.

"I do hope there's nothing wrong, sir," he commenced; but Bruce was already half-way up the stairs. Both he and White guessed what had happened. They knew that poor Thompson's repeated summons at the bedroom door would remain forever unanswered—that the unfortunate baronet had quitted the dread certainties of this world for the uncertainties of the next.

They were not mistaken. A few minutes later they found him listlessly drooping over the side of the chair in which he was seated, partly undressed, and seemingly overcome at the moment when he was about to take off his boots.

On a table near him were two bottles, both half-emptied, and an empty wineglass. Each of the bottles bore the label of a well-known chemist. One was endorsed "Sleeping-draught," the other "Poison," and "Chloral."

The three men were pale as the limp, inanimate form in the chair while they silently noted these details. Bruce raised the head of his friend in the hope that life might not yet be extinct. But Sir Charles Dyke had taken his measures effectually. Though the *rigor mortis* had not set in, he had evidently been dead some time.

Thompson, quite beside himself with grief, dropped to his knees by his master's side.

"Sir Charles!" he wailed. "Sir Charles! For the love of Heaven, speak to us. You can't be dead. Oh, you can't. It ain't fair. You're too young to die. What curse has come upon the house that both should go?"

Bruce leaned over and shook the old butler firmly by the shoulder.

"Thompson," he said impressively, for now that the crisis he feared had come and gone, he exercised full control over himself. "Thompson, if you ever wished to serve Sir Charles you must do so now by remaining calm. For his sake, help us, and do not create an unnecessary scene."

Governed by the more powerful nature, the affrighted man struggled to his feet.

"What shall I do?" he whimpered. "Shall I send for a doctor?"

"Yes; say Sir Charles is very ill. Not a word to a soul about what has happened until we have carefully examined the room."

At that instant Mr. White caught sight of a large and bulky envelope, which had fallen to the floor near the chair on which Sir Charles was seated.

Picking it up, he found it was addressed, "Claude Bruce, Esq. To be delivered to him *at once.*"

"This will explain matters, I expect," said the detective.

"Whatever could have come to my master to do such a thing?" groaned Thompson, turning to reach the door.

"Come back," cried Bruce sharply. "Now, look here, Thompson," he went on, placing both his hands on the butler's shoulders and looking him straight in the eyes, "it is imperative that you should pull yourself together. That sort of remark will never do. Sir Charles has simply taken an over-dose of chloral accidentally. He has slept badly ever since Lady Dyke's death, you understand, and has been in the habit of taking sleeping-draughts. Now, before you leave the room tell me exactly what has happened, in your own language."

"I can't put it together now, sir, but I won't say anything to anybody. You can trust me for that. Why, I loved him as my own son, I did."

"Yes, I know that well. But remember. An over-dose. An accident. Nothing else. Do you follow me?"

"Quite, sir. Heaven help us all."

"Very well. Now send for the doctor, without needlessly alarming the other servants."

Bruce placed the envelope in the pocket of his overcoat, saying to the detective:

"We will examine this later, White. Just now we must do what we can to avoid a scandal. The case between Lady Dyke and her husband will be settled by a higher tribunal than we had counted upon."

"It certainly *looks* like an accident, Mr. Bruce," was the answer, "but it all depends upon the view the doctor takes. And you know, of course, that I shall have to report the actual facts to my superiors."

"That is obvious. Yet no harm is done at this early stage in taking such steps as may finally render undue publicity needless. It may be impossible; but on the other hand, until we have heard Sir Charles's version, contained, I suppose, in this letter to me, it is advisable to sustain the theory of an accidental death."

"Anything I can do to help you will be done," replied the detective. With that they dropped the subject, and more carefully scrutinized the room.

To all intents and purposes Sir Charles Dyke might, indeed, have brought about the catastrophe inadvertently. The sleeping-draught bore the ledger number of its prescription, and there is nothing unusual in a patient striving to help the cautious dose ordered by a physician by the addition of a more powerful nostrum.

His partly dressed state, too, argued that he had taken the fatal mixture at a time when he contemplated retiring to rest forthwith. A fire still burned in the grate. On the mantelpiece—in a position where the baronet must see it until the moment when all things faded from his vision—was a beautiful miniature of his wife.

The detective, with professional nonchalance, soon sat down. There was nothing to do but await the arrival of the doctor, and, having heard his report, go home.

In the quietude of the room, with the strain relaxed, Bruce was profoundly moved by the spectacle of his dead friend. Whatever his logical faculties might argue, he could not regard this man as a murderer. If Lady Dyke met her death at his hand then it must have been the result of some terrible mistake—of some momentary outburst of passion which never contemplated such a sequel.

Poisons which kill by stupefaction do not distort their victims as in cases where violent irritants are used. Sir Charles Dyke seemed to live in a deep sleep, exhausted by toil or pain—sleep the counterfeit of death—while the bright colors and speaking eyes of the miniature counterfeited life. Standing between these two—both the mere images of the man and the woman he had known so well—the barrister insensibly felt that at last they had peace.

It was his first experience of the tremendous change in the relationship established by death. It utterly overpowered him. No mere words could express his emotions. Between him and those that had been was imposed the impenetrable wall of eternity.

A bustle in the hall beneath aroused him from his grief-stricken stupor, and Mr. White's commonplace tones sounded strange to his ears.

"Here's the doctor."

A well-known physician hastened to the room. Thompson had carefully followed instructions. The doctor was not prepared for the condition of affairs that a glance revealed to his practised eye.

"Surely he is not dead?" he cried, looking from the form in the chair to the two men.

Bruce answered him:

"Yes, for some hours, I fear, but we wanted to avoid spreading unnecessary rumors until—"

"I understand. My poor friend! How came this to happen?"

The skilled practitioner merely lifted one of the dead man's eyelids, and then turned to examine the bottles on the table.

"My own prescription," he said, after tasting the contents of one phial. "Ah, this was bad; why did he not consult me?" and he sadly shook his head as he tasted the remaining liquid in the second.

"What do you make of it?" said Bruce.

He looked the other steadily in the face and the doctor interpreted the cause of his anxiety.

"A clear case of accidental poisoning," he replied. "Sir Charles has consulted me several times during the past week on account of his extreme insomnia. I specifically warned him against overdoing my treatment. Change of air, exercise, and diet are the true specifics for sleeplessness, especially when induced, as his was, by a morbid state of mind."

"You mean—"

"That Sir Charles has never recovered from the shock of his wife's death. I did not know of it myself until it was announced recently, and I gathered from him that the manner of her demise was partly unaccounted for. Altogether, it is a sad business that such a couple should be taken in such a manner."

Mr. White was industriously taking notes the while, and the doctor regarded him with a questioning look.

"This gentleman is in the police," explained Bruce.

"Indeed!"

"Yes. We came here by mere accident. Mr. White and I were engaged in an important inquiry—the cause of Lady Dyke's disappearance, in fact—and we hurried here at a late hour to consult with Sir Charles. Hence our presence and this discovery."

"How strange!"

"There is no reason now," broke in the detective, "why the body should not be moved?"

Claude shuddered at the phrase. It suggested the inevitable.

"Not in the least. I am quite satisfied as to the cause of death."

The despatch of telegrams and other necessary details kept Bruce busily employed until two o'clock. Not until he reached the privacy of his own library was he able to break the seal of the packet left for him as the final act and word of the late Sir Charles Dyke.

CHAPTER XXIX

HOW LADY DYKE DISAPPEARED

(Being the Manuscript left by Sir Charles Dyke, Bart., and addressed to Claude Bruce, Esq., Barrister-at-law)

It is customary, I believe, for poor wretches who are sentenced to undergo the last punishment of the law to be allowed a three weeks' respite between the date of their sentence and that on which they are executed. I am in the position of such a one. The difference between me and the convicted felon lies merely in environment; in most respects I am worse situated than he. My period of agony is longer drawn out, I am condemned to die by my own hand, I am mocked by the surroundings of luxury, taunted by the knowledge that though life and even a sort of happiness are within my reach I must not avail myself of them.

There may come a time in the affairs of any man when he is compelled to choose between a dishonored existence and voluntary death. These unpleasant alternatives are now before me. You, who know me, would never doubt which of them I should adopt, nor will you upbraid me because our judgments coincide. There is nothing for it, Bruce, but quiet death—death in the least obtrusive form, and so disposed that it may be possible for you, chief among my friends and the only person I can trust to fulfil my wishes, to arrange that my memory may be speedily forgotten. My virtues, I fear, will not secure me immortality; my faults, I hope, will not be spread broadcast to cram the maws of the gaping crowd.

I do not shirk this final issue, nor do I crave pity. In setting forth plainly the history of my wife's death and its results, I am actuated solely by a desire to protect others from needless suspicion. Having resolved to pay forfeit for my own errors, I claim to have expiated them. This document is an explanation, not a confession.

I have not much time left wherein fittingly to shape my story so as to be just to all, myself included. If I am not mistaken, the officers of the law are in hot chase of me, but my statement shall not be made to an earthly judge. The words of a man about to die may not be well chosen; they should at least be true. I will tell of events as nearly as possible in their sequence of time. If I leave gaps through haste or forgetfulness you will, from your own knowledge of the facts, readily fill them up once you are in possession of the salient features.

Mensmore and his sister were the friends of my early years. We played together as children. Gwendoline Mensmore was two years younger than I, and I well remember making love to her at the age of eleven. Her mother died when she was quite a baby, and her father married again, so her step-brother Albert is her junior by four years. I taught him how to ride and swim and play cricket. My father's place in Surrey—we did not acquire the Yorkshire property until the death of my grandfather—adjoined the estate General Mensmore occupied after his retirement from the army.

We children always called Gwendoline "Dick," to avoid the difficulty of her long-sounding name, I suppose, and I honestly believe that our respective parents entertained the idea that a marriage between us was quite a natural thing. I went to school at Brighton, and Mensmore, being a somewhat precocious lad, joined the same school before I left. The headmaster, the Rev. Septimus Childe, was an old friend of my father's, and when he wished to purchase a house at Putney—the terrible house which has figured in my dreams for the past three months as a Place of Skulls—my parents put pressure on my mother's trustees to make the transaction an easy one. Of course, I knew it well. We regarded it in those early days as a town house, and always lived there during the season.

My father's succession to the title and estates changed all that. We quitted Surrey for Yorkshire, and Wensley House, Portman Square, was a step upwards from the barrack-like building which so admirably suited Mr. Childe's requirements.

When I was at Sandhurst General Mensmore got into difficulties. He quitted Surrey, and we gradually lost sight of him and his children. Afterwards I knew that he struggled on for a few years, placed his son in the army, and then came a complete collapse, ending in his death and the boy's resignation of his commission. Of Gwendoline Mensmore's whereabouts I knew nothing. Her memory never quitted me, but the new interests in my life dulled it. I imagined that I could laugh at a childish infatuation.

Then I married. I did so in obedience to my father's wishes, and Alice was, I suppose, an ideal wife—far too ideal for a youngster of my lower intellectual plane. I know now that I never had any real affection for her. I was always somewhat awed by her loftier aspirations. My interests lay in racing, hunting, sports generally, and having what I defined as "a good time." She, though an excellent horsewoman, and in every sense an admirable hostess, thought Newmarket vulgar, treated Ascot as a social necessity, and turned up her eyebrows at me when I failed to see any utility in schemes for the reclamation of the submerged tenth.

Thus, though we never quarrelled, we gradually drifted apart. She knew she bored me if she asked me to inspect a model dwelling; I knew she hated the people who were the companions of a coaching tour or a week at Goodwood. Unfortunately, we were not blessed with offspring. Had it been otherwise, we might have found a common object of interest in our children.

Insensibly, we agreed to a separate existence. We lived together as friends rather than as husband and wife. We parted without regret and met without cordiality. Do not think we were unhappy. If our marriage was not bliss, it was at least comfortable. I think my wife was proud of my successes on the turf in a quiet kind of way, and I certainly was proud of her and of the high reputation she enjoyed among all classes of society. I even reverenced her for it, and I well knew that the enthusiastic receptions given us by our Yorkshire tenantry were not due to my efforts in their behalf, but to hers.

So we lived for nearly six years, and so we might have continued for sixty had I not met Gwendoline Mensmore again, under vastly changed circumstances. She was a chorus-girl in a variety theatre, earning a poor living under wretched conditions. I discovered the fact by mere chance.

I met her, and she told me her story—how she had married a man named Hillmer, whom her father had trusted, and whom she believed to be able to save them from ruin. Then the crash came. Her father died; her husband also broke down financially, took to drink and ill-treated her; her brother was swallowed up somewhere in the Far West. She had no alternative but to live apart from her husband and try to support herself by the first career that suggests itself to a young, talented, and beautiful woman. But she was already weary of the stage and its distasteful surroundings. Her nature was too delicate for the rude friendships of the dressing-room. She shuddered at the thought of a mild carousal in a bar when the labors of the night were ended.

In a word, were I differently constituted, were she cast in more common mould, there was apparently ready to hand all the material for a vulgar *liaison*.

My respect for my wife, however, no less than Mrs. Hillmer's fine disposition, saved both of us from folly. Yet I could not leave her exposed to the exigencies of a life in which she was rapidly becoming disillusioned. Away in the depths of my heart I knew that this sweet woman was my true mate, separated from me by adverse chance. There was nothing unfair to Alice in the thought. Were she questioned at any time, I suppose, she must have admitted that we were, in some respects, as ill-matched a couple as we were well-matched in others. You will say that I understood but little of feminine nature—nothing at all of my wife's.

How best to help Mrs. Hillmer—that was the question. It was at this stage I made the initial mistake to which I can, too late, trace a host of succeeding misfortunes. I did not consult my wife. Trying now to analyze my reasons for this lamentable error of judgment I imagined that it arose from some absurd disinclination on my part to admit that I went to the stage-door of a theatre to inquire about the identity of a young woman whom I had recognized from the front of the house.

Don't you see, my dear Bruce, it is almost as bad to fear your wife as to suspect her.

As, at that time, my own life was free from the slightest cloud of sorrow, I took keen interest in the troubles of Mrs. Hillmer, and I amused myself by playing, in her behalf, the part of a modern magician. I felt intuitively that she would resent any direct attempt on my part to place funds at her disposal, and I found a great deal of harmless fun in helping her with her consent, but without her actual knowledge.

I am, as you know, a rich man. At this hour I cannot sum up my available assets to within £100,000. Altogether I must be worth nearly a million sterling—yet my money cannot purchase me another day's existence such as I would tolerate. Strange, is it not?

Well, the close of the year before last was a period of unexampled activity on the Stock Exchange, and, by way of a joke, I made some purchases on Mrs. Hillmer's account, with the intention of pretending to pay myself out of the profits, while handing her such balances as might accrue. She is a shrewd woman, and quick at figures, so I might have experienced some difficulty in deceiving her. But the mad record of the past twelve months was in no wise belied by its inception. My purchases were those of a man inspired by the Goddess of Fortune. Stocks which I bought commenced suddenly to inflate. I astounded my brokers by the manner in which I ferreted out neglected bonds, mines which struck the mother lode next week, railway companies whose directors were even then secretly conspiring to water the stock.

Mrs. Hillmer became infected with the craze like myself. Twice we plunged heavily in American Rails and came out triumphantly. To end this part of my story, after five months of excitement I had contrived not only to swell my own deposits to a large extent, but I had secured on Mrs. Hillmer's account a sufficient quantity of reliable stock to bring her in an average income of £1,500 per annum.

My greatest difficulty was to persuade Mrs. Hillmer to break off the habit of speculation once she had contracted it. I found that she perused the late editions of the evening papers with the same eagerness that a bookmaker looks for the starting prices of the day's races. By the exercise of firmness and tact I was able to stop her from further dealings.

At the close of this period I need hardly say that two things had happened. Mrs. Hillmer and I were fast friends, with common objects and interests in life; and, concurrently, the ties between Alice and myself had loosened still more.

I also carelessly made another blunder. Under the pretence that secrecy was requisite for Stock Exchange transactions, I persuaded Mrs. Hillmer to allow me to pass under the name of Colonel Montgomery.

Mrs. Hillmer, of course, was now able to live in comparative luxury. I came to regard her house as an abode of rest. I was more at home in her drawing-room than in my own house. She often spoke to me of my wife, and obviously wished to see her, but here I did a cowardly thing. I represented my married existence as far less comfortable than it really was, and gradually Mrs. Hillmer ceased all allusion to Alice. She misunderstood our relations. I knew it, and did not explain. Not a very worthy proceeding for a man whose sense of honor is so keen that he prefers death to disgrace. But one can deceive no other so easily as oneself.

Occasionally, when opportunities offered, we went out together. It was foolish, you will say, and I agree with you. If folly were not pleasant it would not be so fashionable. But, to this hour, the relations between us are those only of close friendship. Never in my life have I addressed her by other than her married name, never have I touched her arm save by way of casual politeness.

I really think I flattered myself upon my superior virtues. I could see all the excellence but none of the stupidity of my behavior.

About this time, Mrs. Hillmer's husband died. Thenceforth she became slightly reserved in manner. When life was a defiance she fought convention, but with safety came prudence. In fact, she told me that my frequent visits to her house would certainly be ill-construed if they became known. I was seeking for a pretext to introduce her to her own set in society, when a double catastrophe occurred.

My wife discovered, as she imagined, that I was clandestinely occupied with another woman, and Mrs. Hillmer's brother returned from America.

It will best serve my hurried narrative if I relate events exactly as they happened, and not as they look in the light of subsequent knowledge.

Mensmore was naturally astounded to find his sister so well provided for, and gratefully accepted the help she gave him towards resuscitating his own fortunes. But it did not occur to either of us that he would take the ordinary view of the bond existing between us, and I shall never forget his rage when he found out that I was not known to his sister's servants by my right name. It was an awkward position for all three. He was loth to allege that which we did not feel called upon to deny. But between him and me there was a marked coolness, arising from suspicion on his part and resentment on mine, coupled, I must add, with an unquiet consciousness that his attitude was not wholly unreasonable.

Mrs. Hillmer and he discussed the matter several times. He urged that this compromising friendship should be discontinued. She—a determined woman when her mind was made up—fought the suggestion on the ground of unfairness, though, like myself, she would have been glad of any accident which would alter the position of affairs.

He interpreted her opposition to different motives. Finally, as his financial position was a dangerous one, as we afterwards learned, and he despaired of setting things straight in Raleigh Mansions—judging them from his own point of view—he resolved to leave England again.

And now I come to the night of November 6.

It was, as you will remember, a foggy and unpleasant day. I had some business in the city which detained me until darkness set in. I had not seen Mrs. Hillmer for two days, so I resolved to drive to Sloane Square—travelling by the Underground was intolerable in such weather—and have tea with her.

I did not know then that she had gone with her maid to Brighton—intending to return that evening. It was a sudden whim, she told me subsequently, and she had not even informed the other servants of her intention.

The pavements in the City were slimy with the dampness of the fog, and as an empty four-wheeler passed through Cornhill I hailed it, a most unusual choice on my part. The cabman, I noticed, was fairly elevated, but as these fellows often drive better when drunk than sober, I simply told him to be careful, and jumped in. I reached Sloane Square all right, and detained the cab for my intended journey home in time for dinner.

At the door of Mrs. Hillmer's flat I met the cook and housemaid, both going out to do some shopping, probably, in the spare hour before it was time to prepare dinner.

They knew me well, of course, and admitted me to the drawing-room, telling me that Mrs. Hillmer was out, but would surely return very soon.

I had not been in the room a minute before the sharp double knock of a telegraph messenger brought the coachman, whom the girls left in charge of the house, to the door, and I startled the man by appearing in the hall, as he did not know of my presence.

"What is it, Simmonds?" I said, as I correctly guessed the message to be from Mrs. Hillmer.

"The missus is in Brighton, sir," he answered. "She wants the carriage to meet her at Victoria at seven o'clock. It's six now, and I ought to go around to the stables at once, but both these blessed girls have gone out. I'm in a fair fix."

"No fix at all," I said. "I want to see Mrs. Hillmer, so I will wait here until she arrives—or, at all events, till the servants come back."

The man scratched his head, but he could think of no better plan, so he, too, went off, and I was left alone, for the first time in my life, in Mrs. Hillmer's abode. It is the small events that govern our lives, Claude, not those that stand out prominently. The shopping expedition of a couple of servant girls, intent on securing a new cap or a few yards of calico, brought about my wife's death, caused misery to many people, and ends, I sincerely hope, in my own speedy leap into oblivion.

I picked up a novel, "Tess of the D'Urbervilles," hit upon the terrible episode that culminates on Salisbury Plain, and was soon deeply interested, when another knock—this time an imperative summons long drawn out—caused me to hasten to the door.

I opened it, and in the dim light of the staircase landing, for a second did not recognize the lady who stood outside. Heaven help me, I was soon enlightened. My wife's voice was bitterly contemptuous as she said:

"You don't keep a footman, it appears, in your new establishment, Charles."

Had I been suddenly struck blind, or paralyzed, I could not have been more dumfounded than by Alice's unexpected appearance. A thorough scoundrel might, perhaps, have thought of the best thing to say. I blurted out the worst.

"What are you doing *here*?" I stammered when my tongue recovered its use.

"No doubt you resent my appearance," she cried, in a high, shrill tone I had never before heard from her, "but I shall not trouble you further. I merely came to confirm with my own eyes what my ears refused to entertain. Now, I am satisfied."

She half turned with the intention of reaching the street, but, rendered desperate by the absurdity of my position, I gripped her arm and pulled her forcibly into the entrance-hall, closing and bolting the door behind us.

"You have seen too much not to see more," I cried. "I will not allow you to ruin both our lives by a mere suspicion."

She was in a furious temper, but her sense of propriety—for she did not know that the servants' quarters were empty—restrained her until we had both entered the drawing-room.

Then she burst upon me with a torrent of words.

CHAPTER XXX

SIR CHARLES DYKE ENDS HIS NARRATIVE

"A mere suspicion, indeed!" she said, and there was that in her voice which warned me that I had better try unarmed to control a tigress than a wife who deemed herself wronged; "these are pretty *suspicions* that surround you. A house tenanted by another woman where you are evidently master! A mistress who left the ranks of the ballet, or something of the sort, living in luxury on means supplied by you! A married woman who casts off her husband with her poverty, to take up a paramour and riches! Do you think you can blind my eyes further? I have the most convincing proofs of your infamy. Do not imagine that on any specious pretext I will condone your conduct. I despise you from the depths of my heart. Henceforth I will strive to forget your very existence."

"Alice," I said, and if she had not been blinded by passion she must have been affected by my earnestness, "will you listen to me?"

"Why should I? What respect have you shown to me that I should now seem even to accept your excuses?"

"I appeal to you not to do anything in anger. You have good reason to be enraged with me. I only ask you to suspend your final judgment. Hear what I have to say, take time for deliberation, for further inquiry, and then condemn me to any punishment you think fit."

She did not answer me. Her eyes were roving round the room and taking stock of every indication of poor Mrs. Hillmer's artistic aptitude. The place was eminently home-like, much more so than our elegant mansion in Portman Square, and my wife noted the fact with momentarily increasing bitterness. Yet I essayed my desperate task with failing nerve and terrible consciousness of a bad cause.

"Notwithstanding all that you have seen and heard," I said, "I am not guilty of the crime you accuse me of. Mrs. Hillmer is an old friend of mine, whom I have helped from a state of misery to one of comfort and comparative happiness. She is as pure-minded in thought, as spotless in character, as you are yourself. You are doing her a grievous injustice by doubting the relations between her and me. If you only knew her—"

My wife laughed scornfully.

"Pray spare yourself, Charles. I have never seen you so interested before, but you lie badly, nevertheless."

"I do not lie. Before heaven I am telling you the truth."

"You are even willing to perjure yourself, *Colonel Montgomery?*"

My poor armor was ill-fitted for this stroke. I suppose I must have flinched before it, for she went on:

"You see I am well posted. My detectives have done their work well. Oh, Heaven, that I should ever have learned to love a vile wretch like you. I thought you respected me, at least. I tried hard to bend my own wishes to sympathy with yours, and I dreamt even of ultimate success. I knew you didn't care much for me, but the devotion of a slave has at times been rewarded by the affection of her master. Fortunately, I am a slave by choice. It only required experience to break my bonds, and you have supplied the experience."

For the first time in my life did it dawn on me that my self-contained and haughty wife harbored other thoughts than a sentiment of respect for an indulgent and easily controlled husband. It was a shock to me, a deeper humiliation than she dreamed of. How could I expiate the past, wipe out this record of error and folly, but not of ill-doing, and live happily with her so long as Providence was pleased to spare us? While these things ran through my brain she suddenly turned on me.

"You fear exposure in the law courts! You dread your name figuring in a society scandal! How little you know me. You naturally compare me by your own contemptible standard. I left your house to-night determined never to return to it should I find you here, as in all probability, I was told, would be the case. I will go to my sister until I have determined upon my future life. You, at least, will never, by my desire, see or hear from me again. Thus far, I presume, I will fall in with your views."

She would have passed me, but I held fast to the inside of the door. If once she got away from me I might never be able to set affairs even tolerably right. Better, I deemed, have one trying scene in the hope that she would calm down in the face of facts, than allow her to carry the quarrel to her relatives and strengthen her attitude by their natural support.

"Alice," I said, "you shall not go."

"How can you dare to detain me?" she shrieked, and the glint in her eyes showed how thoroughly her passions were aroused.

"You can separate from me if you will. I shall not venture to hinder you. But I swear you shall not do this rash act without knowledge. I tell you you must remain here. When you leave this house you do so in my company."

"And why am I to be kept a prisoner?"

"Mrs. Hillmer will return in less than an hour. You have sought this meeting yourself. Very well. You shall have it. When your charges have been thoroughly thrashed out in the presence of Mrs. Hillmer and myself I will then accompany you where you will, and leave you under the protection of your sister, or any one else you choose, should you still persist in leaving me."

Of course my action was unwise to the last degree. But remember, Claude, that during these last awful five minutes I had seen a side of my wife's nature hidden from me six long years. And I was a man suddenly plunged into a raging sea, drifting helplessly I knew not whither. All that consumed me was a wild desire for such scant justice as I deserved. I had erred, but my faults were not those my wife alleged against me.

If she was angry before she was now absolutely uncontrollable.

"What?" she screamed. "Remain to meet your—your mistress? Never, while I have life!"

She flung herself upon me so suddenly that she tore me away from the door. She was a strong and athletic woman, and I suppose she expected some resistance, for she used such force as to drag me forward into the middle of the room, overturning a chair in the effort. I was so utterly taken by surprise that I yielded to her violence more completely than she expected.

She staggered, let go her hold, and fell heavily backwards, tripping over the fallen chair. I made a desperate attempt to save her, but only caught the end of a fur necklet, and it tore like a spider's web.

Her body crashed against a Venetian fender, and her head came with awful force against a sort of support for the fire-irons that stood up a foot from the ground.

Then she rolled over, her eyes and face undergoing a ghastly change, and instantly became, as I thought, unconscious.

I knelt beside her, raising her head with my right hand, and brokenly besought her to speak to me, when I would at once do anything she demanded. But she gave no sign of animation. In a frenzy of despair, I forced myself to examine her injuries, and my heart nearly stopped beating when I discovered that a large piece of iron had been driven into her brain through the back of her head.

I knew in a moment that she was dead. Although I have not had much experience of that terrible epoch in the human being, I have seen far too much of death in animal life not to know that she who had been my honored and respected wife now lay before me a mere soulless entity—a symbol only of the splendid vital creature who, a minute earlier, was angrily protesting against the supposed faithlessness of her mate.

Looking back now upon the events of that fateful night, I marvel at the appalling coolness which came to my aid as soon as I realized the extent of the misfortune which had befallen both Alice and myself. I can fully understand what is meant by the callousness of a certain class of criminals, or the indifference to inevitable death betrayed by Eastern races. No sooner was I quite assured that my wife was dead—dead beyond hope or doubt—than I regained the use of my reasoning faculties in the most marvellously cold-blooded degree.

The actual difficulties of my position were enormous. I arraigned myself before the judge and jury, and saw clearly that every circumstance which contributed to Alice's suspicions in the first instance were now magnified a hundred-fold by the manner and scene of her death.

Before me, in ghostly panorama, moved the dread crowd of witnesses against me, the degradation of my family, the bitter and vengeful feelings of my wife's relatives, the suffering of poor, unconscious Mrs. Hillmer, the whole avalanche of horror and misery which this unfortunate accident had precipitated upon every person who claimed my relationship or friendship.

My mental attitude was quite altruistic. Could I have undone the past, I would cheerfully have undergone a painful and protracted death forthwith.

But no possible atonement on my part would restore Alice to life. I knew it was quite improbable that I should be convicted of murdering her, strong as the circumstantial testimony against me must be. The mere legal consequences did not, however, weigh with me for a second. From that awful hour I felt that I was doomed personally. My only thought was to seek oblivion, not only for myself, but for all whom Alice's death might affect.

Reasoning in this way, I rapidly resolved to make a bold effort to conceal forever the time and place of the fatality. If I failed, I could tell the truth; if I succeeded, I might, at my own expense, save a vast amount of unnecessary sorrow.

The desperate expedient came to me of carrying off the body to the untenanted house at Putney where my old master had resided until his death, utilizing the four-wheeled cab with its half-drunken driver for the purpose.

If I reached Putney unhindered, I could dispose of my terrible burden easily, for the river flowed past the grounds, and every inch of the locality was known to me.

It occurred to me that perhaps the body might be found and recognized. Our personal linen was never marked, by reason of the fact that our laundry work was done upon our Yorkshire estate, but as a temporary safeguard I resolved to take some different and less valuable outer clothes from Mrs. Hillmer's residence.

Her maid was of a similar build to my wife, so I hastened to the girl's room, and laid hands upon a soiled coat and skirt which were relegated to the recesses of the wardrobe.

I glanced at my watch as I came along the corridor. It was 6.15 P.M. All the incidents I have related to you had happened within a quarter of an hour. Oh, heaven! it seemed longer than all the preceding years of my life.

Having resolved upon a line of conduct, I pursued it with the *sang-froid* and accuracy of one of the superior scoundrels delineated by Du Boisgobey. The door of the flat was locked. If the servants, hardly due yet, returned unexpectedly, I would send them off to Victoria Station on some imaginary errand of their mistress's.

I knelt beside my poor wife's body once more, and with great difficulty took off her costume and loosely fastened on the maid's garments.

In her purse there were some bulky documents, which I afterwards discovered to be the reports furnished by a firm of private detectives, detailing all my movements with reference to Raleigh Mansions with surprising accuracy. But she had concealed her name. These men themselves only knew me as "Colonel Montgomery."

How Alice first came to suspect me I can only guess. Perhaps my indifference, my absence from home at definite hours, a chance meeting in the street unknown to me—any of these may have supplied the initial cause, and led her to verify her doubts before taxing me with my supposed iniquity.

Indeed, her final act in coming alone to Mrs. Hillmer's abode, revealed her fearless spirit and independent methods. She wanted no divorce court revelations. She would simply have spurned me as an unworthy and dishonorable wretch. Her small belongings I put in my pockets; the clothes I made into a parcel and stuffed temporarily beneath my overcoat.

Then I unlocked the door, and went down the few steps to the main entrance. There was no one about, the fog and sleet having cleared the street—a quiet thoroughfare at all times.

I took the risk of the maids coming back, and I ran to the square for my conveyance. The driver had been improving the occasion, and was more inebriated than before. He brought his cab to the door, and I knew, by the appearance of things, that no one had entered during my absence.

With some difficulty I lifted Alice's body into my arms in as natural a position as possible, and carried her to the cab, leaving the door of the flat ajar. Luck still favored me. The cabman supposed that she, like himself, was intoxicated. A man came down the opposite side of the street, but he paid not the slightest heed to me, and, indeed, we were but dimly visible to each other.

Exerting all my strength unobtrusively, I placed my wife on the rear seat, and then calmly gave the driver instructions. He grumbled at the distance, but I told him I would pay him handsomely. Searching in my pockets and Alice's purse, I could only find twelve shillings, so, although it was risky, to avoid a quarrel with the man, I determined to give him a five-pound note.

Thus far, all had gone well.

The notion possessed me that, to all intents and purposes, I had murdered my wife, and that I was now disposing of the visible signs of my guilt in the most approved manner of a daring criminal. Whether I did right or wrong I cannot, even at this late hour, decide. Should my death induce forgetfulness, I am still inclined to think that I acted for the best. My wife was dead; I was self-condemned. Why, then, allow others, wholly innocent, to be dragged into the vortex?

This was my line of thought. If you, reading this ghastly narrative, shudder at my deeds, I pray you nevertheless to weigh in the balance the good and ill that resulted from my actions.

At last we reached Putney, and drew up at the end of the disused lane which runs down by the side of the house to the river.

Here, again, the road was deserted. I lifted my wife out, carried her to the postern-gate, and returned to give the driver his note. The man was so amazed at the amount that he whipped up his horse instantly, fearing lest I should change my mind.

I was about to force open the old and rickety door into the garden when I remembered the drain-pipe jutting into the Thames—a place where, as a child, I often caused much alarm by surreptitious visits for the purpose of catching minnows. I quickly took off my coat and boots, turned up my trousers and shirt-sleeves, and examined the pipe with my hands.

It exactly suited my purpose. In half a minute I had firmly wedged my wife's body beneath it. This was the most horrible portion of my task. The chill water, the desolation of the river bank, the mud and trailing weeds—all these things seemed so vile and loathsome when placed in contact with the mortal remains of my ill-fated Alice.

She had loved me. I believe I loved her, as I assuredly do now when her presence is but a memory, yet I was condemned to commit her to the contaminating beastliness of such surroundings. It was a small matter, in the face of death, but it has weighed on me since more than any other feature of that cruel night's history.

Before leaving Putney I tied her clothes, hat, and furs to a couple of heavy stones and threw the parcel into deep water.

By train and cab I reached home but a few minutes late for dinner. It was not difficult for me to act my part with the servants, nor keep up the farce during the weary days that followed. My consciousness was so seared by what I had gone through that the mere make-believe of my position was a relief to me.

That night, in the privacy of my room, I recollected the broken fender, and feared lest the ironwork would supply a clue should the body be discovered, a thing I deemed practically impossible.

But, for Mrs. Hillmer's sake, I took no risk. Next morning, before I saw you at Tattersall's, I made arrangements for the whole contents of her drawing-room to be transferred to her brother's flat, where, to my knowledge, the articles were needed.

Mrs. Hillmer had gone out early, so the thing was done in her absence. Her amazement was so great that she wired me, using as a signature the pet name of her childhood, and this was the first message you heard the groom refer to when he came a second time with the telegram from Richmond.

I wrote her a hurried note, explaining that I intended the transfer as a sop to her offended brother, but she had telegraphed again, and I had to go to see her, to learn that Mensmore resented the gift, and had gone off in a huff to Monte Carlo.

A little later, I took the supreme step of writing a farewell letter. Since my wife's death I could not bear to meet any other woman. I communed with my poor Alice more when dead than when alive.

I do not think I have anything else to tell you. Step by step I watched you and the police tearing aside my barrier of deceit. At times I thought I would baffle you in the end. Were it not for my folly in bribing Jane Harding I think I must have succeeded.

That poor girl was the undoing of me in the first instance, and she now has brought me my final sentence, for she came to-day and told me, with tears, all that happened between the detective and herself. White, too, put in an appearance.

To-morrow, I suppose, he will bring a warrant, if you do not see him first and tell him the truth.

Do not misunderstand me. I am glad of this release. When you strove to arouse me from my despair I did, for a little while, cherish the hope that I might be able to devote my declining years to the work which Alice herself took an interest in. But the web of testimony woven round my old friend, Mensmore; the self-effacing spirit of his sister, who, to shield me, was willing to sacrifice herself; the possibility that I might involve these two, and perhaps others, in my own ruin—every circumstance conspired to overwhelm me.

I can endure no more, my dear Bruce. It is ended. The past is already a dream to me—the future void. My poor nature was not designed to withstand such a strain. The cord of existence has snapped, and I cannot bring myself to believe it will be mended again. In bidding you farewell I ask one thing. If you take a charitable view of my deeds, if you consider that my penalty is commensurate with my faults, then you might take my dead hand and say, "This was my friend. I pity him. May the spirit of his wife be merciful unto him should they meet in the regions beyond the grave."

And so, for the last time, I sign myself

CHARLES DYKE.

CHAPTER XXXI

VALEDICTORY

Much as Bruce would have wished to inter his dead friend's secret with his mortal remains in the tomb, it was impossible.

Sir Charles Dyke's sacrifice must not be made in vain, and the strange chain of events encircled other actors in the drama too strongly to enable the barrister to adopt the course which would otherwise have commended itself to him. An early visit to Scotland Yard, where, in company with Mr. White, he interviewed the Deputy Commissioner, and a conference with the district coroner settled two important questions. The police were satisfied as to the cause of Lady Dyke's death, and the coroner agreed to keep the evidence as to the baronet's sudden collapse strictly within the limits of the medical evidence.

A wholly unnecessary public scandal was thus avoided.

With Lady Dyke's relatives his task required considerable tact. Without taking them fully into his confidence, he explained that Sir Charles had all along known the exact facts bearing upon her death and burial-place, but for family reasons he thought it best not to disclose his knowledge.

Bruce needed their co-operation in getting the home office to give the requisite permission for Lady Dyke's reburial. The circumstance that the deceased baronet had left his estates to his wife's nephew, joined to the important position Bruce occupied as one of the trustees and joint guardian, with the boy's mother, of the young heir, smoothed over many difficulties.

After a harassing and anxious week Bruce had the melancholy satisfaction of seeing the remains of the unfortunate couple laid to rest in the stately gloom of the family vault.

The newspapers, of course, scented a mystery in the proceedings, but definite inquiry was barred in every direction. Even the exhumation order gave no clue to the reasons of the authorities for granting it, and in less than the proverbial nine days the incident was forgotten.

Sir Charles had made it a condition precedent to the succession that his heir should bear his name, and should live with his widowed mother on the Yorkshire estate, or in the town house, for a certain number of months in each year, until the boy was old enough to go to school.

The stipulation was intended to have the effect of more rapidly burying his own memory in oblivion. Bruce, too, was given a sum of £5,000, "to be expended in bequests as he thought fit."

Claude understood his motive thoroughly. Jane Harding had been loyal to her master in her way, so he arranged that she should receive an annual income sufficient to secure her from want. Thompson, too, was provided for when the time came that he was too feeble for further employment at Portman Square, and Mr. White received a handsome *douceur* for his services.

Mrs. Hillmer did not even know of Sir Charles Dyke's death until weeks had passed. Acting on Bruce's advice her brother simply told her that everything had been settled, and that the authorities concurred with the barrister in the opinion that Lady Dyke was accidently killed.

When she had completely recovered from the shock of the belief that her loyal friend had murdered his wife, Mensmore one day told her the whole sad story. But he would allow no more weeping.

"It is time," he said, "that the misery of this episode should cease. When the chief actor in the tragedy gave his life to end the suffering, we would but ill meet his wishes by allowing it to occupy our thoughts unduly in the future."

Mensmore's marriage with Phyllis Browne was now definitely fixed for the following autumn, so he carried his sister off with him on a hasty trip to Wyoming in company with Corbett—a journey required for the protection and development of their joint interests in that State.

Not only did their property turn out to be of great and lasting value, but during their absence the Springbok Mine began to boom. Even the cautious barrister one day found himself hesitating whether or not to sell at half over par, so excellent were the reports and so extensive the dividends from that auriferous locality.

The two young people were married, a scion of the house had become a lusty two-year-old, Mr. White had become Chief Inspector, and Miss Marie le Marchant had, by strenuous effort, risen to the dignity of double crown posters as a "dashing comedienne"—when Bruce's memories of his lost friends were suddenly revived in an unexpected manner.

Mr. Sydney H. Corbett came to him with measured questionings and brooding thought stamped on his brows.

"It's like this," he said, when they were settled down to details, "I want to get married."

"To whom?" inquired Claude, wondering at the savage tone in which the announcement was made.

"To Mrs. Hillmer."

"Oh!"

"That's what everybody yells the moment I mention it. She screams 'Oh!' and runs off with tears in her eyes. Her brother says 'Oh!' and looks uncomfortable, but refuses to discuss the proposition. Now you say 'Oh!' and gaze at me like an owl at the bare statement. What the dickens does it all mean, I want to know? I'm not worrying about what happened years ago. Mrs. Hillmer is just the sort of woman I require as a wife, and I'll marry her yet if the whole British nation says 'Oh!' loud enough to be heard and answered by the U-nited States."

"That's the proper sort of spirit in which to set about the business."

"Yes, sir; but I can't get any forrarder. There's a kind of rock below water which holds me up every time I shoot the rapids. She likes me well enough, I know. She calls me 'Syd' as slick as butter, and I call her 'Gwen'; but there you are—if I want to go ahead a bit she pulls up and weeps. Now, why the—"

"Steady, Mr. Corbett. Women weep for many reasons. Do you know her history?"

"No, and I don't want to."

"But perhaps that is exactly what she does want. Remember that she has been married before, with somewhat bitter experience. She probably believes that a husband and wife should have no secrets from each other. Above all else, there should be no cloud between them as to bygone events. Mrs. Hillmer is highly sensitive. If she imagined you were under any misapprehension as to the circumstances under which Sir Charles and Lady Dyke met their deaths—do not forget that you were personally mixed up in the affair—she would neither entertain your proposal nor explain her motives. She would just do as you say—run away and cry."

"Well, now, that beats everything," said Corbett admiringly. "That never struck me before."

"It is the probable explanation of her attitude, nevertheless."

"Then what am I to do?"

"Write to her. Ask her permission to learn the facts from me. Tell her you believe you understand the reasons for her reticence, and that your only excuse for the request is that you want to go to her on an equal plane of absolute confidence. It seems to me—"

"That I'd better get quick and do it," shouted Corbett, vanishing with the utmost celerity.

Bruce still occupied his old chambers in Victoria Street. He did not expect to see Corbett again for a couple of days. To the barrister's utter amazement he returned within ten minutes.

"Fire away!" he cried excitedly. "You struck it first time. I just rang her up—"

"Rang her up?"

"Yes; she's staying at the Savoy for a few days, so I telephoned from the Windsor. I could never fix up a letter in your words, you know. But switch me on the end of a wire and I know where I am."

"What on earth did you say?"

"As soon as I got her in the box at the other end, I said, 'Is that you, Gwen?' 'Yes,' said she. 'Well,' said I, 'I guess you know who's talking?' 'Quite well,' said she. 'Then,' said I, 'I've just been telling Mr. Bruce I wanted to marry you, and that you wouldn't even discuss the proposition. He said you probably wished me to know the whole story of Sir Charles Dyke, but felt kinder shy of telling me yourself. He will get it off his chest if you give him permission, and then I can come along in a hansom and fix things. What do you say?' There was no answer, so I shouted, 'Are you there?' and she said, 'Yes,' faint-like. 'Don't let me hurry you,' said I, 'but if you agree straight-away I can catch Bruce at home, for I've just left him.' With that she said, 'Very well. You can see Mr. Bruce.' And here I am."

"Having accomplished the whole thing satisfactorily."

"As how?"

"Don't you see you have proposed to the lady and practically been accepted?"

"Jehosh! It does look something like it. Say, I'm off! This story of yours will keep until to-morrow."

He would have gone, but Bruce jumped after him.

"Not so fast, Mr. Corbett. You must not sail into the Savoy flying a false flag. Kindly oblige me with your attention for the next half-hour."

With that, he unlocked a safe and took from its recesses Sir Charles Dyke's "confession." He read the whole of its opening passages, explaining the relations between Mrs. Hillmer and her unfortunate but abiding friend.

The straightforward, honest sentences sounded strangely familiar at this distance of time. Bruce was glad of the opportunity of reading them aloud. It seemed a fitting thing that this testimony should come, as it were, from the tomb.

Corbett listened intently to the recital and to the barrister's summary of the events that followed.

"Poor chap!" he said, when the sad tale had ended. "I hope you shook hands with him as he asked you to do?"

"I did. Would that my grasp had the power to reassure him of my heartfelt sympathy."

For a little while they were silent.

"So," said Corbett at last, "Gwen thought I would make the same mistake as the poor lady, and suspect her wrongfully."

"No, not that. But naturally she wished the man whom she could trust as a husband to be wholly cognizant of events in which already he had participated slightly."

"She was right. I like her all the better for it. But, tell me, is there any necessity for that wonderful document to be preserved?"

"Not the slightest. It has served its last use."

"Then put it in the fire."

Bruce did not hesitate a moment to comply with the wish. The flames devoured the record with avidity, and the two men watched the manuscript crumbling into nothingness. Then Corbett said:

"I must be off to the Savoy."

"Good-bye, old chap," said Bruce. "And good luck to you, too. I congratulate both Mrs. Hillmer and yourself."